I0668698

For Love's Sake

CARLA HOWATT

Published by By the Book Publishing, 2023.

FOR LOVE'S SAKE

First edition. December 23, 2023.

Copyright © 2023 CARLA HOWATT.

ISBN: 978-1778290626

Written by CARLA HOWATT.

Table of Contents

For my husband, Don.

Our wedding vows should have included a promise to never use what I learned while researching this novel against you.

Chapter 1

Present Day

The battle was ferocious. The two combatants were evenly matched and willing to do whatever it took to win. One minute the girl was on her back being straddled, then in a flash, her legs flipped up and forward, wrapping around his neck and pulling him over backward. He cried out in surprise. A moan rose from the audience as they sat around the living room, watching and shaking their heads. The family was used to the rambunctious antics of the seven-year-old twins, and they often spent time dodging them as the two chased each other around their grandparents' large, sprawling ranch-style home.

"Okay you two, time to break it up," Rose said as she entered the room, clapping her hands to get their attention. "If the adults in the room would stop encouraging this type of behavior, maybe things wouldn't be constantly getting broken around here!"

"Oh Mom, they're young and they need to blow off some energy," Brandon, her son-in-law said as he stood up from the couch. "And they haven't broken anything since that old vase that Aunt Tony gave you for your wedding. You always said you didn't like it anyway."

"That's not the point," she smiled affectionately at him. "They should learn to behave when they are at someone else's house."

"Oh, come on," Brandon said teasingly as he threw his arm around her shoulders and hugged her. "This isn't someone else's house; this is Gram's house!"

Brandon dodged the tea towel which she snapped in his direction. He laughed and then turned to the twins.

"Okay you two, time to settle down, Grams says so."

The twins Jonathon and Bethany pulled apart, but not before Jonathon got in one last swat at his sister.

"Owwwww! Daddy! Jonathon hit me!"

"Jonathon, stop it and leave your sister alone," their mother Kayla interjected.

"It's time for dinner now everyone," Rose spoke to the rest of the room, while at the same time resting her hand on the top of Jonathon's head, holding him gently in place.

The adults in the room slowly began to stand up and work their way toward the dining room. Brandon fell in behind his wife and placed his hand on Kayla's back. He leaned forward and whispered in her ear.

"You're a good Mom, and you have great kids."

Kayla smiled slightly and looked up at her husband with a grateful look. Brandon knew that his wife took every comment about her children's behavior that came out of her mother's mouth to heart as an indictment of her parenting skills. He saw it as his job to counterbalance the negativity that was running around in her head by making sure she heard a lot of affirmations from him.

He didn't think he would ever really understand the tension that sometimes flared up between Kayla and her mom; they were both amazing women who were dedicated, passionate mothers. He didn't think Rose meant anything really critical by her comments, but Kayla still wasn't confident enough to speak up and let her mother know how she felt. Until she did, he would be there for her.

"Oh Mom, it smells so good!" Joshua exclaimed, throwing his head back and inhaling deeply. "You are just the best cook in the world!"

"Say that while you can bro; Sarah won't appreciate it once you're married," Kayla laughed.

"Why would she care after we're married?" Joshua asked, looking at his fiancé Sarah who shrugged her shoulders and raised her hands, palms up.

"Well, when you get married, you'll have to say that Sarah's cooking is the best," Kayla looked at them quizzically, as though she wasn't sure why she was having to explain the obvious.

They pulled back the chairs at the dining room table and took their places.

"I don't think that will be a problem as I don't cook," Sarah said with a smile. "Joshua will be the one doing the cooking in our family, right hon?"

"Yup," Joshua responded, leaning over to kiss the top of his fiancé's head. "I'd fear for my life if she ever put food down in front of me and we weren't at a buffet."

"If you want Sarah, I would love to show you how to cook some basic things before the wedding," Rose spoke up, a smile on her face. She wanted to connect with her daughter-in-law-to-be, but they were such very different women. It wasn't just that they were from different generations —sometimes Rose felt as though they came from different worlds. Rose knew that she was unusual in this day and age, in that she had stayed home to raise her children and never gone back to work. She just had no desire to enter the workforce and she gained a lot of satisfaction from keeping their home immaculate, spending time with her grandchildren, and doing fundraising for causes that grabbed her attention. She knew she was very privileged, and she was grateful for it every day.

"Oh, no thanks Rose," Sarah answered. "I have no interest in learning to cook or, heaven forbid, bake. I would rather go out for dinner or order in. Let the people who are skilled in those areas work their magic and I will appreciate it. Much like I will this amazing spread!" It was hard for Rose to be offended by Sarah's refusal of her offer as she was so earnest in her respect for the work Rose did for her family. She constantly told Joshua, within hearing of the rest of the family, how lucky they were to have a mother like Rose.

"Did your mother ever try to teach you?" Kayla asked, looking a bit befuddled.

"Nope, but she did teach me the difference between compound and simple interest, and how to code," Sarah responded with a grin. She never seemed to take it personally that Kayla found her upbringing so alien. "My mother wasn't exactly domesticated herself, so it wasn't a priority in our family."

David, who sat at the head of the table, stood up and picked up the carving fork and knife. "Well, let's not let things get cold. I'll start carving the roast if you want to start passing the dishes around," he nodded in Rose's direction, and she picked up a bowl and began to pass it around.

"Don't worry about taking too many potatoes, there are plenty more where those came from," she reassured her hungry family.

"When do we get to open Phoenix's presents?" Bethany piped up, reminding everyone that the reason for the gathering was to celebrate the youngest family member's first birthday.

"You know the rules," Kayla answered her daughter. "We have to eat supper first."

Sarah studiously avoided looking at Joshua. If she looked at him after Kayla's comment, she wasn't sure she could keep a straight face. Just that day, as they got ready to head over to his parent's house, they had been laughing about the fact that there always seemed to be a rule for everything in the Slater family.

There was a rule, although unwritten, about what time they were supposed to arrive for dinner, a rule for how long they had to stay after dinner was over, and even for how they planned their upcoming wedding.

Every Sunday, the Slater family gathered for a roast beef dinner. It was a rule that you showed up unless you had a very good reason not to. These Sundays were also the day when the family celebrated birthdays and anniversaries together. According to her fiancé, this tradition had existed for as long as he could remember. Growing up, Sunday dinners were sacrosanct. When he was old enough to go to college, Joshua was still expected to come back for that one meal every week. And he brought her to meet his family for the first time at a family Sunday dinner.

Afterward, the adults began to push away from the table, rubbing their stomachs and groaning with contentment.

"Not just yet" Rose stood, motioning for them to sit back down. "It's time for Phoenix's birthday cake!"

Leaving the dining room, Rose went to the kitchen and was setting a large number one candle in the middle of it when the doorbell rang. "Someone get that?" she called.

She heard Brandon at the front door saying hello. She had just picked up the plate that held the birthday cake when she heard a commotion. Frowning, she cocked her head, trying to hear what the voices talking to Brandon were saying. Unable to hear anything audible, she sat the cake down on the kitchen table and walked back into the dining room.

Standing in the middle of her dining room were two uniformed policemen. David was standing up at the table, a deep frown marring his handsome face. The other adults in the family were still sitting around the table, the shock on their faces almost comical.

Even the twins were speechless as the officers swiftly moved around the table and approached their grandfather.

"David Slater?" one of the police officers asked.

"Yes, that's me," the patriarch of the family responded.

"Please turn around," the second officer approached David and as he turned him around, he pulled his hands behind his back. "You are under arrest; you have the right to remain silent..."

There was an eruption of noise as everyone began to speak at once. Phoenix, the youngest of the family looked around and his bottom lip began to quiver. The twins Jonathon and Bethany began talking rapidly, their voices becoming louder and louder as they demanded answers to their questions from their parents.

Rose stood rooted to the spot, her hand resting on her chest. Her eyes were wide as she took in the scene in front of her.

"What is this about officer?"

"Why are you doing this?"

"You can't just..."

"What's going on?"

As the police officer led David towards the front door, Rose suddenly found herself moving in front of them.

"Excuse me, but can you tell me what is happening? Why are you arresting my husband?" she asked in a shaky voice.

"We have a warrant here for David Slater," the officer answered. "He is being charged with murder in the first degree."

"What?" David yelled. "What are you talking about?"

"Please come with us sir," the police officer slipped her forearm under David's arm as David's legs appeared to give out from under him.

"Dad!" Kayla wailed while her husband put his hands on her shoulders to keep her from running forward and throwing herself at her dad.

"What the hell is going on?" Joshua asked, stepping up beside his mother.

"He is being arrested. He has been read his rights and we are taking him to the local precinct, you can find out more information there," the other officer informed them as they continued to escort David out of the house.

Looking over his right shoulder, David yelled to his wife "Call Terry and ask him to get me a lawyer!"

Chapter 2

Present Day

There was a brief minute after the door shut behind David and the two officers when the only noise in the Slater home was the sound of Phoenix hiccoughing back a cry. Then, everyone seemed to start talking at once.

"What just happened?"

"Why would they do this?"

"There has to be a mistake."

Each family member was asking questions, but no one had any answers. Finally, Kayla turned to her mother, who was the only person in the room who was standing stock still, saying nothing.

"Mom! Dad said to call his Uncle Terry!"

"What?" Rose looked at her daughter, her eyes blank and wide.

"Dad said to call Uncle Terry! Why aren't you calling him?"

"Oh, yeah, I'll call Terry, he'll know what to do," One minute Rose was standing there quiet and unmoving and the next, she was all action. She ran into the kitchen, grabbed her phone, and called Terry, her husband's lifelong friend. She rested the phone between her shoulder and her chin as she began putting food back into the refrigerator.

"Hi Terry, this is Rose. Can you call me as soon as possible? Something horrible has happened and I don't know what to do," She hung up after leaving the message. A second later she picked up her phone again and sent a follow-up text.

"Sorry about the cryptic message," she wrote, "no one died." She didn't want him worrying and thinking the worst after hearing her voice message. A giggle erupted from her throat as she realized that the strangest thoughts were hitting her. Why was she worried about Terry right now? Her husband had just been arrested. And arrested for murder. She shook her head, staring out the kitchen window, the phone still in her hand.

She jumped when the phone rang and she almost dropped it in the kitchen sink.

"Hello, Rose? What's going on?" Terry sounded concerned. It wasn't like her to contact him out of the blue. He had been friends with David for many years and Rose would jokingly comment that David brought Terry into their relationship with him. He was very much David's friend. Sure, they socialized and had even hoped their wives would become friends, but it never seemed to work out that way. Even when Terry changed wives, it just didn't seem to be in the cards. And so, most of the time, it was David and Terry who called each other.

"It's David," Rose said, her voice catching. "He's been arrested."

"Arrested? Whatever for?" Terry asked, incredulous. "When?"

"Just a few minutes ago; the police came to the house and arrested him," Rose choked out. Saying it out loud was making it even more real and she didn't like it. She didn't like it one bit. "They arrested him for murder!"

There was silence on the other end of the phone as Rose struggled to keep her composure. "He said to call you and tell you to get him a lawyer."

There was silence on the other end of the phone.

"Terry?"

"Yeah, yeah, I'll give a buddy of mine a call. I don't know if he handles this kind of case, but he can help until we can find someone else," Terry mumbled, as though speaking to himself. "He can help David out at this point at least."

"Okay," Rose felt a hollow sensation in her stomach. She hadn't digested what was happening right now, today, never mind at any other point down the road. No, she wouldn't go there right now.

"I'll take care of this at my end Rose, don't worry. Can I get a hold of you at this number once I find out anything?"

"Yes, I'll keep the phone with me, please let me know the minute you know anything more," Rose asked him. She reached out for the kitchen countertop, looking for support as her legs weakened. She was more relieved than she let on that someone else was stepping up and taking charge.

Just as she hung up, Kayla came into the kitchen.

"Is Terry getting a lawyer?" she asked her mother.

"Yes."

"How long will it take?"

"I don't know, I didn't ask," she answered her daughter.

"Did you ask if we can go see him?"

"See him?"

"Yes, see him," Kayla frowned at her mother. "Can we go to the police station and see Dad, try and find out what is happening?"

"I didn't ask him."

"You didn't ask? Why not?" Hands on her hips, Kayla stood in front of her mother, demanding an answer.

"Because it never crossed my mind," Rose responded, becoming annoyed with the interrogation from her daughter. "I'm sorry but I haven't read the instruction manual on what questions to ask when your husband is arrested and hauled out of your home!"

Joshua walked into the kitchen, running his hands through his light blond hair.

"What's going on in here?" he asked, frowning as he looked from his sister to his mother. They seemed to realize it was rhetorical and he continued.

"Did you get a hold of Terry?"

"Yes," Rose answered. "He's going to have a friend of his who is a lawyer help your dad. He's going to keep us posted."

"Okay, that's good," Joshua bobbed his head up and down. "Yeah, that's good."

"Well, I for one am not going to sit around and wait for something to happen," Kayla threw her brother and mother a disparaging look. "I'm going down to the police station to find out what is happening."

"I don't think that's very helpful Kayla," Joshua told his sister. "You'll just end up sitting around and waiting."

"Well, it beats doing nothing; we have no answers and we don't know what's happening. This has to be some kind of huge mistake and the sooner we figure things out, the sooner we can get him out of there."

"And how are you going to do that Kayla? Descend on them with two kids and a baby in tow and hope they get so annoyed they let Dad go?" Joshua rolled his eyes at his sister.

"Mom, if you're just going to sit around, I'm going to leave the kids with you and go and see if I can get this straightened out," Kayla informed her mother as she turned to leave the kitchen.

Throwing his arms up and shaking his head, Joshua followed his sister.

Rose stood, leaning up against the countertop, phone in one hand. She knew going down to the station was futile. If they weren't going to give her any information here, she doubted very much they would tell her what she needed to know if she showed up and said please. This was a job for a lawyer, who knew how to navigate the system. She didn't move to stop her daughter or explain any of it to her. She knew her daughter well enough to know that if she stayed here with the rest of them and just waited, she would go crazy. Rose didn't mind watching the kids, and once Kayla spent some time cooling her heels at the police station, she would be ready to come back.

Hopefully, she would hear back from Terry soon and he would have some answers. What on earth was going on? Surely it was a case of mistaken identity or something. Maybe there was another David Slater and they had confused the two men? There had to be a reasonable explanation. Men like David didn't just get arrested for murder at their grandchild's first birthday celebration. And the look on his face; God she would never forget the shocked and horrified look on his face as they hauled him away. If the family was upset and confused, imagine how he must feel.

Just then, Sarah entered the kitchen with a pile of dirty dishes.

"Sorry, hope I'm not intruding, but I figured I might as well clean up the dinner table," she said, uncertainty on her face as she glanced at her future mother-in-law. Just what was the etiquette in these situations? Nothing had prepared her for what to say to a woman whose husband had just been arrested for murder.

"No, that's very kind of you Sarah, thank you!" Rose looked genuinely pleased. She motioned for her to put the dishes down on the island. Opening the dishwasher, she began to load the machine with the dishes Sarah had brought in.

"I can do that if you want to go and talk to the family," Sarah suggested, reaching for a plate. "I may not be much of a cook, but I excel at dishes!"

"No, that's okay hon, I need to keep busy, and I think Kayla is mad at me so I should stay here."

"I don't think she's mad, she's just in shock."

Rose looked at her, one eyebrow raised. "We're all in shock but Kayla is the only one who lashes out."

Sarah smiled and began scraping off the plates that needed it.

"Are the kids okay?" Rose asked Sarah. She wasn't feeling ready to see her grandchildren just yet. They would have so many questions and she had no answers for them. She needed a bit more time to gather her thoughts and calm her nerves.

"I think so; they're confused, as we all are of course," Sarah answered. "Except of course for Phoenix who is now lying on top of Uncle Josh. They should both be snoring in no time."

"That's nice," Rose said distractedly as she glanced down at the phone still in her hand. How long was it going to take them to know something? Although it had been less than half an hour since she first called Terry, she felt herself becoming even more anxious, if that was possible. Surely it wouldn't take very long to realize there had been a terrible mistake? A mistake they could look back on years from now and laugh about. They would tell stories about the time Grampa was hauled away and charged with murder because they had him mixed up with someone else. David would mime being behind bars and their grandchildren would laugh and shriek. Their kids would shake their heads and remind them all that it was fine to laugh now but it had been scary at the time.

"Did Brandon drive Kayla?" she suddenly asked. "She didn't go alone, did she?"

"Brandon drove her, yes. Although he didn't look too thrilled about going. He tried to talk her out of it, but she was determined," Sarah told her. Saying she was determined was an understatement. If Brandon hadn't agreed to drive her, Sarah had no doubt that Kayla would have peeled off the driveway and driven herself to the police station. It was a good thing he had gone as Sarah didn't think that having Kayla driving while so upset and agitated was a good idea.

"Look, do you want Josh and I to take their kids to our place so you don't have to worry about them?" Sarah asked. She really wanted to be helpful but wasn't sure what Rose needed.

"No, no, that's okay, they'll help me keep my eyes off the clock. I'm going to go and see how they are doing," Rose pushed herself away from the counter and walked out of the kitchen. Sarah looked at the pile of dishes that Rose had left on the counter when she stopped loading up the dishwasher in mid-stride. Rose seemed to have forgotten what she was doing and simply abandoned the task. Not that anyone could blame her, Sarah thought as she took over the task.

Chapter 3

The Past

The locker door slammed, the sharp metallic sound echoing down the empty hallway. Stifling a sob, the locker's owner ran towards the exit doors.

"Rebecca, wait!" the sound of feet hitting the tiled floor followed her.

"Leave me alone!" she flung over his shoulder. "I don't want to talk to you!"

Standing in the exit's doorway the teenage boy watched her run to her little red Nissan in the parking lot.

Slapping the door with the palm of his hand, he cursed under his breath. Turning around he retraced his steps down the hallways.

~~~~

"I don't know what to do," Rebecca cried into the receiver. "He says he isn't going to come and if he doesn't want to see me, I can't make him."

"Now you're being silly, Rebecca," her friend said. "It's not that he doesn't want to see you."

"Bottom line is, Ashley, if he wanted to see me this summer, he would make it happen," Rebecca wailed.

"I know you don't want to hear this right now but not everyone has the options in life that you do."

"Yeah, yeah I know, I'm a spoiled brat, everyone keeps telling me that. I don't need to hear it from one of my best friends too!"

Ashley let her friend's words hang in the air. She knew Rebecca was hurt and was lashing out. She knew Rebecca was hurting and didn't know how else to process her emotions. She was used to getting everything she wanted, something Ashley found hard to deal with. It was something that she talked over with their other friend Kim quite often. Kim, like Ashley, didn't understand why Rebecca was being so unreasonable about David working this summer. In fact, she related more to Rebecca's boyfriend right now. He was faced with either working all summer, so he had money to go to college in the fall, or to spend time with his girlfriend at her cabin by the lake.

Love makes the world go round but you need money to eat and go to college.

"I'm sorry," Rebecca said quietly. "I'm just so upset with him."

"I know, but I really think you need to look at it from his point of view and not take this so personally."

"You're so nice and understanding Ash, maybe you should be David's girlfriend instead of me," Rebecca sighed as she rolled over onto her back.

Ashley felt as though her heart was being squeezed into a vice. Her best friend, the one she had grown up with, shared secrets and late-night sleepovers with had no idea the pain those words caused her.

She took a deep breath, pushing thoughts of David away, as she always did. She couldn't think about him that way. He was her best friend's boyfriend.

And even if he wasn't, there was no way he would have ever given her a second look. She was just Rebecca's quiet, slightly chubby shadow. She was under no illusions; she knew that standing next to Rebecca with her glowing skin, slim hips, and cute giggle, she paled in comparison. She didn't begrudge Rebecca for being the one that everyone wanted to be around. She loved her for it. She was proud to call Rebecca her best friend.

"Hello, Ash? Did you hear what I said?"

"Sorry, what was that?" Ashley started as she realized she had zoned out.

"I said, do you think he might change his mind and spend the summer with me instead of killing himself at some forestry camp?"

"I don't think it's an option for him. He has to make money to pay for college," Ashley explained once again.

"But he has scholarships, and this is our last summer before we have to be adults, why rush it?"

Ashley knew it was useless to try and make Rebecca understand. She didn't know what it was not to be rich. She had little concept of money and what things cost. She had tried to explain to her that having your college tuition covered didn't mean it was all clear sailing afterward. But Rebecca had always had someone there to pay her rent, to make her dinner every night, to pay for her when she went to the movies.

"David has made up his mind, so why don't you just enjoy the time you have together until summer is here? Then it will be time to hang out at the cabin and Kim and I will come visit you," Ashley decided to try and steer her away from the topic of David. Sometimes Rebecca could ruminate and obsess about things, especially if it was something that made her unhappy.

Chapter 4

Present Day

Pulling up to the police station, Rose pulled into an empty parking spot to the right of the front door. Throwing the car into park, she reached over and grabbed her purse, pulling it onto her lap. And then she sat there, unmoving. How did one prepare oneself for talking to the authorities about your husband's unexpected arrest? Did she just go up to the front counter and demand to see him? Or was there a form she would have to fill out, maybe called "The WTF Form"? She suppressed a giggle as the absurd thought came to her that this situation could be so common, that they had a form specially designed for it.

Taking a deep breath, she lifted the purse and opened the car door. She had to resign herself to the fact that she was in unchartered territory and would have to just take things as they came. It wasn't a comfortable place for her to be, but she didn't have much choice.

She approached the front door, just as an officer dragged an obviously intoxicated man out of the back seat of his patrol car. The man was cursing the officer and his mother, and the officer continued to maneuver him toward the door to the precinct. The expression on the cop's face said this was not his first time in this situation and he didn't anticipate it being his last. Long-suffering was the expression Rose would have used to describe him.

She opened the door so the officer and his handcuffed prisoner could more easily enter the building.

With a nod of his head, he addressed her "Ma'am." She smiled weakly and wondered if his reaction would have been less respectful if he knew she was there to check on her alleged murderer husband. She mentally shook herself, trying to escape these surreal and morbid thoughts. She had received a phone call about three hours after David was taken from their home. It was Bruce Hivers, the lawyer that Terry had called. He had rushed down to the precinct and spoken with both the police and David. He didn't know a lot more than she did, and could only tell her that yes, he had been charged with murder and he was at the precinct. They had wanted to talk to him, but although criminal law wasn't the lawyer's area of expertise, he knew enough to shut it down. By the time he had arrived, David was in an interrogation room and had answered a few preliminary questions. Once they began to ask him more specific questions, he asked for his lawyer.

Bruce Hivers had called her and let her know that David was okay and holding up well. They were in the process of booking him and then he asked if she could come down to the precinct to talk to him about what was happening. He didn't want to leave just yet until he had a better idea of what was going on. He also wanted to talk to her about finding a criminal lawyer who would be able to take over. She suspected he wanted to find out how much money she was willing to pay before he decided which lawyer to call.

Kayla had returned to the house after cooling her heels at the precinct for a couple of hours. They had refused to tell her anything and ignored her demands to see her father. She had called to let Rose know she was returning just before Bruce called. It was just as well that Kayla didn't know there was a lawyer there talking to David and the police or she would probably have jumped all over him, demanding answers. Right now, Rose was not up to the hyper energy that would no doubt be rolling off her daughter. She needed to remain calm and to do that, she needed calm people around her. While she was tempted when Joshua offered to come with her, in the end, she sent him and Sarah home with a promise that she would keep them up to date whenever she learned more. She had insisted that Kayla and Brandon also pack up the kids and go home. That was harder to pull off, but in the end, Brandon stepped in and reminded Kayla that the kids would need to be put to bed soon and that they would be happier in their own beds. It was not the first time since her daughter had married that Rose was thankful for Brandon's calm demeanor. She often thought he was more like her than her own daughter as Brandon preferred calm and peace just as Rose did.

Her worries about what to do once she entered the precinct were unfounded as Bruce Hivers was waiting for her arrival and approached her as soon as she entered the lobby area.

"Mrs. Slater?" he asked as he extended his hand to shake hers.

Wow, she thought to herself, she must have a distinctive "my husband was just arrested for murder and I don't know what is happening" look on her face. Then she glanced around the waiting area and realized many people were either much younger than her or obviously high on either drugs or alcohol.

"Mr. Hivers, thank you for coming down so quickly," she said as they sat in the only two chairs that were next to each other. "I have so many questions, I don't know where to start."

"Don't worry about it, we will take this one step at a time," he reassured her with a pat on her forearm. He was an older gentleman with a receding hairline and kind eyes, and she immediately felt better knowing he was in charge of things right now. "I have a few questions for you first and we will go from there. It's my understanding that the police knocked on your door and arrested your husband, promptly, taking him away, correct?"

"Yes."

"Okay, and they told you that he was being arrested for murder?"

Rose took a deep breath, still not used to hearing those words about her husband. "Yes, that's correct."

"Okay, I've spoken to the police and then I had a few moments with your husband," he continued. "The police have indicated that he is being arrested on a cold case that they have recently re-opened. They have used new technology and as a result, they have decided to arrest your husband."

"But what murder? When? Who?" Rose's head was swirling with a million different thoughts and questions.

"A former girlfriend of David's was found murdered the summer after they graduated from high school," Bruce consulted his notes. "Her name was Rebecca Evans."

"Rebecca? Oh my God," Rose exclaimed. Of course— why wasn't that the first person she thought of when this happened?

"Did you know her?" Bruce asked.

"No, no, I didn't meet David until many years after she was killed," Rose explained. "But he told me about her and how her death has always haunted him."

"So, you know of her, but you never actually knew her?"

"That's right; what kind of testing did they do?"

"I don't have all the particulars just yet I'm afraid. Right now, I think it is more important that we get your husband an attorney who is more familiar with this area of law."

"Okay."

"Now, I have to ask you about your ability to pay," Bruce said. "Not because I'm worried about it myself but because we need to know if you will need a public defender or not. I can certainly recommend a good criminal lawyer, but if you can't afford one..."

"No, no, we can afford one, I don't want to leave this to chance. I think it's best if we hire the best lawyer we can right now so we can get this cleared up as soon as possible."

"Okay, I have someone in mind," said Bruce, "but I need to check and see if he is available first." He rose and when she made to follow him, he put his hand on her shoulder. "Wait here and I'll make some phone calls."

She watched him walk away from her as he pulled out his phone. She was still overwhelmed and uncertain but at least there were things they could do now. Now that she knew what they were facing, or at least some of it, she could take some control over the situation. They would get a lawyer who would help them get to the bottom of things and help put this behind them. She walked over to the front window of the precinct and glanced out. The wind had died down a bit and the darkness of night had settled in. She wasn't sure what time it was and the sense of unreality that had fallen over her when David was first taken away only deepened. She couldn't believe she was standing in a police precinct talking to a lawyer about her husband's murder charge. Her husband of 29 years. Her loving husband and devoted father. The man who had kissed Kayla's skinned knee and held the back of Joshua's bike when he was learning to ride.

"Mrs. Slater?" Bruce Hivers was back and standing behind her. She turned around and he handed her a business card. "This is the lawyer I would recommend. He can take this on and I told him you would call him."

She took the card from his hand and looked down at it. It was a plain card, white with black printing. Barry Lorman, JD, Criminal Defense Attorney, and a phone number, email address, and office address.

"So, I have to call him? I thought maybe you would just ask him to come here."

"There isn't much he can do here tonight; they will be doing paperwork with David and getting him booked in," Bruce explained gently. "Give Barry a call tonight and set something up to go in and talk to him tomorrow, then go home and try to get some sleep. There is nothing else anyone can do."

"You said you saw David? Is he okay?" Some part of her was hoping he would have sent a message to her through the lawyer. Something that would reassure her and tell her if there was something he needed or anything more she could do.

"Yes, he is fine—a bit stunned, but he'll be fine," Bruce told her.

"Can I phone him?"

"No, not tonight. To be honest I'm not sure when you will be able to contact him. That is why it's so important you get a criminal lawyer lined up. That way the lawyer can keep you informed about what is going on and when and how you can see him," Bruce explained. "Look, I know it must be really hard to feel so excluded from something that affects you so radically, but I'm afraid that's just the way it will be for a bit."

"Okay." She tried to take in what he was saying but it seemed so unbelievable that she couldn't talk to her own husband. That she couldn't see him. That she had no idea when she would be able to talk to him again. She took a shaky breath and closed her eyes briefly.

"I'm going to go now, is there anything else I can do for you?" The lawyer seemed unsure if he should leave her alone or not.

"No, no I'm okay. I'll make that phone call and go home," she reached for his hand and began to shake it. "Thank you so much for everything."

He left the precinct, and she watched as he got in his car and pulled out of the lot. She couldn't help but envy the fact that he could just leave the situation. She wished she could too. She reached into her purse and grabbed her phone. Punching in the number on the business card, she dialed Barry Lorman's phone number. He answered immediately and they planned to meet at his office in the morning.

Disconnecting the call, she left the building. Once in her car, she hesitated for a moment while her phone connected to the Bluetooth in her car. She brought up her son's number and dialed. She was reversing and pulling out and Joshua answered so quickly she wondered if he had been holding his phone and staring at it.

"Mom?"

"Hi Josh," she answered, weariness rolling over her like a wave. The stress of the last several hours was finally catching up with her. "I'm just leaving the precinct."

"Is he okay? What's going on?"

"I haven't seen him, but the lawyer Uncle Terry sent has and he said your dad is doing good. He gave me the name of a criminal lawyer and I'm going to meet him in the morning," she explained.

"But why have they arrested him? What murder are they talking about? Do they have the right David Slater?" The questions rolled out of Josh's mouth as though they had been pent up and were begging for release.

"One question at a time, hon. They arrested him because when your dad was a teenager his high school girlfriend was killed. They seem to think they have evidence that it was your dad who killed her. Yes, they have the right David Slater but obviously there has been some type of mistake."

"No kidding! A murder from when he was in high school? What possible reason could they have for thinking it was Dad?"

"I don't know exactly—they did some kind of testing," she said, rubbing her forehead wearily as she waited at a red light.

"That's so crazy."

"I know; part of me wishes I could just bury my head in the sand and pretend none of this was happening."

"Well, that sounds nice, but have you ever known anything in life to go away just because you ignored it?" Joshua asked, his voice lightening somewhat.

"No, but sometimes it's nice to pretend it would," she said. "I'm almost home now so I'm going to let you go now."

"Okay, is there anything I can do? I feel so helpless," Joshua asked.

"You could call your sister for me and fill her in," Rose said, only half joking. She knew her daughter would take it as a slight if she didn't call herself, but she also wished that someone else would deal with her drama. Rose wasn't sure she had enough left in her to deal with Kayla as well.

"I can do that if you want Mom," Joshua responded quickly. "But you know she won't be happy until she has had a chance to pump you for information herself."

Rose smiled and even though they couldn't see each other, she knew he would be smiling too. Their family was close-knit and loving but that didn't mean they didn't see each other's weaknesses. The moment of normalcy was just what she needed in the midst of everything that was happening.

"I'll call your sister once I get home," Rose reassured her son. "She's not going to be happy that she can't talk to Dad."

"Did they give you any indication when they are going to let him come home? Or when we can talk to him?'

"No, I think the lawyer that Uncle Terry sent was just there to make sure your dad didn't say anything incriminating to the police and to be the one to talk to us. Once I talk to the criminal lawyer tomorrow, I'm hoping to have more information."

"Poor Dad. If the lawyer doesn't know what's going on, then Dad probably doesn't know either—that would drive me mental," Joshua said, as the reality of the situation seemed to sink in.

They were silent then, as each of them processed what was happening. For David to go from participating in a happy family birthday celebration to being in jail and having no freedom or control over what was happening; to not being able to see or even talk to family members when he wanted to. As difficult as all this was for them, their hearts ached for him and what he must be going through.

The silence was broken when Rose's call-waiting on her phone beeped.

"I have to go, Josh. It looks like Kayla is on the other line."

"Okay, good luck with that," he chuckled.

"Hi Kayla," Rose answered the other line. "I've just left the precinct."

"Is Dad with you?" Kayla asked.

"No, they didn't release him," Rose explained. "I have a—"

"Why not? I thought the lawyer was sent to help him. What did the lawyer do? When are they going to let him come home?"

"Kayla, give me a minute to explain everything as I understand it." Rose waited to make sure Kayla wasn't going to ask more questions before she continued. "The lawyer Uncle Terry sent came and spoke with me. He has seen your dad and spoken with the police. He also gave me the name of a good criminal lawyer and I have an appointment to see him tomorrow."

"So, you didn't even get to see Dad?" Kayla asked, sounding distressed.

"No, the only person he is allowed to talk to right now is his lawyer."

"When is he allowed to talk to us then?" Kayla demanded.

"I'm not sure. I'm hoping to have more answers after talking to the criminal lawyer tomorrow."

"This isn't right—you only hear of these types of things happening in Communist countries. The police come and grab someone from their home and whisk them away and their family isn't allowed to see them."

"I know it seems unfair right now Kayla, but we need to just take things one step at a time," Rose explained patiently.

"Did the lawyer know why they were charging him? Who do they say they think he killed?"

"When your dad was in high school, a girl he was dating was killed and now they seem to think it was him," Rose repeated the story to her second child. "So, they don't have the wrong David Slater."

"His high school girlfriend? But that was, like, decades ago!" Kayla sounded both confused and a bit incredulous. "Why would they suddenly think he murdered some girl from when he was a kid?"

"I don't know Hon, something about some new kind of testing they did. We really don't have all the facts just yet. I'm hoping to learn more soon."

"This is just crazy," Kayla murmured.

"How are the kids? Were they able to settle down?" When Rose had left the house, Kayla and Brandon were busy gathering their children and preparing to take them home. The job was made harder as they were keyed up and distracted as they watched their Gramma prepare to leave. They wanted to know where Grampa was and if they could go and see him too. If Mom and Dad and Gramma got to go and visit Grampa, why couldn't they?

"Yes, it took a bit of work, but we got them settled," Kayla responded absently. "I want to come with you to see the criminal lawyer in the morning."

"No Kayla, that isn't necessary, I will be fine going myself."

"I know you'll be fine, but I have some questions I want to ask too," Kayla insisted.

"No Kayla. If you have questions let me know and I will see what I can find out, but I am going alone." It wasn't often that Rose put her foot down when it came to her daughter; she had learned over the years that sometimes it was best to pick her battles. She didn't need Kayla peppering the lawyer with questions and demanding answers. She needed to handle this herself and not worry about trying to protect her daughter's feelings. She had some questions that her daughter might not like to hear the answers to.

There was silence at the other end of the phone as Kayla realized that she was not going to get her way on this. She knew the tone of voice her mother was using and there was no point arguing with her.

"I'll text you questions as they come to me then," Kayla conceded. "What time is your appointment?"

"It's mid-morning so send me any questions you have by around 9-9:30." Rose felt bad that she didn't feel comfortable telling her daughter the exact time of the appointment, but she didn't want to find her daughter on her doorstep as she was getting ready to leave. Sometimes Kayla tried to just bull-in-a-China-shop her way through life.

They said their goodbyes, with Rose promising to let her daughter know if she heard anything more. For the rest of the drive home, Rose drove on autopilot. If someone had asked her about the road conditions or what lights had been red, she wouldn't have been able to provide any specifics.

All she could remember was driving through the night and thinking that there was a storm building, and that she was going to have to dig deep to find the strength required to take care of her family.

Chapter 5

The Past

"Damn it Jimmy, quit'cha crying or so help me god, I'll give you something to cry about," Nancy Kowalski yelled out the back door into the yard that was surrounded by a rickety fence that at one time had been blue. Now it was a washed-out color full of nicks and scratches and missing slats.

Little Jimmy was lying in the dirt, holding his knee to his chest, and trying to stifle a sob. There was a cut on his knee about half an inch long. He had gotten it when he went down the rusty slide that had been nailed to a half-dead tree. A piece of metal was sticking out and he hadn't noticed it until he felt the burning tear and the pain that followed.

He pulled his shirt towards his knee and tried to stem the flow of blood that was dribbling down his calf. He knew there was no point in asking his mother for a bandage as she would just laugh and ask him if he thought they were rich or something. Then she would tell him to use his shirt and to quit dripping blood all over the kitchen floor, had he been born in a barn or something?

That was one of his mother's favorite topics—where he had been born, how he had been born, and whether he was worth loving or not. He wasn't sure why she found it such a fascinating topic, but he knew she must, or she wouldn't keep bringing it up as much as she did. As always, he concluded that it must not have been a very happy event for her. In fact, he was sure of it. That was probably why he didn't have a birthday like the other kids in kindergarten. His mom told him that when he grew up and showed his mettle then, and only then, would he have earned a proper birthday.

It didn't make much sense to Jimmy and try as he might, he couldn't figure out what a mettle was anyhow. The blood had slowed to a trickle and he inspected the cut a bit closer. It wasn't too bad, as far as cuts go. He had seen worse. Like the time Tommy down the street had fallen and hit his head while he was riding his bike. There was so much blood, that Jimmy swore someone could swim in it. And the cut on his head was twice as long as the one on his knee. It was so deep Jimmy could see bone, and boy, did Tommy scream. Jimmy didn't think he had ever heard anything that loud before or since. But everyone knew that Tommy was a wimp. Not like Jimmy—he was no wimp. He could take a cut or a thumping and barely cry at all. He had learned to grit his teeth and swallow real hard so he could keep the cries way back in his throat. No one was going to be able to call Jimmy Daniels a pussy.

Of course, that didn't stop his mom from telling him he was a baby. She said he got his feelings hurt at the drop of a hat. When she saw his bottom lip quiver, even if he managed not to cry, she made sure he knew that she had noticed. "Be a man, Jimmy!" she would berate him. "No one is going to look out for you in life, so you better learn to grow a thicker skin than that."

Jimmy stood up, stretched his leg, and then shook it a bit to see if it started bleeding again. When he knew it wouldn't bleed all over Mom's kitchen floor, he headed back towards the house. He would go in and not say anything about the cut. Maybe Mom would notice he wasn't crying about it and tell him he was growing up to be a big man. She might even tell him she loved him and give him a kiss on his cheek like she did after she had been out with her friends.

Chapter 6

Present Day

The sun's rays peeking through the bottom of her bedroom blinds managed to find Rose's eyelids and it felt as though they were piercing a hole in her retinas. Groaning, she rolled over, pulling her duvet up over her head. For a split second, her mind was a blank slate but then it all came crashing in on her consciousness. David. Arrest. Murder.

"Shit," she exclaimed as she pulled the duvet down to her sides and laid still, arms straight. She glanced at the clock at her bedside, grimacing when she realized she had overslept. Flinging back the sheets, she stood up and headed to the bathroom. She had an hour before she had to leave for the lawyer's office.

After she had showered and dressed, she went into the kitchen to make some breakfast. While she was waiting for the bread to toast, she checked her phone to see if Kayla had sent her any questions she wanted Rose to ask the lawyer. There were several. She read over them and realized that there was not one question that Kayla had texted that Rose was not also wondering about. One of the things that was on her to-do list before she left this morning was to jot down the questions she wanted to ask the lawyer, just so she wouldn't forget anything. Now she could just use the texts as her notes. Smiling, she sent a text to her daughter, thanking her for taking the time to put down the questions in writing. It would help her immensely.

Once again, Rose mused that life had an odd symmetry to it; everyone had their own strengths and weaknesses and sometimes you needed to back off and let what you perceived as someone else's weakness strengthen you.

She drove to the lawyer's office with a to-go coffee mug beside her and the radio blasting out classic rock songs. The station had been one of Rose's favorites for years now because they had never once, to her knowledge, ever played a rap song. It was rare that they didn't play a song that would take her back to a happier time in her life; one that was more carefree and seemed so much simpler than the present, no matter what was going on. And today, she needed all the positive thoughts she could muster.

She was belting out the last chorus of "I Love Rock and Roll" with Joan Jett when she came to a red light in front of the office building that housed Barry Lorman's legal office. As the song faded, the announcer's voice came on with breaking news: a local man had been arrested the previous night for a murder that dated back to the early 1990s—more details on the hour.

Rose froze and the saliva in her mouth evaporated as her stomach lurched. She hadn't considered the possibility that the media would become involved, especially before they even knew what was going on. She wondered if they would use David's name when they provided more information. She imagined their friends hearing about it on their drive to work. Once again, the feeling from the previous night returned; a feeling of everything being out of control, of her not having any say over what was happening to her or her family.

The sound of cars honking behind her jolted her into action as she realized the light had turned green. Shaken, she drove through the intersection and turned into the office parking lot. She was going to have to get a hold of herself before she inadvertently caused an accident.

~~~~

"Hi, I'm Rose Slater. I have an appointment with Mr. Lorman?" She told the smartly dressed receptionist who had been typing something on her computer when Rose walked in. At least she assumed that is what the girl had been doing, although how she was able to do so with her claw-like nails, Rose had no idea.

"Yes, Mr. Lorman is expecting you. Follow me."

She followed the receptionist to the left of her desk and down a long hallway. There were windows into mostly empty rooms with glossy, expensive-looking tables that had remote controls and what looked like complicated but fancy-looking boxes of buttons.

"Can I get you something to drink Mrs. Slater?" The receptionist asked as she opened one of the doors and ushered her in.

"No, I think I'm okay, thank you."

"No problem, let me know if you change your mind. Mr. Lorman will be with you shortly."

Rose sat down at the highly polished table and ran her hands along the top of it. She wondered if she had done the right thing by telling Mr. Hivers not to worry about how expensive the criminal lawyer he recommended to them might be. It was obvious that no expense had been spared in furnishing the office.

"Mrs. Slater!" A man who was much younger than she anticipated entered the room. He was perhaps in his mid-thirties, with a youthful, boyish appearance. His light brown hair was cut short and showed his slightly thinning scalp. He was smiling broadly as he shook her hand.

"Please, call me Rose," she insisted.

"Great, if you don't mind calling me Barry."

She smiled at him, feeling anxious to move things along and find out what was going to happen.

"Do you mind if I record us? It won't be used for anything except to help jog my memory of our conversation," he asked her. She nodded for him to go ahead, and he reached over to the control panel she had noticed earlier and pushed a button.

"Okay Rose, you are here to chat with me because your husband was arrested and charged with murder yesterday, is that correct?"

"Yes."

"Okay, and you are interested in retaining me to represent your husband?"

"Yes, I am. Bruce Hivers recommended you."

"Right, great guy Bruce."

Rose smiled faintly. She wasn't feeling capable of engaging in a lot of small talk right now.

"Bruce outlined the basic situation for me and I will be in touch to make sure the courts know that I will be the lawyer on record for your husband."

"Thank you."

"Now I know in cases like this, things can seem overwhelming and this is a system you are not used to dealing with, so I want you to feel free to ask any questions you have, and I promise I will try to give you the best answers I have. However, I can almost guarantee that you have questions I won't be able to answer just yet." He smiled at her, as though to soften the truth he was outlining for her.

"My biggest question is: what now?"

"Well, your husband has been charged. That means they have gone through the necessary paperwork to put your husband in jail and start the process. They will have fingerprinted him, taken his picture, taken his personal items, and issued his jail clothes. He will have slept in the jail last night, waiting to hear about his first appearance in court and his bail hearing." He spoke slowly and in a calm voice. She knew he must have gone through this explanation many times, but she was grateful he wasn't rushing or acting as though this was something she should already know.

"He will appear in court, and we will ask for bail so he can be released and go home."

"How soon will that happen?"

"That usually happens within about 48 hours of someone being arrested, unless it is a weekend or they are really, really busy."

"Okay, so probably by tomorrow sometime? He will have to spend another night in jail?"

Barry was silent for a moment as he looked over the table at her. He seemed to be weighing his next words carefully.

"I think it's only fair to let you know that when the charge is murder, obtaining bail can be very difficult."

She stared at him as what he had just said began to sink in. She took a deep breath. "Go on."

"Part of my job is going to be explaining to the judge why he should receive bail, and that's what I'm going to be working on today," he continued to explain to her.

"When will we be able to talk to him or see him?" she asked.

"I will have to speak to the officers at the jail, but I suspect we'll need to wait for the outcome of the bail hearing. The best thing you can do right now is work with me to build a case for bail."

"I can do that!" Rose felt as though she was reaching for a lifeline. She wanted to do something, anything, to help her husband.

"I need to know everything there is to know about your husband: how many children you have, if he's a little league coach, does he volunteer for anything? We will want to show the court he is a stable and upstanding citizen and how he is no danger to the community or a flight risk."

"We have two adult children and three grandchildren," she told him. "He isn't a little league coach, but he volunteers at the homeless shelter once a week." As she spoke it struck her as odd that he just sat across from her and nodded; then she remembered that their conversation was being recorded.

For the next hour, they went over David's life—from the number of years they had been married to his career path, where they had lived, and if he had received any awards. What did his grandchildren call him? Grampa? Pappa? Pop-Pop? Some of the questions seemed random and Rose would raise an eyebrow in his direction but he reassured her that even if he didn't use everything, it would help paint an accurate picture of David's life.

At the end of the hour, Barry wrapped things up and asked her if she had any further questions.

"Bruce mentioned that they had arrested him because of some new testing. Do you know what that is all about?"

"I'm afraid I don't have those kinds of details just yet; that will come as we go through this process. There will be a time when they have to turn over all the evidence to us and we will get a chance to go through it. But I have to warn you, this is a long and arduous process. The answers to your questions will never seem to be there when you want them and things will move slower than you ever thought possible."

Rose sat back in her chair, feeling as though the wind had been completely knocked out of her sails. Barry watched her reaction but didn't say a word, he just let her process what he had said. He had watched many people sit in the chair she was in right now and everyone had a different reaction, but he knew it was a pivotal point in their relationship. They would either choose to trust him or they would run out screaming and demanding a different lawyer.

It didn't take long for him to see which direction this conversation would take as a look of resignation slowly came over Rose's face. She sat up straight in her chair, reached for her purse, and then stood up. She reached her hand out to shake his.

"Well, then I better not keep you from getting this moving, Mr. Lorman."

He smiled to himself and decided he liked this woman. She was smart and strong and that was exactly what she was going to need to be in the days and months ahead.

Chapter 7

The Past

David slammed the tailgate shut and walked over to his friends who were gathered by the fire.

"Want a beer?" He held out a bottle and his friend Chris gratefully accepted it.

"Thanks, dude," Chris said as he tossed his empty into a nearby bush. There were four of them standing around the fire tonight. The mood was subdued as they all gazed into the flames.

Suddenly, David let out an ear-splitting "Whoopee!" and raised his beer in the air as though to toast his friends. "Here's to our future!"

The boys began to laugh and throw back their beers as they all started talking at once. They were at a strange point in their lives, teetering on the precipice of adulthood. They wanted to leap forward with all they had but they seemed to realize that this night and this time in their lives was special, and they would never be able to return to it.

They would be heading their separate ways in a couple of weeks and having experiences and living a life without each other.

They had been together for as far back as they could remember. Growing up in each other's homes fueled by homemade cookies, orange soda, and Spiderman Band-Aids. David could close his eyes and see the water stain pattern that was on the ceiling of Chris's bedroom. Wade knew the sound Chris's sister made when her father walked up and changed the channel on their TV set. Terry knew that Chris's mother made meatloaf every Sunday night and that his dad drank a bit too much most Fridays after work.

By ten that evening, they were all perched on logs, leaning into the fire, elbows resting on their knees, trying to warm their chilled hands.

As Wade peeled back a piece of the label on his bottle, he asked Chris who was sitting to his right, "So, when are you leaving?"

"Next Friday. Gonna drive down and get settled in for a couple of days."

"Your parents taking you?"

"Of course, they'll hang on to me until the very last second."

The boys smiled as they thought about their families and the difficulty they were having in letting their boys grow up.

"When do you start?" Chris asked.

"Monday morning," Wade said, referring to his new job as an apprentice electrician. "I'm a bit stressed by it."

"Why?" Chris was surprised to hear Wade say this.

"I know, it's stupid. I'm not like you guys going off to college, moving away and everything but if I screw up, what am I gonna do then?"

"You're not gonna screw up Wade; you got brains, you work hard so you'll be fine."

"You freaking out about having to do some work, buddy?" David chimed in.

"No, I was just saying I don't know how I'm gonna handle all the pretty young ladies in town once you fools leave!"

The boys laughed and David tossed a beer cap in Wade's direction.

"Do you think we'll ever be back here like this again?" Chris suddenly asked.

"What do you mean? Of course, we will. Why wouldn't we?" David responded with surprise in his voice.

"Well, everyone says once you're finished with school and go to college and work, you never really come back; you say you will, but you don't," Chris spoke quietly and shuffled his feet in the dirt.

"Not us!" insisted Wade. "We're not like everyone else!"

"Can't argue with that," Terry chimed in, a smirk on his face.

David leaned over to grab another beer while declaring, "Oh, we'll be back!"

"Damn right," they all shouted in unison and then burst out laughing.

They spent the next few hours reminiscing and sharing stories of their exploits throughout the years. Sparks snapped into the black sky as the boys added broken twigs and fallen logs to the fire to keep the cold night at bay.

By the time the stories slowed down and the moments of silence became longer, the thick smell of burning wood was clinging to their clothes and hair.

Just before midnight, they threw dirt and sand on the fire to put it out.

After exchanging back slaps and good-natured air boxing, Wade jumped into Terry's pickup. After some back and forth, Chris finally convinced David to let him drive the LTD.

"So, has Rebecca calmed down yet?" Chris asked David almost as soon as they pulled out.

"She'll be fine," David responded with a sigh. "She'll come around eventually."

"I don't know man, she's pretty pissed. I talked to her at school today and she was pretty twisted. I think she figures you might still come round to her way of thinking."

"I don't know how to get through to her. I don't know why she can't understand that I need to work this summer," David said, the frustration evident in his voice. "To tell you the truth, it's got to the point where I'm beginning to look forward to leaving because every day it's the same thing. She just keeps on at me about it, she won't let up."

"Remember when you guys first started going out—I warned you she was a handful," Chris chuckled. "Can't say you didn't know what you were getting into."

"Thanks for the sympathy, Bud," David shook his head as he looked over at his friend. "Easy for you to laugh."

"Hey, she's Rebecca. It's the price you pay," Chris elaborated.

"Ha! I'm thinking that's not how relationships are supposed to work," David protested.

Chris laughed and playfully jabbed at David's shoulder. "Well, they do say that relationships are give and take."

The two drove along in companionable silence, the sound of the road humming under the Ford's tires. Chris slowed down as he approached the turn-off to take them back into town.

"Hey, why don't I go by the ball diamonds before I drop you off?" Chris asked quietly.

"Sure," David agreed, the abundant amount of beer he had consumed all evening had dulled his senses and so he didn't question his friend. Chris took the first left after the high school and entered the parking lot of the recreation grounds. Pulling up behind the bleachers, Chris put the car in park and David turned towards his friend.

"What's up?"

"Let's go for a walk, I need some fresh air," Chris responded.

"Sure, but I gotta get going soon, I have to be up early in the morning."

"Yeah, no problem." Before opening the door, Chris nervously rubbed the palms of his hands on his jeans.

The two boys passed under the bleachers and walked toward the baseball diamond. David was quiet, walking slowly and deliberately to make sure he didn't weave. He was beginning to wonder why his friend wanted to come here and waited patiently for his friend to bring up whatever was on his mind. He tried not to show his impatience, but he was anxious to find out why they were here. After a couple of minutes, Chris spoke up, his voice quiet and low.

"Do you think you can ever truly know someone?" His question caused David to momentarily stop walking.

"Why? What makes you ask that?" he asked Chris.

"Just wanted to know what you thought."

"I don't know. I guess you can to a certain extent, but you can't get in someone's mind completely, right?"

"Right."

"What's this about, Chris?"

Chris kept walking as though he hadn't heard the question. He thrust his hands deep into the front pockets of his jeans. He tipped his head back and looked up at the stars, twinkling in the night sky. "Do you think people can choose whom they love?"

"I don't know, I never really thought about it," David said. "Why?"

"I just..." Chris seemed at a loss for words and David waited patiently for him to say more.

After a couple of minutes passed and it became obvious that Chris wasn't going to say anything, David decided to try to lighten the mood.

"Wait, don't tell me, let me guess: you've fallen in love with Miss Haustmeir, haven't you?"

"You got me, I tried to hide it, but true love needs to be expressed!" Chris exclaimed and they both burst into laughter. Miss Haustmeir was the school librarian who was about 80 years old and lived with her cats in the house she grew up in and inherited from her parents. There had been a rumor going around when they were in elementary school that she had had her parents stuffed when they died and that they were sitting in her front living room, keeping her company when she returned from work every day.

The laughter seemed to break the tension and finally, Chris spoke up and told David that he had been wondering if it was a good idea to ask Ashley out.

"Ashley? Really? That surprises me, man," David said. "I thought you just saw her as a friend all these years."

"Well, yeah. And I do. I was just thinking about it, but I don't know if it makes sense what with us all going off to college and stuff soon,"

Chris elaborated. "Never mind, it's not a big deal, I'll probably just leave it be."

"Well, that's up to you, of course, but frankly I think you should count yourself lucky if she agreed to go out with a degenerate like you," David said, keeping his face as poker straight as possible.

"You're probably right," Chris said with a broad smile.

"Now if that is all, how about we get going?" David asked.

"Sounds good, I'll beat you to the car," Chris said as he broke into a sprint, taking David unawares.

It was only later that night, as he lay in bed going over the evening's events that David realized that Chris's initial question about whether we can choose whom we love didn't align with him wondering if he should ask Ashley out. He hadn't talked about Ashley as though he was in love with her. As he felt the room spin around him, he had an uneasy feeling that he had let his friend down somehow. But for the life of him, he couldn't figure out how.

Chapter 8

The Past

"Hit him! Hit him again!" the crowd roared as the two fourth graders rolled around in the dirt. Michael grinned as he pushed Jimmy's face into the dirt.

"Down in the mud just like you like it," Michael said.

"Oink, oink, oink" the other kids began saying, their voices all joining as one. There was rarely a school day that went by when Jimmy didn't hear an "oink" being tossed in his direction. The kids at school took pleasure in the fact that he often showed up in dirty clothes and smelly, greasy hair.

Jimmy looked around at the ground and spied a small rock, a pebble really. It would have to do. He reached for it and bringing his arm to the side and backward, he swung out at his assailant.

"Hey!" Michael cried out as the hard edge of the pebble connected with his cheekbone. A small red line appeared where the pebble had broken skin. "What the hell do you think you're doing, piggy?!"

Where before he had been having fun terrorizing Jimmy, now he was mad. He swung his elbow at Jimmy, aiming wildly. He didn't connect but managed to throw himself off balance and his opponent made the most of it by landing a punch to Michael's solar plexus.

"Ooooph," the noise Michael made sounded like a leak from an air mattress. He gasped and tried to inhale air into his lungs.

"What on earth is going on here?" Mrs. Klein strode towards the boys. The children who were gathered around them scattered before the fifth-grade teacher. "Jimmy and Michael, what are you doing?"

"He hit me, Mrs. Klein!" Michael was clutching his stomach and showed his face to the teacher.

"Did you hit him, Jimmy?" Standing next to him, she put her hands on her hips and frowned down at him. Jimmy stood, his head down. "Look at me!" She reached out and lifted his head by grasping his chin.

"Answer me, Jimmy: did you hit Michael?"

"Yes."

"Get inside now," she pointed angrily to the front door of the school. "Wait for me at the office."

~~~~

"Michael told me what happened, Jimmy, and I want you to know that I am not going to tolerate such behavior from a student in my school."

"Yes sir," Jimmy said, his head down, eyes on the ground.

"What do you have to say for yourself?" Mr. Masterson demanded. "Look at me Jimmy!"

Jimmy tried to force himself to look at the principal, but no matter how much he willed them, his eyes remained fixed on the floor. He knew that if Mr. Masterson saw his eyes, he would see the darkness in them and he couldn't let that happen.

Frustrated, the principal placed his hand on Jimmy's shoulder and pushed him down to sit on a chair. Then he reached out to push a button on his phone and told his secretary to send in the school nurse.

"Mrs. Gravlin, Jimmy here decided to start a fight with Michael Schmidt. I would like you to take a look and make sure he doesn't have any cuts, scrapes, or broken bones that we need to tell his parents about when they come and get him."

Jimmy's heart sank and he felt the back of his throat constrict. He knew there was no way that he would be able to talk the principal out of calling his parents. Everyone knew that the principal was a hardnose and did what he said he was going to do, and that nothing could change his mind—not tears and no amount of promises or cajoling could change his mind.

Nurse Gravlin told him to stand up and, slipping her hand under his chin, she raised his head to inspect his face for cuts or bruising, then she asked him if any part of him hurt. He told her he was okay, and that nothing hurt. She lifted his hands and turned them over to inspect them, then she reached for his shirt sleeve, to push it up to check his arms. He jerked his arm away from her and quickly backed up.

"Jimmy Daniels!" The nurse admonished him, reaching for his arm.

"I'm okay, you don't have to check me," Jimmy protested.

"Well, Michael didn't fare so well. He has a cut on his face and a very sore stomach," she said.

Jimmy crossed his arms across his chest as he backed up against the wall of the principal's office. He felt trapped and his heart was pounding through his threadbare shirt. His parents were on their way and Jimmy only had to fend these people off until they arrived.

A moment earlier, the thought of his parents being called had struck fear into him but now he was waiting anxiously for them to arrive and save him from being exposed by Nurse Gravlin.

The nurse threw up her arms in frustration and looked at the principal who raised his shoulders in resignation. "Just leave him be. I've got to get these minutes for the school board written up and I've wasted enough time on this already."

The school secretary popped her head in and said, "Principal Masterson, Jimmy's father is on his way here."

"Thank you, can you please have Jimmy sit outside the office while we wait?"

The secretary jerked her head toward the hallway as she looked at Jimmy, her lips pursed and a frown between her brows. Jimmy moved quickly out of the office and sat on one of the hard wooden chairs in the hallway. After a few minutes, he began to swing his legs

back and forth under the chair, causing the chair to wiggle and the
screws holding it together to squeak in rhythm with his legs.

"Stop that, Jimmy," the secretary glared at him from her desk. He
stopped swinging his legs and stared at the picture hanging on the
wall on the other side of the hallway. It was a picture of a farmer's
field and a small red barn. The sky had wisps of white clouds floating
in the sky and Jimmy wondered why the artist would paint a picture
of a field. Weren't there more exciting things to look at than a field?
Why would he decide to paint something so boring? Maybe he
knew it was going to be hung in a school principal's hallway and he
wanted to make sure the kids who were waiting there wouldn't be
entertained by his art.

He had been sitting there for about 20 minutes when his father
walked in down the hallway. He passed Jimmy without saying a word
or acknowledging him and stopped at the secretary's desk.

"Mr. Daniels for Mr. Masterson," he announced.

The secretary buzzed the principal's office and told him that Jimmy's
dad had arrived.

"You can go in now Mr. Daniels," she told him.

The door to the principal's office closed with a bang behind his father
and both Jimmy and the secretary jumped in their seats. There were a
few quiet moments when they began to hear shouting coming from
the principal's office. The secretary looked up from her work and at
the principal's door, then at Jimmy. After making eye contact briefly,
he resumed looking at the picture on the opposite wall and she went
back to her work.

A few minutes later, his father came stomping out of the office,
grabbed Jimmy by the arm, and hauled him out of the school. His
father didn't allow Jimmy any time to stand up so he could follow
him. Jimmy knew if he could just plant his feet firmly on the ground,
he would be able to run to keep up with his father, but he could feel

his shoulder beginning to burn from the force of being pulled across the parking lot and he continued to stumble.

His father opened the back door of the car and threw Jimmy unceremoniously in the backseat. He opened the driver's door and sat down behind the wheel. Pulling out of the lot, his father remained quiet, and Jimmy knew this was bad. Real bad. When he was angry, his father yelled. When he was past angry and was just scary mad, he didn't say anything. Jimmy focused on his bladder. Whatever he did, he had to make sure he didn't pee his pants. He had done that once when his Father was mad at him and had been forced to sit in it for two days. Then he had to go to school that Monday still wearing the pants. They were dry by then, but the stink was obvious and the kids never let him forget about it.

His father looked straight ahead as he turned off the road and onto their driveway. When he pulled up to the house, Jimmy opened his car door and stepped out. His father grabbed him by his ear and pulled him toward the house.

"Get. In. The House. Now." he spat out.

Jimmy walked as fast as he could while trying not to trip over anything. Because his father had his ear, his head was turned to the side, and he couldn't completely see where he was walking. He made it in without tripping and his father threw him forward and he landed near the coffee table in their living room.

"Don't. Move."

He heard his father open the dresser drawer in his parent's bedroom and he knew what was coming. He could only hope this was all his father had planned. If it was, he could bear it. He would grit his teeth and try not to cry, but he could do it. He had done so many times before.

Entering the living room, his father had the well-worn belt in his right hand.

"Why the hell can't you behave?" his father asked, his voice ominously low. Jimmy wasn't sure if he was supposed to answer or not. It was usually best to wait and see.

"Answer me, boy!" his father snapped the belt towards him, and he winced.

"I'm sorry Father, but Michael started it." He felt the sting of the belt across his lower legs before he had finished speaking.

"Don't lie to me, boy! The principal told me what happened! Not only fighting in the schoolyard but disrespecting the school nurse!"

"I wasn't disrespecting her, I promise Father!" Jimmy knew better than to argue, but the injustice of it wouldn't keep him quiet. "She wanted to roll up my sleeves and I didn't want her to see—"

"See what boy? What didn't you want her to see?" His father reached forward grabbed his son's forearm and squeezed tightly. Jimmy winced from the pain. "Maybe you didn't want her to see just how bad of a boy you really are, huh?"

Jimmy knew there was no correct answer and so he kept quiet. The pain from where his father was pressing down on his bruises kept him focused on his breathing and the rhythm of the clock in the hallway.

"Now pull your trousers down and lean over the couch." He suddenly let go of his son and pushed him towards the sofa.

"Yes Father," Jimmy did as he was instructed, knowing that the sooner he complied, the sooner it would be over. His father had hit him with the leather belt about five times before Jimmy heard his mother's voice.

"What is going on here?" she asked indignantly.

The knot in Jimmy's stomach tightened and he knew the belt was only the beginning. There would be no escape for him today.

Chapter 9

Present Day

Rose lay on her bed and stared at the ceiling. She had phoned both her children and filled them in on what Barry had to say and what the next couple of days would look like. Of course, they were both frustrated that they couldn't see or even call their dad and they had questions about the evidence and why the police had arrested him in the first place. All questions Rose had no way of answering. Now, with the afternoon stretching ahead all she could do was wait to hear about the bail situation. She tried to remember everything David had told her about his high school sweetheart. She knew that it had broken him up when it happened and that the entire town was left reeling. His friendship group was never the same afterward, although David could never really say if it was a natural parting of ways as they all headed off to their lives or whether it was because of the girl's sudden and violent death. Her death. That was something David hadn't talked much about. All he had said was that she had been found dead in a remote area near her parents' lake cabin.

Rose's stomach felt queasy. This is what they were accusing her husband of doing. What possible evidence could they have found so many years after the event? David had told her that when it happened, they thought it might have been someone who was transient and just moving through the area. They had questioned David, but he had been working at a camp at the time she was killed and a group of them went to watch a movie at the local theatre the day she was murdered. None of this made any sense.

Apart from his alibi, her husband was simply not a violent man. He had never lifted a hand to her in the 29 years they had been together. There was no way, never.

She hadn't slept much last night, and the stress and tension were beginning to catch up with her. Her eyes grew heavy, and she nodded off.

She was running through the woods, the branches slapping her face and her bare legs. Her heart pounded in her ears, keeping time with her ragged breathing. Someone was behind her, feet slapping at the underbrush with every step. She felt a sound tear from her throat, erupting into a blood-curdling scream. Hands touched her skin, grabbed her by the shoulders and she screamed louder, batting at the hands holding her...

Waking up with a start, Rose saw a dark figure lean over her and she scrambled back towards her headboard.

"Wake up! Mom, wake up!" As her eyes focused, Rose realized it was Kayla in her bedroom, shaking her violently.

"What? What?" she asked her daughter, looking around the room, bewildered.

"Mom! What were you dreaming about? You were screaming at the top of your lungs!"

"I don't know." Breathing hard, Rose pressed her hands to her chest, "I didn't hear you come in."

"I figured that. I rang the doorbell a couple of times, and you didn't come," Kayla explained. "I knew you had to be home because the car was here, so I came in."

"I must have really crashed, I didn't hear a thing," Rose ran her hand through her hair and rubbed the sleep out of her eyes. "What time is it?"

"It's almost three," Kayla said as she pulled back the curtains on the bedroom windows.

"Oh, my goodness," Rose scrambled to her feet. "I had no intention of sleeping that long."

"Well, you must have been really tired, to zonk out like that," Kayla said. "Were you having a nightmare? You were really screaming, I thought someone was attacking you."

"Yeah, it was a nightmare. Not surprising I guess considering the last 24 hours."

"Come on, let's go to the kitchen and I'll make us some tea," Kayla suggested.

"Was there a reason you came over?" Rose asked as she followed her daughter out of the bedroom.

"I wanted to talk to you about our plans for Dad."

"Our plans?"

"Yes, plans. Now come sit down and let me get some tea into you. Do you have a snack we can have with it?"

"There's still some leftover birthday cake." Most of Phoenix's birthday cake had gone home with him and his parents last night, but Kayla had insisted on leaving some with her parents.

"I'm thinking we need to sit down and figure out a game plan for Dad. He is going to be counting on us to get him out of that awful jail and home with us,"

"I understand that Hon, but I don't know what else we can do." Rose sat down at the kitchen table and played with the salt and pepper shakers that were sitting in the middle. She was still feeling a bit groggy and wished she could just sit in silence for a while until she was completely awake.

"Well, for one, I am going to do some research on this lawyer you talked to. I want to make sure that he is good at his job," Kayla said, sounding slightly skeptical.

"I looked him up online last night and he seems very well regarded and he was recommended by Uncle Terry's friend," Rose found herself getting defensive at the idea that she hadn't done due diligence. "And anyway, I put down a retainer and have already signed paperwork for him to defend your father."

"Hmm," was Kayla's only response as she plugged in the kettle.

"Kayla, you are going to have to trust me on some things, and having your father's best interest at heart is one of those things."

"Oh, I know that! I didn't mean to make it sound like I didn't, I'm just so aggravated," Kayla dished up two slices of birthday cake and practically threw them on their plates. "What are we supposed to do now?"

"Sit down hon," Rose pushed out the chair across from her and gestured for her daughter to sit down. They sat across from each other and picked at their desserts. "If it's any consolation, I feel like pulling out my hair and screaming in frustration too."

"Maybe that is what your nightmare was really about," Kayla smiled at her mother over the kitchen table and Rose was pleased that her daughter was still able to find some humor in the situation.

"It probably was," Rose chuckled.

They sat in silence until the kettle began to whistle and Kayla prepared their tea.

"I'm sorry to have to mention this but..." Kayla looked down at her mug and her spoon clinked against the side as she stirred. "The case was mentioned in the news. They didn't mention Dad's name but I'm sure that will come out soon."

"I know, I heard it on my way to the lawyer's this morning. That is one thing you can do if you want to keep busy."

"What's that?"

"Figure out how we handle any media calls that come our way. We should make sure we know what to say so we don't make things worse," Rose explained.

"I can do that! Gwen, my friend from college who does media relations for a big utility company can probably give me some tips," Kayla reached for her phone and began to tap away on the screen.

Rose needed to pick up some groceries and she pulled out her phone to make a list of items she didn't want to forget. What should one get to eat when one's husband was in jail for murder? She couldn't remember the last time she had to cook for one. She had just decided to stick to the usual when the doorbell rang at the same time that Kayla's phone began to buzz. She left her daughter talking to her friend and went to answer the door.

Without a thought, she opened the door wide and was shocked when she came face to face with a wall of bodies, pushing and shoving to get in front of her.

"What do you have to say about your husband?"

"Did he do it, Mrs. Slater?"

"Did you know?"

Microphones were thrust in her face and huge camera lenses from what she assumed were video cameras stared at her with great, intruding eyes. She was frozen on the spot, unable to make her legs move.

Kayla came up behind her and grabbed the door, pushing her mother out of the way.

"Get back!" she commanded. "You are trespassing, and the police have been called."

"We just want to know how the family is holding up!"

"The family will give a statement later today; you will all be notified when that will be, Now get off our property!"

Rose watched in surprise as the crowd backed away and began to disperse. The door slammed behind Kayla as she turned to face her mother. "What were you thinking Mom? You can't just open the door to media like that!"

Staring at her daughter, the magnitude of what was happening washed over her and both her face and her body began to crumple. She leaned up against the hallway wall and slid down it, sobs wracking her body.

"I'm sorry, I'm sorry," Rose heard herself say repeatedly. She wasn't sure why she was apologizing, but it seemed as though she had failed somehow. It was all too much, and she couldn't help but feel like she should have a better handle on things than she did. The shock and stress of the last day seemed to rest on her shoulders and beat her down to the ground. She felt Kayla slide down the wall beside her and wrap her arms around her shoulders.

"Shhhhhh..." Kayla ran her hand down her mother's hair, soothing her as if she was a young child. "It's okay Mom, it's okay."

It took a few minutes, but eventually Rose's crying was reduced to the odd sniffle and a ragged, involuntary hiccough. Finally, she leaned the back of her head against the hallway wall and stared up at the ceiling. Her daughter had handed her a tissue at some point, and it was balled up in her hand, a soggy mess.

"Feel better, baby?" Kayla asked and the two women burst into laughter. When Joshua was very small, he had suffered from some type of stomach bug and his mother had asked him when he had finished vomiting if he "felt better, baby?" He was so confused and wanted to know what a better baby was. His toddler's voice made it sound like someone saying butterball and everyone laughed. It had become a running family joke. One of those things where an outsider would wonder why they thought it was so funny, but for them, it was a piece of their history as a family and filled them with warmth and a sense of connection to each other.

"Yes, I do feel better baby!" Rose patted her daughter's arm where it lay wrapped around her shoulders. She began to rise and wipe off her pants which were dusty from sitting on the floor.

"Why did you tell them we would be making a statement?"

"That's what my friend Gwen said to do. She explained that if the news started to hound us, it was best to just give one statement, let them take their pictures ask a couple of questions, and be done with it. Depending on how big this thing gets, she said it might not keep them away for long, but it should help for a bit."

"I had no idea it was going to be this crazy." A shudder passed through Rose as she thought of the horde of reporters on her front step. "I wonder when they released your father's name."

"I don't know, but it must have just happened. When I was driving over here the radio hadn't used his name yet," Kayla mused. "They sure move fast."

Just then, the landline started to ring.

"Let me answer that in case it's media." Watching her daughter head for the phone, Rose was amused by how easily she had taken control of the situation. She saw so much of herself in Kayla; she only felt good when she had a job to do and a purpose.

"Mom, it's Stacey," Kayla passed her mother the cordless phone.

"Hello?"

"What the hell is going on Rosie?" No one got away with calling her Rosie except her best friend of the past ten years. "I just flew back into town and what do I hear on the radio on the way home from the airport? The entire world has blown up."

"It feels that way Stace," Rose confided. "Are you too tired to come over? I could use a friend right now. Kayla is here but—"

"Say no more, I just have to pick Roger up from the kennel and we'll be over." Stacey was the only woman that Rose knew who had her poodle named Roger so that he would stay humble. Although her friend doted on her dog, she was quick to tell people that Roger was a bit of a snob who thought mighty highly of himself. Apparently, he came from a long line of very well-bred canines and had an illustrious pedigree. By naming him Roger, she was able to keep his ego in check. That was one of the things that Rose adored about her friend; while she was extremely smart, beautiful, and sophisticated, she didn't take herself, or her dog, too seriously.

Going to the washroom, Rose splashed some water on her face and applied mascara and lipstick. While she knew she didn't have to put on a brave face for Stacey, she knew she would feel better if she freshened up.

Kayla appeared at the door to the bathroom, holding her purse and phone in her hand.

"I'm going to meet with Gwen, and we are going to go over what we should be saying to the media," Kayla informed her. "I will call you when we are done and let you know what we have planned."

"Just don't go doing anything like talking to the media without talking to me first Kayla. I want to make sure that whatever we say goes through our lawyer first," Rose warned her.

"Why does it have to go through the lawyer? We aren't the ones who are being accused of a crime," Kayla frowned in confusion and Rose was reminded that contrary to the way she acted sometimes, her daughter was still a young woman.

"Because we don't want to say anything that might hurt your father or his... his case," Rose stumbled over referring to her husband's situation as a "case." What had started as a misunderstanding was quickly turning into something so much more. A case. Her husband had a case.

"I guess that makes sense. I promise we won't do anything rash," she gave Rose a peck on the top of her head as though she was a young child.

"Are you sure you don't want me to go with you?" Rose asked.

"No, you spend some time with Stacey and maybe even open a bottle of wine. Try to relax a little," Kayla gave her a quick hug and headed for the front door. Just as she was about to open the door, she stopped in her tracks and stared at the doorknob.

"What's wrong?"

Kayla turned on her heel and walked toward the back of the house. "Might be better if I didn't announce my departure by opening the front door. I don't know if they are still out there, but I'm going to slip out the back door."

Rose went to the living room and carefully pulled the blind on the window down. She peeked out to see if any media was lying in wait for her. There were two vans and a couple of cars with people standing around, looking bored. Sighing, she left the room and reached for the phone to call Stacey and warn her to pull up the driveway as close to the house as possible, or she might get ambushed.

Chapter 10

The Past

"David! Get down here right this minute!"

Rolling over and pulling the pillow over his head, David groaned out loud. It was Saturday morning; couldn't they give him a break just this once? As long as he could remember, his parents had one strict rule about weekends. He had no curfew, but he had to be ready to get up in the morning to do chores. If he whined and complained about it, they told him that maybe they should make him come home earlier so he would be well-rested in the morning. While many of his friends were jealous and thought his parents were cool, both he and his parents knew it wasn't that they weren't strict, but they felt strongly that their children needed to learn consequences. Stay out late? Pay for it in the morning. Drink too much beer in the sand hills? Well, you can look as green in the morning as you want, but you aren't going to get out of any work.

David mostly respected his parents for their logical parenting style, but this morning? Every muscle in his head seemed to ache and throb. His mouth and eyes felt as dry as the Sahara. Why did he have those last couple of beers with Terry and Wade? Then he smiled to himself as he recalled Chris falling off the tailgate of the truck as David and the others convulsed with laughter. While he had no recollection as to why they were laughing so hard, he did know they had a great time together.

He threw back the covers and slowly swung out of bed, placing his feet on the floor. He waited for the blood to stop pounding in his head and then stood up. He knew from experience he would just need a few over-the-counter painkillers and a load of water, and he would begin to feel human again.

A few moments later, he walked into the kitchen and was met with the tantalizing aroma of his mother's pancakes.

"Mmmmm... what's the occasion?" David sat down at the kitchen table and perused the counter with hungry eyes. He noticed there was a pile of bacon heaped on a plate.

"Nothing really, I was just thinking I won't have many more Saturday mornings to pamper you before you leave home," she said quietly, her back to him as she flipped a pancake in the frying pan.

"Mom?" When the seconds ticked by and she didn't answer, he called her name again.

"What?" she answered, her voice quivering.

"What's wrong? You aren't crying, are you?"

"Now why would I be crying," She laughed as she wiped at her eyes with her apron. "My only son leaves home all the time, no big deal."

He got up and approached her, turning her around to face him. He wrapped her in his arms, chuckling under his breath. For the past six months, she had been acting as though he was moving to another planet.

"I'm going away to work for the summer and then I'll be home for a week before I head off to college. Even then, I'm moving away from home, not out of your life!" he reassured her.

His mother was a petite woman, short in stature but big on emotion. Her thick brown hair was pulled back in a ponytail with stray tendrils loose around her ears. She was a beautiful woman with big, brown almost haunting eyes and clear, wrinkle-free skin, a color that made her look tanned year-round.

"She having a 'my baby's leaving me' meltdown again?" David's father teased as he walked into the kitchen, grabbing his favorite mug off the tree that held the family's coffee cups.

"Oh sure, laugh all you want, but you two will never know what it feels like to let a piece of yourself go," her voice cracked, and his dad leaned against the sink while reaching out to rub her back.

"Now Helen, you know he won't be gone for good; he'll be just a phone call away. And anyway, you'll have Jessie here!"

"Of course, I do, but a son isn't the same as a daughter, everyone knows that," Helen said. David's younger sister was an introverted young girl six years his junior who rarely asked for any attention, and spent hours immersed in the latest novel she was reading.

"Hey Dad, now that I'm pretty much an adult, why don't you pour me a cup of coffee?" David asked. "I'll take mine with some cream and sugar."

"Ha! Not until you decide to drink it black as God intended," his dad said with a smile. It was an ongoing family joke. For as long as David could remember, his dad would call out "Who wants a coffee?" when he poured himself one. While the question was intended for his wife, little David would always say "I want one!" His Dad decided one day to call his bluff; the taste of the bitter black coffee was enough to stop David from taking up drinking coffee.

"Sit down you two," his mother said, shooing them towards the table and gathering herself together to dish up a plate for each of them.

~~~~

Later that day, David jumped on his bicycle and rode down the driveway and out onto the road that ran east to west in front of his house. He had worked hard the summer he turned fifteen so that he could afford to buy the bike. He knew there was no way they could afford to buy him a car when he turned sixteen and got his license, but that didn't stop him from getting around and to where he needed to go. David had always been a pragmatic boy who didn't spend a lot of time worrying about things he couldn't control, and while he would have loved to have a used Camaro or something, he realized there was no sense in yearning for what he would never have. The Cannondale Road bike, with its shiny blue aluminum frame, was his pride and joy. While other boys his age were still dreaming of their first car, David was cruising up and down the roads, whipping from one friend's house to work, then to school, and back. The only drawback was when he started dating Rebecca; it was inconvenient not to be able to drive her home from school. The weekends were usually okay as his dad let him use the family car, but even he had to admit being picked up for a date in an old navy-blue Ford LTD was not particularly romantic. But Rebecca didn't seem to mind. The difference in their family's wealth had never presented a problem until they were making plans for this summer.

David pumped harder and faster on his pedals, leaning into the wind. When he had something on his mind, nothing was more soothing than a good, hard bike ride. And his mind was busy. He knew there was no way he could blow off this summer by joining Rebecca and her family at some plush cabin. He had to work, or his future would be in jeopardy and he couldn't understand why she didn't understand. She was a smart girl; she knew his family didn't have money to pay for all of his education. And there was no way they could have the life they dreamed about if he didn't get a degree. As much as he loved his mom and Dad, he wanted more out of life than settling down at a young age and having a family like they did.

~~~~

"I think tonight is the night," Rebecca whispered. Her two best friends in the whole world looked up in surprise from their place on her bed. Kim, with her bright red curly hair piled high on her head looked up, her mouth forming a small 'o' and Ashley, who was sitting cross-legged stared at her in surprise.

"THE night?" Ashley's eyes widened.

"WHAT?" Kim's lanky legs swung over the side of the bed as though ready to spring into action.

"Sssshhhhh! Do you want to alert the neighbors? Yes, THE night."

"But why tonight? I thought you wanted to wait until you and David were away from home and at college." Ashley asked.

"Yeah, what happened to not wanting the first time to be in the back seat of that stinky old Ford of his?" Kim joined in. The three girls had been best friends for the last two years of high school and their friends knew that where one of them was, the other two weren't far behind. Where Rebecca was slim and shapely, Kim was skinny, where Ashley was a friend to all the boys, Kim was shy and awkward. And where Rebecca was unreasonable both Ashley and Kim were guided by reason and logic.

"Well, there are worse places, I guess. After all, girls have been doing it for years in all sorts of places," Rebecca stated as she applied her lip gloss, smacking to make sure evenly over her lips. "This is going to be the last time we see each other alone before the summer comes and he heads off for some god-forbidden work camp."

"It's a forestry work camp Rebecca, not the army during wartime." Ashley rolled her eyes.

"Ha, ha," Rebecca grabbed the belt that was lying over the back of the chair in her bedroom and began to thread it through her high-waisted jeans.

"Are you worried about something Rebecca? You're going overboard about David working this summer." Kim asked quietly.

There was silence in the room and after a minute, Kim leaned over and tapped Ashley who had started flipping through the latest copy of Sassy magazine. Ashley looked up to see Rebecca standing in the middle of her bedroom, tears rolling down her cheeks.

"Oh honey, what's wrong?" Ashley jumped up and wrapped her arms around her best friend. Steering her towards the bed, they sat down.

"He's going to leave me!" she began to wail. "He's going to go away and meet someone else and decide he likes her better and he's going to leave me!"

"What? As if! David is crazy about you. And even if he wasn't, where is he going to meet a girl when he is working in a forestry camp all summer? It's not exactly the kind of work they hire girls to do. He's going to be around sweaty, stinky boys all summer."

"But what if he does meet someone? What if the cook is some beautiful young, skinny girl and he forgets all about me?"

"Because all camps have beautiful cover girls as cooks. Not!" Kim said with a laugh. "It's more likely to be an old lady of forty with rollers in her hair and a Marlboro hanging out of her mouth. They'll have to check their meals for ashes."

Rebecca smiled through her tears, hiccoughing at the picture her friend had drawn.

"Is that why you've been so crazy about him working?"

"Well, not the only reason. I wanted to spend the summer with him," Rebecca insisted weakly. "But yeah, that too."

"You better get it together or you are going to ruin the little time you two have left together before he leaves. And if you are so worried about him finding someone else, you had better not let him go while he is mad at you."

"That's why I thought tonight might be THE night," Rebecca said with a smile. Ashley gave her a playful punch in the arm, and the three of them flung themselves back onto the bed, breaking into giggles. They had been friends for so long, that it was hard for Ashley to believe that soon they would all be moving on to another stage in their lives. It was an exciting and kind of scary time for them all. She felt as though she was standing on the edge of a very high and steep cliff, looking over the edge. There were butterflies in her stomach, but she couldn't help but look forward to the future because it was so bright and promising.

~~~~

That night, headlights bobbed along trails and barely-there roads in the sand hills of Morgan County. It was as though the setting sun was a siren call to all the teenagers within a ten-mile radius who had access to a car. They came from the north, the south, east, and west. Cars full of underage teenagers, cans of beer, and bottles of cheap wine. The girls were in their jeans and matching denim jackets, a cloud of body spray wafting around them. The boys with their freshly shaven and slightly raw faces, the smell of their liberally applied Brut and Drakkar Noir competing with the smell of burning wood from the bonfire.

The music was loud as teenagers moved in the ever-expanding circle around the fire, the size of both increasing every hour. For the last couple of generations, teenagers had visited this area, started a bonfire, and participated in stories that became more and more dramatic as the night wore on. Small disagreements became life-impacting slights, and an innocent look grew to become evidence of cheating that threatened to ruin a young woman's life, or at least her evening. Raging hormones and cheap alcohol, fueled by throbbing music, and hurt feelings could make these teenagers pretty vulnerable. The sparse bushes around the campfire were littered with small groups of girls, comforting one of their own, while at the same time vowing to never again speak to the offending peer. Occasionally throughout the evening, small scuffles broke out amongst a couple of the boys. They were quickly pulled apart by friends who took them to one of their cars, opened a fresh can of beer, and encouraged him to enjoy the evening and stop bugging out about some girl.

Rebecca wanted to make sure there was no drama for her and David tonight. She sipped on her drink and kept close by his side, holding his hand. David was happy to keep things low-key and calm. He wasn't much for drama, and he had been a bit concerned that

Rebecca would use the opportunity to gather her friends and create a stir. Not that he was sure what she thought she would have accomplished by doing that.

Close to midnight, someone tossed a cracker into the fire, causing everyone to jump back in surprise. The offender was quickly subjected to some harsh criticism and hung their head, promising to never do it again. While the group was drinking while underage and breaking all sorts of trespassing laws, they drew the line at summertime fireworks and crackers. They respected fire and made sure when they left that the bonfire had been liberally doused. Of course, the girls were not participants in that part of the evening. As soon as the boys began to unzip to put the fire out, the girls ran giggling and shouting 'Ewww!" towards their vehicles. No matter how old they became, the boys were still little boys at heart.

Having risen and moved back as soon as the cracker exploded, Rebecca and David found themselves almost alone. The rest of the party had returned to the fire or were circling the cracker thrower.

"There always has to be one in the crowd, huh?" David murmured as he drew Rebecca close, resting his chin on her head. "You smell so good tonight."

"You do too," she snuggled into him, pressing her face against his chest. "You always smell so good."

"I figured by now I would smell like a bonfire," David chuckled.

"A little bit, but that isn't a bad thing," she reassured him. "I know it's silly, but I want to remember everything about this night, including your smell."

"It's not silly," David told her, holding her even tighter. Now that she wasn't harping on at him about the summer, he was free to enjoy her company and feel nostalgic as their school years were almost over. They had so many memories together that he found it hard to distinguish his memories from hers. She was either in most of them or something about it would remind him of her. Sometimes he wondered if it was healthy that they had been so inseparable for most of their lives. How did he know whether he loved her, like the forever kind of love? How much of it was just that she had always been there and all his years were wound up so tightly with her? She was the constant thread that ran through everything.

"Why don't we go find someplace with a bit more privacy so we can talk," Rebecca said as she tugged on his hand, pulling him along with her.

"I like privacy," David said with a grin.

~~~~

Half an hour later, David and Rebecca were parked along the side of an abandoned driveway. The driveway led to an old derelict farmhouse that was littered with bottles and graffiti. At one time it appeared as though a mattress had been hauled into the house, but it now hung half in and half out of the entrance, stained and filthy. The two of them often joked that if the police ever came and used their forensic lights, the place would light up like the Fourth of July and require sunglasses.

They had been down this road often, simply parking there at the end of a Friday or Saturday night bonfire. But tonight, they just sat, staring out the windshield at the night sky.

"How many lovers do you think those stars have shone down on?" Rebecca asked. "Oh, the stories they could tell."

"Some pretty dirty stories," David laughed as he nuzzled her neck. She tilted her head back to give him better access and began to run her hands through his hair. A wash of sadness rolled over her and she pulled his lips to hers. His tongue entered her mouth, and she felt a small thrill. She never got bored of kissing David.

Time seemed to stand still and then he placed his hand at her side, as though to cup her back. His hand moved up and down, the thumb slowly caressing the slight curve of Rebecca's breast. This was the part she loved more than anything. The point in time when they first started kissing and she felt needed and wanted. She felt as though they were the first two people who had ever felt this way. She felt loved.

"Why don't we move to the back," David asked, his breath coming fast and his voice husky.

"Okay."

They opened the front doors and then the back doors. David grinned to himself as, for not the first time, he appreciated the big old car. No cramming in the back seat for them. Half an hour later, with the windows fogged up, Rebecca lay on her back, her top discarded and panting heavily. David lay beside her, running his hands up and down her body, his bare chest heaving. They both still had their jeans on, although both were undone.

"David?"

"Mmmm?"

"I think tonight is the night."

David's head lifted, his face showing his surprise. "You mean THE night, the night?"

Rebecca giggled and nodded her head. While David had never pressured her into having sex for the first time, she knew he was more than ready. He respected her feelings on the matter, and it had never been an issue between them.

"Are you sure?"

"Of course, I'm sure, I wouldn't say so if I wasn't sure."

David lifted himself, resting most of his weight on his two hands that were placed on either side of her. He looked into her eyes and then lowered his head to kiss her deeply. He had known this day would come; it was inevitable. But she had always insisted it wouldn't be in the backseat of some car. He felt an uneasiness wash over him. This didn't feel right.

"Why now?" he asked her, his brows furrowing.

"What do you mean, why now? Isn't this what you want?"

"Of course, it is, but I'm just surprised."

"I don't know why you're so surprised. You are going to be gone for months and I want to make sure you have something to remember me by," she smiled up at him.

"You mean you want to have sex for the first time to make sure I remember you?"

"Come on David don't say it like that. I love you and I want to please you. And myself."

David was quiet for a minute and then he heaved himself up and into a seated position.

"What's wrong?"

"It just doesn't feel right. I feel like you want to have sex just to manipulate the situation."

"Don't be ridiculous David! You're making way too much out of this," Rebecca insisted. She moved to draw him back down to her, but he shook himself free.

"If the last couple weeks hadn't been all about your insecurities with me leaving, I might believe you, Becky."

"Insecurities? Who said anything about insecurities? I just wanted to spend the summer with my boyfriend, why is that so wrong?"

"Come on Becky, you know what that was all about. I've known you for too many years not to understand you."

"Oh, you think you know me that well, do you?" Rebecca didn't know why she was arguing with him about this. He had hit the nail on the head so why was she denying it? It just bugged her so much that he thought he knew everything about her. And he was so damned noble that he was going to give up having sex with her because of it. Did that mean he wasn't that attracted to her after all? Could he just turn it on and off like that?

They gathered their clothes and moved back to the front seat, Rebecca creating a wide chasm of space between them.

"Oh, come on Becky, don't be like this," he pleaded. "I want our first time to be special, just like we talked about. I don't want it because you're afraid I don't love you enough to keep it in my pants for two months."

Rebecca continued to stare out the window, not answering him. Finally, he started up the car and did a U-turn next to the house. He drove without saying a word. He was feeling confused and upset without being completely sure why. He knew most boys his age would think he was insane for missing out on screwing Rebecca Evans, the popular cheerleader. But he didn't like feeling manipulated, as though she was pulling the strings and he was her puppet. He always knew that Becky had that side to her; the side that would stop at almost nothing to get something if she wanted it. Over the years he had watched her bat her eyes at her parents and play the innocent little girl if she wanted something from them. She could butter up a teacher by using flattery. But he couldn't recall ever being the one she was trying so hard to get to do something. Had she maybe even thought if they slept together that he would ditch all the plans for his life and join her at her family's cabin? It was bad enough if she was trying to "cheat-proof" him.

When he pulled up in front of Rebecca's home, he turned towards her, his wrist resting on the steering wheel. "We both have exams this week and I'm going to be packing up; I won't be able to see you much, except at school," he began. "I don't want this to be hanging over our heads. Can we please talk about it?"

"There is nothing to talk about David," Rebecca said as she reached for the door handle. "You go and do your thing and I'll do mine this summer. We'll meet back up at college and see how things go."

"What does that mean?" David asked, jumping out of the car as she did. "Becky!"

He banged the top of the car as she strode up the steps to her front door. He knew better than to follow her. Her parents would not be impressed with teenage drama on their steps. And he certainly didn't want to have to explain what it was about. Hell, he wasn't even all that sure himself what it was all about.

Jumping into the car, he sped away. He had had enough for one night. After weeks of haranguing, he was done. She could work through whatever it was that was making her so buggy. He didn't have any energy left to play these games. He had a lot of studying to do, he had to pack up and get ready to go to work. And that didn't even take into consideration the emotional toll his mother was bound to take on him this week.

Chapter 11

Present Day

When Stacey arrived an hour later, the media onslaught was down to one car and she was able to enter the house without being bothered. Rose opened the door and let her in before throwing her arms around her and hugging her tightly.

"Oh, Rosie, I can't imagine what you are going through, this is horrible," Stacey murmured.

Determined not to break down again, Rose pulled away and gave her friend as genuine a smile as she could muster.

"It's not fun, but now that you are here, I know I'm going to be fine."

"Uh-huh," Stacey responded with a rueful smile. "Glad to know I have such magic powers."

"And how are you Mr. Roger?" Rose bent down to give Roger a scratch behind his carefully coiffed ears. "Did you enjoy yourself at the kennel?"

"Now, now Roger, don't listen to her, we all know it's a spa, not a kennel. You went away for a few days at the spa," Stacey winked at Rose in jest. Her sometimes-over-the-top treatment of her pet was the butt of many jokes from her friends.

They walked into the kitchen where Rose had a bottle of her favorite red wine open to breathe, alongside two wine glasses. Pouring the wine, Rose sighed deeply and plunked herself down at the table.

"Okay, I know you're probably sick of this already, but I need you to tell me what happened, right from the very beginning," Stacey demanded. "I need to have the whole picture so I can help."

Rose went through what had happened over the last 24 hours, beginning with the police barging in and interrupting her grandson's first birthday party. She finished up by talking about her conversation with the criminal lawyer this morning.

"And now Kayla is meeting her friend who does media relations to decide how to handle the media," Rose wrapped up. "She told them we would make a statement later today."

"Wow, Rosie," Stacey sat back, took a long sip from her wine glass, and stared at her friend while shaking her head from side to side. "You've been through the wringer."

Rose raised her wine glass as though in a toast and Stacey clinked her glass against hers.

"So, you say it was his high school girlfriend, huh?"

"Yeah, it's so frustrating because this is so obviously a mistake, but I don't know what we're up against right now. They don't have to tell us anything yet, simply that he has been charged. They ran some new kind of testing that wasn't invented back in the 90s when she died."

"Huh," Stacey twirled the stem of her wine glass between her fingers.

"I keep thinking of him in that jail and the injustice of it all just makes me want to cry," Rose's voice cracked on the last part of her sentence. "Of all people, David sitting in a jail cell? He is the last person who should be there. He's like the kindest man I know, a great father and a doting grandfather. I couldn't ask for a better husband and now here he is locked up like an animal."

"I know it must be frustrating, but that is the way the process works. They must have had some kind of evidence to get a warrant for his arrest. If it was enough for his arrest then it is enough for them to hold him in jail until he goes through the process," Stacey's voice was low and steady, as though explaining something very complicated to a child.

Rose stared at her friend, her eyes wide. "You sound like you think he should be locked up, Stacey! This is David we're talking about!"

"I know, and maybe I worded that badly. I'm just trying to say that there is a process that has to be followed. It isn't personal to David, it's just the process," Stacey explained. "I don't want to sound harsh or uncaring, but the truth is that we can't dwell on that, we just have to move forward."

Rose nodded her head and sat staring at the wine in her glass as she swirled it around.

"And anyway, David is a strong man, he knows how to adapt and make the most of any situation he's in—he'll be fine."

"I guess you're right."

"You know I am."

The two friends sat in companionable silence for minutes, each of them deep in their thoughts.

Stacey finally broke the silence by asking a question that set Rose back a bit.

"How have things been with you and David? I mean before all of this?"

"What do you mean?" A frown marred Rose's face.

"I know we haven't talked about it much, but I was just wondering if you two had managed to recover from, you know, last summer," Stacey took a sip from her glass.

"Oh, yeah," Rose shifted uncomfortably in her chair. "It's good, everything's good."

Stacey stared at her friend from across the table and Rose met her eyes almost defiantly.

"If you say so," Stacey finally relented.

"I do."

With the topic off-limits, Stacey began telling Rose all about her business trip, regaling her with tales of poor airline service and overly friendly salesmen who tried to convince her to ignore their wedding rings. By the time the wine bottle was empty, the best friends were relaxed, and Rose felt as though a large amount of the tension had left her body.

Her phone rang and she looked down at the cordless phone to see that it was Kayla who was calling. Answering it, she listened for a few minutes and then put her hand over the receiver.

"Kayla and her friend Gwen are going to come by, can you stay and be a second set of ears for me?"

"Of course," Stacey responded quickly. She reached down and stroked Roger, murmuring to him about how nice it was to be at Auntie Rosie's again.

Disconnecting the call, Rose explained that Kayla and Gwen were going to come over and go through the game plan for handling the media. Gwen wanted to talk to Rose directly and was offered to coach her in dealing with being interviewed. The wine in Rose's stomach felt sour as she sat at the table, staring at her phone.

She felt Stacey's hand cover hers and she looked up into her friend's eyes. "You're going to be okay Rosie,"

"I know," she responded with a wry smile. "I just can't believe this is happening. How could anyone think such a horrible thing about him?"

Stacey pulled her hand away and leaned against the back of her chair. Turning her head to one side, she looked at Rose and asked. "I get the impression you think this is particularly shocking because it's David—why is that? I mean, I get that it's shocking and comes out of left field, but anyone can be accused of something at any time, so why is it particularly shocking to you because it's David?"

A frown formed between Rose's eyebrows as she pondered the question. She wasn't sure why it felt so shocking that it was David of all people, except that he was a good person and didn't deserve this to happen to him.

"I'm not sure, it just seems so unfair. David has done everything by the book; he's supported, provided for, and loved his family. He doesn't cheat on his taxes, and he gets up every morning to go to the office and he never complains."

Looking at her, Stacey said matter-of-factly, "Don't you think that is the bare minimum that should be expected of anyone?"

"Well, I mean, yeah, but..."

"Think about it Rose, you have just listed things that any adult should be doing working, paying taxes, and loving his family. He's a man Rose, not a saint."

Rose wasn't quite sure what to say in response, but she was saved from having to worry about it by the sound of Kayla coming through the back door.

"They're starting to gather out there again," she stated as she walked into the kitchen and threw her purse on the table. "Hi Stacey."

Stacey raised her glass in Kayla's direction and took another sip.

"Mom, Gwen. Gwen, my mom," Kayla said as she opened the fridge and pulled out a cold bottle of pop. "Stop it with the wine now, Mom, this is no time to have your faculties dulled."

"Aye, aye captain," Rose rolled her eyes and raised one eyebrow towards Stacey.

Gwen was an attractive woman with a head full of beautiful auburn hair who stood a hair's breadth over five feet. She had a preoccupied look on her face that spoke of extreme concentration and a mind that was working rapidly.

"Okay, it is almost eight, so we'll need to get out there pretty quickly to issue a statement. That will give them the time they need to make the late news," Gwen stated as she sat down and pulled out a notepad that was full of writing.

"And why do we want it to be on the late news? Isn't it better if we just put it off as long as we can?" Rose asked.

"Absolutely not. We need to give the media what they want, or they will go looking for it elsewhere. And that means someone else's messages are getting to the public instead of David's. We want to keep the media on our side."

"But I have nothing to say. I don't know what is happening or why or what is going to happen next," Rose protested.

"That's not true from what Kayla has told me," Gwen flipped through the pages in her notebook and began to read some of her notes. "You know that within 24 hours you will know if he is going to be released on bail or not, you know that he was arrested because of a new technology that was used to solve a cold case. But most importantly, you know your husband."

"Okay, but do we have to tell them all of that? Won't that just make them more curious and ask questions I don't have the answer for?"

"It probably will, and that is why you're going to answer the questions honestly and say you don't know the answer and you're doing your best to be patient and wait for the system to work. If you give me a few minutes, I am going to jot down a statement I think might work."

The three women got up and left Gwen writing furiously at the kitchen table. They wandered into the living room and Stacey lifted one of the slats in the blind.

"Holy shit, there are a lot more there," she exclaimed. Rose stood beside her, looking out. She was right. There were maybe 20 more vehicles in front of their home and stretched down the block. Rose felt her stomach tighten and she had to breathe deeply in order to settle her stomach.

"Where have they all come from? I didn't think we had that many media outlets in town!" Stacey said.

"Gwen was telling me that these types of situations are getting out of hand because news spreads so fast on social media. And true crime is a big thing online and everyone thinks they're a detective. She said it is probably a combination of legit media and a bunch of bloggers and YouTubers out there.

"Oh great," Rose pressed the palm of her hand up against her forehead. Just what she needed, every lookie-loo in the city coming to her front steps.

"It's going to be okay Mom, you'll do great," Kayla reassured her.

Gwen walked into the living room. "Okay, I think I have an outline which is going to be short and sweet. We just want to give them the basics. I will then let them know that any further updates will be made at Stanley Horowicz Park."

"Why there?" Stacey asked.

"Because we want to get the media off the front doorstep and not turning up here every time something is up. The more we make this house the place for updates, the more they may camp out next time," Gwen explained.

Rose looked over the notes Gwen had made, she asked a few questions for clarification and then said she was okay with it.

"Perfect, now when you get questions, and you will, please wait for me to moderate. Their impulse will be to shout out questions to you and I don't want that to fluster you. Just wait and I will point to someone or call on them to ask the question. We don't want this to be any more nerve-wracking for you than it needs to be. I don't want you getting overwhelmed and blurting something out you shouldn't. Do you understand?"

"Yeah, I do," Rose looked down at the note again and then raised her head. "Only one question."

"What's that?"

"What shouldn't I be blurting out?"

"Don't go saying you think he did it and you hope he rots," Gwen said and the four women burst out laughing. Not because what she had said was so hilarious but because the whole situation was so alien to them and they needed the tension broken somehow.

"Just remember, the message we want to get across to them is that his family stands behind him; that you have a limited amount of information, but you are trusting the system." Gwen went on to explain. "Now, do you want to run this by your lawyer?"

Rose thought for a moment but then shook her head. "I don't think so. It's pretty innocuous and it isn't telling them anything that isn't actually public knowledge."

"Good, that will speed things up then; just remember to let me lead things. Once I introduce you, you read your statement and then I will ask if there are any questions and I will select the person to ask the question. You answer in a way that is honest but short and to the point. This is not the time to ramble or provide more information than they ask for."

"I'll be right there beside you Mom," Rose felt her daughter's reassuring hand on her shoulder. Suddenly, she realized that they had not asked Joshua to join them when they spoke. "We should have given Josh the chance to be here," Rose said, her voice distressed.

"There is no time Mom, this has to happen now, we will talk to Josh about him joining us if we do this again," Kayla responded.

"Kayla's right, there is no time now, I'm going to go out and let them know that you will be issuing a statement in a few minutes, that way they can get ready," Gwen said as she turned around and headed for the door. When she opened the door and walked onto the front deck, the media who had been waiting surged forward. Gwen stepped off the deck and held the group at bay.

"Please listen," she announced in a loud voice. "The family will be coming out in a couple of minutes to make a statement, then they will answer a few select questions. Please respect their space and stay on the ground here. They will be on the deck and that way everyone can see and hear them."

Members of the group began to shout out questions, but Gwen raised her hand to stop them. "We will begin in a couple of minutes."

Chapter 12

The Past

Rose's hands shook as she held the statement between her hands. Looking down, she read it in a quivering voice.

"This arrest comes as a shock to our family. We strongly believe that time will show that a grave mistake was made, and that David will be exonerated. David is a loving husband, a proud father, and an outstanding member of this community. We as his family stand behind him, unified in our faith in him. We will patiently wait for the system to work the way it was intended and hope that he will be home with us soon. During this time, we ask that you respect our privacy. If we have anything further to say, we will give you notice and make a public statement. We will not consider speaking to members of the media who intrude on our property or who harass and stalk us. We trust you understand our position on this matter."

Rose felt numb as she finished the statement and looked up. Microphones were thrust in her direction and the eyes of cameras were blinking and clicking at her. She blinked rapidly, as though looking at an overly bright light.

Gwen stepped forward and asked the crowd if they had questions to please raise their hands. Most of the people gathered began to wave their hands frantically and shout out questions. Gwen ignored them and pointed at someone in the middle of the pack who had their arm raised and was waving their hand.

"You, what is your question?"

"What evidence do they have against your husband, Mrs. Slater?"

"I have very limited knowledge of what the case is that they think they have against him," Rose answered as calmly as she could muster.

"Our lawyer tells us we must wait for the process to unfold before we will have a clear picture."

"Mrs. Slater! Mrs. Slater! Rose!" the crowd shouted to be next.

"You!" Gwen pointed at a diminutive woman who was at risk of being crushed at the front of the pack.

"Who was this girl he killed Rose? Did you know her?"

Before Rose could respond, Gwen stepped forward and reminded the group that allegations had been brought against David Slater but that he had not been convicted. "I believe what you meant to ask was: 'Who is the girl he is alleged to have killed?'"

The woman colored a deep red and Rose couldn't help but think that Gwen had not made a friend with that chastisement.

"She was his high school sweetheart and although I didn't personally know her, David has often spoken of her with fondness," she responded before any further damage could be done.

A tall and lanky man stepped forward, thrusting his microphone aggressively in Rose's face "Is it true that he raped and brutalized her before he killed her, Mrs. Slater?"

"As has been stated, we are unaware of the particulars of the case," Gwen once again stepped forward to intercept the question. Rose was beginning to become annoyed with the woman. She was perfectly capable of handling pointed questions tactfully without being rescued or handled. Something in her posture must have given her away to her daughter as Kayla, who had been directly behind her, slid further to her right and stood closer to Gwen. Rose's assumption proved correct when the next questioner asked that if the police had enough to arrest him, surely she was concerned that he may be guilty? Gwen moved forward as though to answer, and Kayla discreetly held on to the bottom of her jacket to hold her back.

Rose stepped forward and said "No, just because he has been arrested there is no presumption of guilt. It simply means he has been accused. From what our lawyer has explained, they now have the burden to prove him guilty, and that is a high burden."

"Will he be released on bail?" someone at the back of the group shouted.

"As I said, we have no additional information," Rose stated with a tone of finality. "Thank you for your patience, goodnight." She turned on her heel and headed into the house with Kayla and Gwen close behind.

"You did great Mom!" Kayla threw her arms around her mother's neck. "I'm so proud of you!"

Rose closed her eyes and reveled in the warm touch of her daughter. It was a welcome gift after the onslaught of questions and the hostile crowd outside.

"Yeah, there is no way my mom would have been able to keep it together that well Mrs. Slater. I apologize if I got a bit protective of you a couple of times," Gwen's lips twisted and she looked embarrassed.

"Never underestimate my mom," Kayla declared in an overly jovial tone that sounded jarring to Rose. While she appreciated her daughter's support, it sounded a bit forced. Perhaps the tension was getting to her now that they had gotten past the first hurdle.

Stacey, who had stayed in the house, listening at the front window, approached Rose, a full glass of wine in her hand. "Drink," she said.

"Hey, where's mine?" Kayla demanded.

"You have two feet and a heartbeat, help yourself," Stacey told Kayla and they both burst into laughter. It was a standing gag between them that went back so far that no one was quite sure what had given rise to it. But after many years and shared history, they both still found it hilarious.

The four of them spent the next couple of hours finishing off the bottle of California Merlot and discussing what had happened. At some point they had run out of ways to express their shock and dismay and had resorted to just staring into their glasses, shaking their heads. Rose began making notes on what she needed to do over the next few days. She had to call his work and explain what was happening if they didn't already know. She wasn't sure what happened in situations like this. After all, he was accused of a crime, but he hadn't been found guilty. Surely, they would have to make some type of accommodation, wouldn't they?

Chapter 13

The Past

The next week was as busy as David had predicted. He stayed up late at night cramming for his exams, cleaning out his locker, saying goodbye to friends, and going shopping with his mother for what she considered "proper" work clothes.

The forestry service told him he needed a pair of steel-toed boots, four work shirts, four pairs of pants, and several pairs of wool socks. It sounded like pretty hot gear for working in the summer sun and he was fast realizing the tan he had imagined he would come away with might not happen. He would have been content to take jeans and T-shirts but his mother insisted he needed more durable clothes. He felt guilty having them buy him all these clothes, but both his mom and his dad had insisted. His dad said that he would thank them once he was there and realized a t-shirt and jeans just weren't going to cut it.

"When you're tramping through thick forest, digging holes and dodging brambles, believe me, you need something that can stand up."

While he thought his mother was being over-protective, he took to heart his father's words. He knew that if anyone knew the best way to dress for hours of labor, it was his dad.

By the end of the week, he had a bed overflowing with clothes, shoes, his Sony Walkman, a case of cassettes, a notebook and pen (his mother told him he had to write), and an assortment of snacks. He had enough cash in his pocket for incidentals that weren't covered by the camp, and he was ready to go.

It was Saturday night and Chris was going to come over to watch a movie. He had rented Indiana Jones and the Last Crusade. It had taken a couple of months before he was able to snag one at the Blockbuster in town, but he had no doubt it would be worth it. He was looking forward to popcorn, a good movie, and the uncomplicated friendship he had with Chris.

The movie had barely begun when Chris commented on the young actor who played the young Indiana Jones.

"He's a pretty good actor. And with those looks, I bet he has a long career ahead of him."

"Hmmmm."

"So, umm, how are things going with you and Rebecca?"

David looked over him in surprise as the question seemed to come out of the blue.

"Okay I guess," he answered, looking at Chris and raising one of his eyebrows questioningly. "Why are you asking?"

Chris looked at him with a bashful look on his face. "Ashley said that Rebecca is pretty upset, and she wanted me to talk to you and tell you that you should call her."

"I'm not calling her, she knows where to find me," David said, taking another long draw on his bottle of Coke. He turned back to the movie, annoyed that his evening had been interrupted by a reminder of their fight. He just wanted to watch the movie and enjoy his last Saturday night. A few minutes later, a piece of popcorn landed on his lap. He looked up and Chris shouted "Boo-yah! I'm still the king of hoops!"

David grabbed a handful from the bowl and threw it back at him. "Boo-yah yourself!" They laughed and settled back down to watch the rest of the movie. He wished all his relationships were as easy as the ones he had with his friends. They could get annoyed with each other, and they didn't have to have a big talk to make everything okay.

A well-placed shot of food and they understood they had apologized to each other, and they moved on.

~~~~

Rebecca paced back and forth in her bedroom. She had her phone pressed to her ear and was listening to Ashley as she tried to reassure her that everything was going to work out.

"You and David are meant to be Rebecca, this is just a bump in the road, you wait and see."

"I wish I could believe you, but I haven't heard a word from him. Even on days when we are both busy, he would at least call me at the end of the day. Here it is Sunday night and I haven't heard anything from him since Friday!"

"But didn't you tell him to go do his thing and you'd see him when he got back? I can see why he would think you were blowing him off."

"He knows me better than that, he knows I was just hurt and upset. I didn't mean it. What if he goes off to his job thinking we are broken up? What if he thinks I don't care?" she wailed.

"If you want to clear the air between the two of you, then call him."

"But why should I be the one to call him? He has my number too."

Ashley took a deep breath and tried to stay patient. Her friend was going through a bad time, and she needed to be supportive. But from what she could tell, sometimes relationships just didn't appear to be worth the hassle.

"Rebecca, if you want to talk to him, call him."

"He can call me. He's the one who said I was trying to manipulate him—he owes me an apology!"

"But you were trying to manipulate him! Why are you mad when that is exactly what you were trying to do!"

"Whose side are you on? I wanted to send him off to his job with a special memory of us, how is that manipulative?"

"It is when your reason for doing it is to try to control his behavior," sometimes Ashley felt as though she were speaking to a child.

"I don't want to argue about this. You're my friend and you're supposed to be on my side," Rebecca was beginning to sound as though she were pouting. "And Chris said he didn't say anything? Nothing at all?"

"He said he resented me asking him to get involved, that he brought it up and David said everything was fine," Ashley relayed. "Look, why don't you just give him a call and work this out? You know you'll be miserable if you don't and he's leaving for two months." She didn't want to add that if Rebecca was miserable, they would all be miserable. "Or do you want me to give Kim a call and we can come over and keep you company?'

"No, I'm okay," Rebecca said in a tone that told Ashley she could be talked into it but Ashley was growing tired of the drama and decided to take her at her word.

They ended their conversation with Rebecca promising to seriously consider calling David. Of course, Ashley knew she wouldn't. Rebecca was far too stubborn and used to getting her way to give in and call him. Ashley thought the world of her, but she also was very aware of her weaknesses. Rebecca rarely wanted something that she didn't get, somehow. She wasn't spoiled or bratty, but she knew how to approach people. She knew with her parents she could act sweet and innocent, and they would concede to whatever she wanted, as long as it wasn't something dangerous. She knew if someone would respond well to logic, negotiations, or even outright bribery. She often wished she had the same ability, and she would watch Rebecca closely, trying to learn from her. While she did pick up some things, she concluded that, for the most part, Rebecca simply went through life using her intuition about people.

Chapter 14

Gwen and Kayla exchanged a look that Rose caught but was unable to read.

"Umm, Mom, I would talk to your lawyer about that before you talk to Dad's work."

"Why? What are you thinking?"

"Well, it probably depends on the work contract he has but I don't think whether you're incarcerated or not is a protected class that requires them to hold his job for him," Gwen interjected. "What I mean is, I think they can let him go simply because he has been arrested."

Rose felt her stomach drop. How were they going to manage if David didn't even have a job to come home to? The unfairness of the situation hit her again. An innocent man was accused and although he was supposed to be innocent until proven guilty, the world was treating him as though it was a done deal.

"But if he ends up without a job and everyone in town thinks he's guilty, where will that leave us?" Rose lamented. "I could tell by the way the media asked their questions that they already assume he is guilty and that's the way they will report it."

"We need to take one step at a time Rosie," Stacey reached out and patted Rose on the knee. "No need borrowing trouble."

"I suppose you are right, but I also have to prepare myself, right?"

The women were silent as each thought about the thin line between understanding what might happen in the future while also remaining optimistic.

Just then the landline rang, and Kayla reached to answer it. Handing the receiver to her mother, she mouthed "Josh."

"Hi Josh," Rose answered.

"How did the interview go?"

"It was okay, I imagine there will be something on the late news," Rose told her son. "How are you holding up?"

"This whole thing is stressful and upsetting of course, but what can you do?"

"What is Sarah saying?"

"What can she say? She keeps telling me silly jokes to make me laugh and to show her love, she ordered a nice dinner," Josh laughed.

"I'm glad to hear she is supportive. I would hate it if this caused her any concern or anxiety."

"What do you mean? Of course, she's concerned, we all are," Josh sounded confused by his mother's comment.

"Yes, I know; she just doesn't know your dad like we do and I would hate it if she thought maybe she was marrying into a horrible family. Or that she didn't want to be linked to us," Rose explained.

There was an extended pause at the other end of the line before Joshua finally responded.

"Mom, Sarah loves me. Whether my family is a mess or not isn't something that is going to change that."

"No, no, I understand that I just meant that I hope she doesn't see it as a reflection on you or your character."

"Mom, I think you're making this sound even worse. Worst case scenario, it turns out in some weird world that Dad is guilty of murder." He heard his mother begin to protest on the other end of the line, "I know, I know that isn't the case but let's suppose it was. Sarah loves me. She knows and understands me. She appreciates my character. Dad has nothing to do with that, even if he happened to be guilty."

Rose felt as though she were being reprimanded by her son and she didn't like the sensation.

"Of course, she does Josh, I didn't mean to imply she didn't, it's just... oh, I don't know. I must be more tired than I realized, I'm not able to say what I mean," she ran her fingers through her hair, weariness overcoming her.

"It's okay Mom, I just wanted to check in and see how you were doing. Please keep me posted on anything you hear about Dad," Joshua said goodbye and hung up.

Shortly after Joshua's call, Gwen gathered her things and said her goodbyes.

"If you need any help at all, please don't hesitate to call me. Kayla has my number," she told Rose. "And just so you know, you are doing great."

"Thanks, Gwen and thank you so much for your help today."

After she had left, the remaining three women began to tidy up the kitchen, putting away the wine glasses.

"Do you want me to stay and watch the news with you Mom?" Kayla asked. "I can stay if you want."

"No, no that's okay hon, you go home to your family. I'll let you know if there are any developments," Rose told her.

"I'll stay with your mom," Stacey reassured Kayla.

"Make sure you give those kids a hug and smooch from me too. I don't want them to think I have forgotten about them in all of this." Rose usually talked to her grandchildren every day for at least a couple of minutes. She would call and catch up with Kayla and then Kayla would put the twins on the phone to say their hellos. She had completely missed the chance to do that today and she didn't want them to feel their lives were even more unstable.

"Don't worry Mom, they've barely noticed anything is amiss. Once we explained that Grampa was just going with the police because they needed his help, they didn't blink," Kayla grabbed her coat and slipped into her shoes. "We'll just have to be careful they don't see the news in the next couple of days until we get this figured out."

Once Kayla had left and it was just the two friends left, Rose was determined to change the topic of conversation.

"Tell me something interesting that is happening in your world," she commanded Stacey.

"I wish I could, but nothing is as upsetting or momentous as your life right now."

"Exactly the point," Rose chuckled.

"Well, my trip went well, I managed to secure the contract with the pharmacy. That means we will now provide one of the largest pharmacy chains with our leading blood pressure medication," Stacey announced. "That also means I will get an awesome bonus this year, I imagine."

"That's incredible Stacey, I'm so proud of you!" Rose gushed. "I knew you could do it; didn't I tell you?"

"Yes, yes you did,"

They sat in companionable silence, each of them lost in their thoughts. Roger jumped up on the couch next to Stacey and she scratched his belly. This was a scene that had played out in their lives many times over the years of their friendship. Rose wanted to stay in that room and in that minute. She wanted the outside world to stay away and let her be. This was familiar and comforting and made her feel grounded.

"So, you have to wait to hear from the lawyer about bail?" Stacey broke the reverie by returning to the topic.

"Yes, they will set a hearing which could be as soon as tomorrow. That hearing will determine how much his bond will be or if he gets it at all. The lawyer seemed to be trying to prepare me for him not getting bail."

"Why wouldn't they give him bail?" Stacey asked.

"Apparently in murder cases, it's generally denied."

"I could understand that if the murder had just happened or something but even if they think he did it, he has been a law-abiding citizen ever since. What do they think he's going to do—go on some murder spree after, what, twenty years?"

"I don't know, I don't. I also don't understand why they won't let me talk to him on the phone. What is he going to do, tell me to go and move a weapon or a body? This happened so long ago."

"So many questions," Stacey murmured.

"Oh yeah," Rose agreed.

Turning on the TV, Rose began to flip through the channels, finally landing on a local station. She expected to wait until the evening news came on to hear anything and was surprised to hear a breaking news story being announced. Turning up the volume, she leaned in to catch what was said.

"Breaking news: a local man has been arrested for the murder of a young woman who died more than 20 years ago. More on this story from Brian Jeffries. Brian?"

The video cuts to a reporter standing in front of their home, his young face impassive and earnest.

"Thanks, Jane. Tonight, David Slater has been charged in the cold case murder of Rebecca Evans, Slater's high school sweetheart. Police are keeping quiet about the details, only saying there is some type of DNA evidence available, and his family claims to be confident in his innocence. However, Mrs. Slater, his wife of 29 years, did tell us that her husband spoke of the young girl often. Was this a case of obsession? Has unrequited love gone wrong? We will keep you posted as we learn more. Back to you, Jane."

Rose sat as still as a statue on the living room couch.

"Well shit," Stacey said, her voice deadpan.

Out of everything she had said, they focused on the fact that he had mentioned the girl to her. She had heard that the media could turn things around, but this was ridiculous. She grabbed the remote and flipped to a national channel. She was hoping nothing was being reported and that only the local news had covered the case.

On a national channel, she came face to face with a picture of David. It had been taken a couple of years ago at a business event. His hair was disheveled and he had a slightly absent look on his face. The quality of the picture wasn't great, and its graininess gave David's face a sinister appearance. The caption beneath the picture read "Cold Case Closed?" The news reporter was talking about how the police had DNA evidence that would place David at the scene of the young woman's death. He then turned to a man who had joined him virtually. He introduced him as a DNA expert. This expert proceeded to call DNA evidence the smoking gun of evidence. Once they had DNA, there wasn't much a defense attorney could do to convince a jury that their client was innocent. The next expert was a forensic psychologist who began to explain the type of mental illness someone who would murder may be suffering from.

"Okay, that's enough, turn the TV off," Stacey said in a firm voice. "This type of tabloid coverage is not helpful."

Rose turned off the TV and sat on the couch, staring straight ahead. "How do I face people now?" she asked. "Everyone thinks I'm married to a murderer."

"That's the least of your worries right now Rosie, we need to get more information on what is going on. We're flying blind right now."

"They won't give me any more information," Rose said quietly. She lay down on the couch and brought her knees up to her chest. "Even though he's innocent, our lives are ruined."

Stacey sat still in her chair. How could she argue with her friend? She wasn't entirely wrong that the media coverage was going to make it very, very difficult for David Slater to come back from this, even if he turned out to be innocent. How could she reassure her friend when she agreed?

As they sat in the living room, the sky outside dimmed to a dark shade of grey. The clock in the hallway made an old-fashioned, lulling tick-tock sound. Stacey knew there was nothing she could say or do that was going to help her friend except to bear witness to what she was going through. To be here, to listen, and to comfort was all she could do at this point. She must have fallen asleep because she suddenly woke up with a start and realized that the room was completely black. Disorientated, she quietly rose and felt her way out of the room and towards the kitchen.

In the kitchen, she found Rose sitting at the table, her laptop open in front of her.

"I thought you were still asleep on the couch," Stacey said.

"No, I got up a bit ago. I'm just doing some poking around to see what I can learn about the legal process," Rose explained.

Grabbing her phone off the table, Stacey was shocked to see she had been asleep for almost two hours.

"Wow, I passed out, didn't I?"

"It's been a trying day. I slept for a bit, but my brain won't give me a break and I had to do something," Rose explained. "Why don't you head home? I fed Roger, but it would probably be nice for him to be in his own home after being at the spa" She made air quotes when she said the last two words.

"You're probably right, are you sure you'll be okay here by yourself?"

"Of course, I will, I'm a big girl."

"I know you can take care of yourself, but that doesn't mean you have to be alone or that you can't want company," Stacey probed.

"I know, but really, I'm good. I'm just going to finish up here, go have a hot soak in the tub and get to bed," Rose reassured her friend.

"You will call me the minute you need company, comfort, or just someone to talk to, right?"

"Of course, I have you on speed dial," Rose said.

"Speed dial? Is there even such a thing anymore?"

"Yes, on my landline!"

"I'm just saying, that's showing your age a wee bit," Stacey raised her hands and shrugged and Rose laughed.

They said goodbye in the front entryway and Rose leaned up against the heavy wooden door as it closed. She felt as though she had been to hell and back. How was she going to be able to deal with what was coming?

Chapter 15

Present Day

"Kayla? It's Mom here, I wanted to let you know the lawyer called and your dad's arraignment is scheduled for this afternoon at two. I know it's short notice so I'll understand if you can't make it. I'll be there and I'll see if I can talk to him so if you have a message to pass along, let me know."

Rose hung up after leaving the voice mail message. Her mind was racing, and she went over in her head all the things she had to do before meeting the lawyer at the courthouse. He was going to explain to her the approach that they would use in trying to convince the judge to give David bail.

She had to make some phone calls and see if she could round up some people who would be willing to vouch for David. Meantime, the laundry was piling up and she had no idea if she had anything to wear that was clean enough for the court.

She jumped out of bed and threw on her sweatpants and an old holey T-shirt. She wasn't going to get anything done by lying around thinking of what needed to be done. She threw a load of clothes in the washing machine and then grabbed a pen and a piece of paper and began writing down the names of people who she was certain would speak up for David.

Once she had about fifteen names, she began calling. The first call was to their pastor. She wanted to call him first because she figured it would bolster her confidence to call some of the other names on the list. Asking for help was not something she relished doing.

Once the receptionist at the church put her through, they exchanged hellos and Pastor Kevin expressed his concern for her and David as he had heard about the arrest on the news.

"That's actually what I was calling about, Pastor. David's lawyer has asked me to put together a list of people who are willing to speak favorably about him. The judge must see that he is a positive, contributing member of the community." Rose waited, hoping he wouldn't make her elaborate but would just volunteer to put in a good word. After a few seconds ticked by, Rose continued, "I was wondering, if you could, as his pastor, help us out with that?"

"Oh, Rose, I, uh... I've never been asked for this type of thing before. I don't know what the church's policy around that might be," Pastor Kevin stammered.

"What do you mean, policy?"

"Well, I'm sure you understand Rose, that as a representative of the church, I have to be, uh, careful about how my name is perceived by the public as that would be a reflection on the church."

"I'm confused Pastor. How would standing up for an innocent man be a problem for the public's perception of the church?"

"Well, it isn't quite that straightforward, there is so much that we don't know yet," he continued. "I mean, I don't even know anything about why they arrested him or anything. But of course, you know we'll be praying for him and for you and the kids. You just need to hang onto God and have faith he will turn this to good no matter the outcome."

Rose felt as though she had been sucker-punched. All the years of participation in their church, the hours of volunteer work, and the financial support apparently meant nothing.

"So let me get this straight," she said. "You want us to keep the faith in your prayers and the church, but you have absolutely no faith in David?"

There was a bloated moment of silence at the other end of the line before the pastor gathered himself and responded.

"Rose, I know this is a difficult time and you must be so full of questions and conflicting emotions—"

"Don't patronize me, I don't have conflicting emotions, my emotions are very clear. Goodbye," she hung up, grateful she was on her landline because angrily hanging up felt so much better when you could physically slam the receiver.

Well, so much for the first call being a sure thing. She took a moment to calm herself down before she picked the phone up again. She didn't have time to waste being upset, she needed to gather some names.

By the time she made it through the list, she had left five voice messages, and had four people tell her it was a really bad time and could they call her back? Three told her they would speak up for David and two others said no and hung up.

She had heard that it was only during tough times that you learned who your friends were and now she was receiving first-hand experience. Although she was shocked by those who told her no and hung up, at least they had the decency to be honest. She had a pretty good idea that she would never hear from the ones who said they would be calling her back. While she hoped she would hear back from the people she'd left messages for, she wasn't feeling optimistic. It appeared that people had either made up their minds he was guilty or decided they wanted to stay as far away as possible from the situation just in case he ended up being guilty.

By the time Rose arrived at the courthouse after lunch, her mood was black, and she was fighting to hold back her tears. She felt conspicuous as she paced the hallway, as though people knew who she was and were whispering about her. There was the woman whose husband was in jail. What kind of woman can be married to a killer and not know it?

She had always prided herself on being a good woman, a good wife, and a good mother. But she had also prided herself on being a good community member. Someone who volunteered and helped others, not someone who was involved in court cases and bail issues.

"Hi Rose, I have a meeting room just around this corner for us to chat." Barry Lorman had walked up behind her while she was deep in thought and she started a bit as he rested his hand on her shoulder.

They sat at the table in the non-descript meeting room and the lawyer opened his briefcase. Drawing out a sheaf of papers, he sat them on the table and then he grabbed a notepad.

"Do you have the names I asked you to try to round up?" he opened.

"Yes, but I was only able to get three on such short notice," she answered, her eyes on the table.

"That's not unusual, especially in a murder trial. Don't take it personally, many people just don't want to get involved."

"Oh, some of them are going to get back to me and I wasn't able to get a hold of others." She didn't know why she felt the need to try and save face over this, they had much bigger fish to fry.

"So, what my approach is going to be is to ask for bail based on the fact that this murder happened ages ago, and that David has shown no sign of getting into any type of trouble since then. Even if he is guilty, letting him go home to his family is no different than him being free for the past thirty years. Also, because he has a family and is rooted in the community, he is a low flight risk. He isn't about to walk away from his children and grandchildren. Do you have any questions?"

"Oh, umm, well... will I have a chance to speak to him? And if they grant him bail, how long will it take them to release him?"

"I will try to arrange matters so you can at least have a couple of words with him, but to be honest, there is going to be a lot going on and I have to focus on some other things," Barry explained. "As for the bail issue, I want to reiterate that it is very rare for them to grant bail in such serious cases."

"Yes, I know, but if they do?"

"If they do, he should be able to come home tonight as long as you are able to post his bail and get the paperwork done quickly." Barry hesitated, looking as though he had something to say but he wasn't sure what words to use. "Look, the judge that has been assigned today is up for re-election and is known to be a hardass when it comes to both bail and parole; he's not a fan of either and I just don't want you to be disappointed."

Rose nodded, feeling any remaining hope die in the context of his words.

"Let's go to the courtroom now," Barry said gently as he watched the woman shrink before his eyes. In the years he had spent as a criminal defense lawyer, he had never gotten used to the pain and destruction that occurred not just to the victims and the accused, but their families.

~~~~

In the solemn courtroom, Rose felt small and insignificant. The ornate insignia of the state mounted behind the judge's chair simply emphasized his power. This was the judge's domain. One man held the fate of her husband in his hands. The lawyers walked in and gathered at their tables, speaking in hushed tones to each other. Rose took a seat behind the table where Barry had placed his briefcase. She looked around and realized that the people who were already seated were either blatantly gawking at her or stealing glances out of the corner of their eyes. She sat with her back rigid and her eyes cast towards the floor, avoiding looking at anyone.

A couple of minutes later, she sensed someone sit down next to her and she moved over slightly to give them more room. The person raised their arm and placed it along the seat behind her. Looking up, she looked into the familiar eyes of her son. If she had been standing, she would have probably fallen over as she felt her knees go weak.

"Oh Joshua, I'm so glad you made it!" she whispered.

"Of course, I made it. How could you think I wouldn't?" Josh looked surprised and a bit confused by her reaction. "I would think a bail hearing for my father should be considered an all-hands-on-deck kind of situation." It was then that she noticed Sarah sitting next to him.

Before she could say anything else, Kayla and Brandon slid in and sat next to Sarah. She felt tears come to her eyes; she was not alone.

The sound of a door opening, and chains clinking caused them to swivel their head to the far side of the room. A group of uniformed men entered surrounding a prisoner who had shackles on his feet and hands. Rose swallowed a lump in her throat as she watched the father of her children walk into the courthouse. Kayla made a motion as though she was about to stand up and go to her father but Brandon reached out and held her back. He whispered in his wife's ear, and she quickly sat back down again.

David looked the same as he always did and yet completely different. He stood tall and rigid, his back straight and his head held high. She wasn't sure if it was her imagination or not, but he seemed thinner. He passed the prosecutor's table and was walking towards his lawyer when he caught sight of his family in the first row. If the guards had not been pulling him forward, he would have stopped completely. Tears filled his eyes before he averted them and focused on his lawyer. Kayla cried quietly into her husband's shoulder and Josh reached over to hold his mother's hand. Rose took deep cleansing breaths and squeezed her son's hand in reassurance. While she appreciated them being there and they were a source of great strength for her, she wanted them to know she was there for them as well. She was still their mother, and they could count on her.

They all stood when the judge was announced, and the hearing began with announcing the case of the State vs. David Slater. The judge asked David to stand as he read out the charges.

"David Slater, you are hereby charged with murder in the first degree that carries with it a life sentence without a chance for parole for the murder of Rebecca Evans. Do you understand this charge?"

"Yes sir," David responded.

"And has your lawyer explained to you the options you have today and the consequences for each option?"

"Yes, he has."

"And how do you plead to this charge?"

"Not guilty your honor."

"You are also charged with the kidnapping of Rebecca Evans that carries with it a sentence of 20 years imprisonment. Do you understand this charge?"

"Yes sir."

"And has your lawyer explained to you the options you have today and the consequences for each option?"

"Yes, he has."

"And how do you plead to this charge?"

"Not guilty your honor."

As each charge was read, Rose felt herself shut down. The judge's voice became a sound happening far away. She had come prepared to hear her husband charged with murder, but for some reason, although the other charges didn't hold as severe a penalty, the piling on of one charge after another made Rose feel nauseous.

She realized she had been holding onto Joshua's hand too tightly when he shifted his hand to loosen her grip.

"Sorry," she murmured.

David sat back down next to his lawyer, his back straight and stiff. Barry stood up and spoke to the court, requesting his client be released on bail. The judge and the two lawyers began talking and

Rose struggled to follow what was happening until everyone sat down. Barry picked up some of the notes off the table and moved to the podium in front of the judge.

"Your honor, the crime that my client is charged with occurred 30 years ago. In the years since Rebecca Evans's untimely death, David Slater has lived an exemplary life. He is a loyal husband and the father of two adult children as well as the grandfather to three. He is involved in his church, coached his son's little league team, and is a valued employee at the firm where he is an architect. David Slater has deep roots in the community and has many reasons not to flee. I have the names of people in the community who are willing to speak to his character that I can provide to the court and we anticipate receiving even more in the coming days. In addition, Mr. Slater has an unblemished record, having been charged with no crimes during his lifetime and poses no risk to the community. We are requesting you set the bail at $100,000."

"Thank you, Mr. Lorman. Does the State want to address the issue of bail?" The judge looked over at the prosecution's table.

"Yes, your honor." A woman wearing an impeccably tailored matching skirt and jacket set approached the microphone. Adjusting it down, because even in the high heels she was perched on, she did not come close to Barry Lorman's height, she spoke. "The state opposes the granting of bail. There is DNA evidence from the victim which places him with Rebecca Evans when she was killed. The evidence is irrefutable. While Mr. Slater may not have posed a threat to the community over the last several years, we suggest that was because he thought he was safe from discovery. He walked around as an innocent man, afraid of nothing. Now that he knows we have evidence that shows he murdered an innocent young woman, he certainly poses a danger to others. Our community is not safe if he is released, free to walk amongst law-abiding citizens."

The judge looked towards the defense table as the prosecutor took her seat. Barry Lorman stood up and began to address what the prosecutor had said.

"The evidence mentioned by the State is not new evidence and it has only recently come to light that they believe they have a match; Mr. Slater is confident there has been a mistake in the DNA analysis which will vindicate him. To say that he is dangerous simply because he has been charged is a supposition that is not backed by any facts. Every case that comes before this court could be based on the same argument for denying bail and is simply unreasonable."

The judge scribbled down something and then addressed the courthouse.

"We're going to take a ten-minute break while I make some notes and we will return here with my decision," he stood up and walked out of the room. The noise level in the courtroom immediately rose as people in the gallery stood and began talking loudly to each other. Rose couldn't keep her eyes off the prisoner sitting in front of her, her husband.

She leaned over the railing, "Barry, can we have a moment?" she nodded her head toward David.

"We can't leave to give you privacy right now, but..." he glanced toward his client. David turned in his chair and for the first time since he entered the room, he met her eyes. Rose's breath caught in her throat. The pain she saw in his eyes took her breath away. She reached out to hold his hand, but the uniformed officer stood up and stepped forward.

"Please, no contact Ma'am," he instructed her.

Feeling chastised, Rose quickly nodded and addressed her husband "How are you holding up?"

"As well as can be expected, I think I might still be in shock," he smiled wryly. "Thanks for coming, kids," he lifted his chin as he acknowledged Joshua and Kayla as well as their partners.

"We wanted to see you sooner Dad, but they wouldn't let us," Kayla leaned forward, her upper body moving over the wooden railing that separated them. "What can we do for you Dad, what do you need? Can we phone you? Or can you phone us?"

"Gotta have some faith, Sunshine. I haven't given up hope that I'll be coming home today," his voice held a note of disapproval at her assumption he would be remaining in jail.

"Of course, Dad," Kayla smiled. "We've just been struggling with not being able to talk to you and see how you are doing. To make sure you are okay."

"I'm okay, and I can talk to Barry here pretty much whenever we need to," he reassured them. "If I wasn't okay, he would know about it."

"What do you want for dinner?" Rose asked, deciding to follow his optimistic lead. "Anything you want, I'll make sure it's ready when you get home."

"I have a hankering for some of your Beef Wellington," he told her, grinning.

"I'll grab the groceries for it when we're done here," she grinned back at him.

"What do we have to do to pay the bail?" Rose turned and asked Barry. She wanted David to see that she had complete faith in him coming home.

"Once they determine the amount, I will walk you through the process," Barry told her.

"If the bail is higher than we anticipate, I want you to contact Barry and get some instructions from him," David lowered his voice as though the only family member he wanted to hear was his wife.

"It's okay, I've spoken with the bank and there will be no problem getting the money; we will just have to use the house as security," she explained to him, happy she had been able to make the arrangements herself this morning. She was proud he wasn't going to have to worry about such details; he had enough on his plate already.

"How much have they approved it for, though?" he wanted to know.

"For the 100," she explained, uncertain why he was so concerned.

"If it's more, let me know and I'll give you some more banking information," David told her.

"But why? I don't understand."

"I don't want to be in here any longer than I have to and if you have to go back to the bank, it could take days. I have more easily accessible sources," he continued in a low tone as he spoke to her.

Before she could ask him any further questions, the bailiff announced the judge's return, and everyone turned toward the front of the courtroom.

"I've taken a look at the information on this case and considered both sides as presented to this court," the judge began. "Based on the severity of the crime and the evidence against the accused, I hereby deny bail and instruct the accused to be remanded into custody until trial. There will be a preliminary hearing in ten days, on the fourteenth of this month." He banged his gavel and stood up to leave again.

Rose stood up without thinking, as shock coursed through her body. In less than a few seconds, all their hopes had been dashed. They would not be welcoming David home tonight.

His lawyer stood up as the guards approached David to take him away. A cry was ripped out of Rose's throat as she watched her husband being led away. Kayla was crying softly, and Sarah had her arm tightly around Joshua's waist. They stood there for a minute while the courtroom began to clear.

"I'm sorry," Barry had turned to them. "I tried to warn you, it was a longshot."

"I know Barry, you told us, it's just the reality is..." she let her sentence hang as the words to describe how she was feeling escaped her.

"I want you all to follow me as we leave," Barry instructed them. "There are going to be media people outside who will want you to talk. Please don't say anything except that you're disappointed and then keep moving."

They huddled together and moved quickly to keep up with Barry as he made his way out of the courtroom, down the hallway, and out of the building. On the courthouse steps, a group of media representatives waited for them.

"Did you expect him to get bail?"

"What about the DNA evidence?"

"Will you be standing by your man?"

"Mrs. Slater! Mrs. Slater!"

It took all of Rose's self-control to keep walking. She was brought up to be polite and not ignore people, so refusing to stop and acknowledge these questions went against her fundamental instincts.

The mood at Kayla and Brandon's house, where they gathered, was somber. Joshua and Sarah sat on the couch; her hand tucked in his. Kayla shooed the twins upstairs and checked on Phoenix, who was down for his nap. Rose sent a text to Stacey to let her know that David had been denied bail.

"So, what's next?" Josh asked, looking at his mother.

"The state has to turn over any evidence they have to our lawyer, so then we'll know why they're so convinced he's guilty," Rose explained. "Then there'll be the preliminary hearing and at that time they need to convince the judge that their evidence is sufficient to proceed to trial."

"And that's happening on the fourteenth?" Sarah asked.

"So, if the judge decides there is enough to go forward, he will set a date for the trial itself. From what Barry has explained to me, there are a lot of things that happen between the preliminary hearing and the actual trial that involve what evidence gets admitted and stuff like that but those are the two main dates."

"Dad has to be in jail all that time? That's so unfair!" Kayla wailed. "How can they do this to an innocent man!"

"Honey, they don't know that he's innocent," her husband spoke in a calm voice, his arm around her shoulders. "We wouldn't want the courts to let every person accused of a violent crime walk around freely until their trial, would we?"

"But it's my dad!" Kayla broke down sobbing quietly, hiding her face in her husband's shoulder. Using his hand to rub her back, Brandon held his wife. The rest of the family was quiet and lost in their thoughts.

The silence was broken by Rose's cell phone ringing. She looked at the display and the number was shown as unlisted. "Hello?" she answered hesitantly, worrying that the media had gotten a hold of her mobile number.

"Hello?" Rose listened to the sounds on the other end of the line. Someone was there, but they weren't speaking. "Hello? Who is this?" Joshua and Sarah looked up from their chairs and Brandon looked at her over Kayla's head. When no one responded, Rose hung up in frustration and shrugged in her kid's direction. She got up and walked into the kitchen without saying a word. What was the point in wondering who was calling her when it could be any number of different media people or just some random person wanting to annoy her? She grabbed a glass from the cupboard and poured herself some water. The adrenaline she had been running on since court this morning had taken a toll on her body and her mouth was dry and felt as though it had been coated with something.

When her phone rang again, she contemplated not answering. Anyone she cared to talk to right now was in this house, except maybe Stacey or the lawyer. Then she realized it could be Barry with news and she reached and answered the phone.

"Hello?"

The line was full of static, and it cut in and out before Rose heard a woman's voice.

"Rose? Is that you?"

"Yes?"

"It's Jessie."

"Jessie?"

"Yes... bad connection... coming home... tomorrow..."

"You're coming home tomorrow?"

"Yes... later..." The line cut out and went dead.

"Was that Aunt Jessie?" Joshua asked, standing in the kitchen doorway.

"Yeah, it was a horrible connection, but I think she's coming home tomorrow,"

"Wow, things must be dire if Aunt Jessie is coming home," Joshua chuckled. "She usually only comes around for really major celebrations or deaths."

"Well, I'd hope your brother being incarcerated would qualify as a good enough reason to come home," Rose agreed. "Do you know where she is now?"

"No, last I heard I think it was somewhere in Africa where there was a drought," Joshua responded. "But that doesn't mean that's where she is now."

The traveling exploits of David's younger sister were an ongoing source of speculation and interest in her family. As a photojournalist, she flew from one corner of the globe to another covering natural and man-made disasters. They rarely knew when they were going to see her or for how long.

"Wherever she's coming from, I'm sure we'll hear from her as soon as she has a better connection and will let us know when to expect her," Rose said. "But for now, I think I'm going to head home. I'm exhausted."

"Are you sure Mom? Sarah and I could come with you, so you don't have to be alone."

"No, I'm okay. I think I need to have some alone time before your aunt arrives."

"Okay, just so that you know if you need us, we are just a call away," Joshua leaned over and wrapped his arms around his mother, squeezing her tightly.

She relished the feel of him and the comfort he provided. She knew her son was concerned about her and wanted to help. The problem was, she didn't know what could possibly help.

~~~~

Rose woke with a start, her heart pounding and sat bolt upright in bed. What had she heard? It was dark outside, and her bedside clock showed that it was three minutes after four in the morning. She slipped out of bed and padded across the room to the door. Standing completely still, she turned her head to the side and strained to hear something. A creak from the downstairs kitchen floor cracked through the air and Rose's knees went weak. Suddenly, she heard the clicking sound of a light switch, and a soft glow of light came up the stairs. Who was in her house? And turning the lights on?

A feeling of relief washed over her, and she grabbed her housecoat that was draped over her bedroom chair. She made her way down the stairs and to the kitchen.

"Hope I didn't wake you, Rose."

Rose's sister-in-law was sitting at the kitchen table, a glass of juice and a cell phone sitting in front of her.

"You damn near gave me a heart attack, woman!" Rose opened her arms wide, and Jessie stood up to give her a big hug. The two women stood in a silent embrace in the middle of the kitchen, offering unspoken comfort to each other. After a minute, they parted, Rose patting Jessie's shoulder.

"How was your flight?"

"Long and tiring, the usual," Jessie said.

"Where have you come from?"

"I was covering some flooding in South Africa and flew out from Johannesburg and then through Zurich. I booked a flight as soon as I heard what happened."

"You must be exhausted."

"Yeah, traveling is always exhausting," Jessie agreed.

"Why don't we get you settled in then?"

"Rose, I'm tired but I'm used to jetlag. Can we talk about David?"

"Of course, what would you like to know?"

"Oh gee, I don't know, why don't we start with why the hell my brother is locked up and charged with murder?"

"You always did like to get to the point, didn't you?" Rose laughed.

"Life is too short to waste time," Jessie raised her glass of juice as though in a toast to her sentiment.

Rose went over the last couple of days, starting with the shocking incident of his arrest at Phoenix's birthday party, right up until the arraignment this afternoon.

"Wow," Jessie said in a quiet, almost whispering voice. "And for Rebecca Evan's murder."

"Yup."

"And all we know at this point is that the evidence they have against him is some type of DNA match," Jessie confirmed. "Do you know if that is everything they have against him?"

"We're not sure; that is just what they used at the arraignment to make him sound like he was a danger to society. Over the next week or so they will have to share everything with our lawyer, so we'll know what is going on by the date of his preliminary trial—it's called discovery."

"Then I guess we don't have much time," Jessie said and Rose looked at her questioningly. "We need to see what we can find out about all of this and find a way to prove what happened, one way or the other."

"No, Jessie. Barry, our lawyer, said the prosecution have to prove his guilt. They have the burden of proof to show that he is guilty, it isn't up to us to prove that he is innocent." Rose shared with her sister-in-law everything she was learning about the judicial system.

"That is fine for him to say, but we both know that if they have arrested him, there is a presumption of guilt. We can't just sit back and wait for the chips to fall where they may," Jessie waved away the idea that they should sit and wait around for the process to play out.

"And what did you mean we need to find out what happened 'one way or another'?" It suddenly dawned on Rose what Jessie had said. "You can't possibly be suggesting that David might be guilty?"

"I just meant we need to look for the truth, no matter where it leads us. We need to be prepared for whatever we find," Jessie shrugged her shoulders but Rosie couldn't help but notice she was avoiding her eyes.

"What could we possibly do anyway? She died thirty-some years ago. I don't know how we could possibly find anything out."

"I don't know either, but even if it was thirty years ago, there are plenty of people from that time who we should be able to find and talk to. I want to get a sense of what was going on when she died."

"But you were there too," Rosie pointed out. Jessie raised one eyebrow and cocked her head.

"Yeah, and I was all of about eight years old. I have no idea what was going on around outside my preoccupation with my treehouse and my caterpillar collection."

"Oh yeah, I keep forgetting you are just a baby," Rosie grinned over the table.

"How is he doing?" The question was quiet and there was a note of sadness in her voice. The idea of her brother being locked up was almost too painful to think about.

"He is doing pretty well," Rosie reassured her. "He's looking tired and stressed of course—who wouldn't be?"

The two women sat at the table, looking at each other sadly but fondly. The two had always had a great deal of respect for each other. Jessie wondered sometimes how David had been so lucky to find such a stable, smart, and capable wife and Rose admired her sister-in-law's ability to grab life by the horns, no matter what anyone thought. Jessie lived her life on her terms and damned what anyone else thought.

"Well, I had better get some shuteye; the spare room hasn't moved since the last time I was here, has it?"

"Nope, it's right where you left it."

"I'm going to sleep for a few hours and then when I get up, I'm going to put together a list of people I remember from when we were young. And we should maybe also consider going back to where this all began – Meadowland.

They stood up, placed Jessie's cup in the sink, and walked towards the stairs. As Rose expected, Jessie only had a small bag and was able to handle it on her own.

"Thank you so much for coming, Jessie, you don't know what it means to me," Rose flung her arms around her sister-in-law and drew her in close. Although nothing had changed, she felt as though she wasn't in this alone anymore. They parted and as Rosie had one hand on the doorknob to her bedroom, she suddenly turned around.

"Hey Jessie, did you happen to try to call me before we talked on the phone?"

"You mean other than the bad connection call? No, why?"

"Oh, no reason. Someone had the wrong number, I guess. Goodnight."

Chapter 16

The Past

"Do you have your thermos?" His mother asked him, looking around the kitchen frantically as though she expected it to magically appear. "Yes Mom, I have my thermos," David said patiently. "And I have my bag lunch, my booklet of stamps, my suntan lotion, and my first aid kit."

"Don't fret Helen, he has been ready for hours," his father squeezed his mother's shoulder as he walked by her. He opened the fridge and grabbed his brown paper bag that held a sandwich, an apple, and a juice box.

"We're going to get going now."

"What? It's early, you have another half an hour," his mother looked startled. "Why are you leaving so early?"

"So, we can try and save some of our sanity and yours," he kissed the top of his wife's head and turned to go out the back door.

David was grateful for the decision to leave early. His mother was driving him crazy. He was excited about starting this job and being away from home for two whole months. He was packed up and ready to go, he had said goodbye to Jessica before she went to her room last night so everything was set. But there was still a part of him that was a bit nervous. And those few nerves were being frayed by his mother's anxiety.

They walked out to the car with his belongings packed in a large duffel bag. Once his possessions were stored away in the huge trunk, he turned to his mother and wrapped his arms around her.

"Don't worry about me Mom. I'll write, and if I get a chance, you might even get a collect call from me. You don't have to answer but it'll let you know I'm okay," he said the last bit with a lightness in his voice, making sure the moment didn't get too serious.

"Oh, you! We may not be rich, but that'll be the day I don't accept a collect call from my own son!" She smiled at him through the shimmering tears that rested on the lower lids of her eyes. "You just use your head, be safe, and don't forget who you are."

His mother had used that phrase with him for as long as he could remember. When he was young, maybe six or seven, he asked her what she meant by that? After all, he wasn't about to forget his name. But she explained that it meant he should remember what she and his dad had taught him and remember that no matter what, they were people of honesty, integrity, and compassion. It had stuck with him and become a kind of mission statement or mantra for him. He tried to live his life according to it. Part of the reason he did that was because it just seemed to make sense to him; that would be a good way to live his life. The other reason was that he had heard it so many times and since such a young age that it was now a part of him.

When they were finally on the road, his dad turned to him and smiled.

"You did good with your mom; I know she can be a bit dramatic about things sometimes but some people are just born with a tendency to see trouble around each corner. Your being patient and understanding with her shows me the type of man you have grown into and I'm proud of you."

David sat there, stunned. His father rarely talked in such a serious manner to him, and he was certainly not a man to throw around praise. It wasn't that he didn't know his father was proud of him or that he loved him. But generally, he experienced it through how his father acted, not the words he said. He felt a lump form in his throat as he realized that this job and the new life he would have at college were a turning point for him, not only for his independence and his relationship with Rebecca and his friends but with his parents as well. He was becoming a man and his father recognized that and wanted to let him know he was ready.

Miles and miles of highway rolled out under the car and the two men sat in silence, listening to the radio, caught up in their own thoughts. Eventually, they passed the sign that pointed east toward the lake where Rebecca was going to be for the summer. He had a moment of regret that he hadn't reached out to talk to her before he left. It wasn't in his nature to just leave things as they had. In the past, he would have pursued her and tried to work things out. He knew he would have to write her while he was at the camp and let her know he was okay and that as far as he was concerned, they were okay too.

About thirty miles down the highway, they pulled into a gas station that was in a small town called Rutledge to top off the car's gas, use the washroom and pick up some snacks. His dad laughingly commented that David's mom didn't need to know they hadn't stuck to just their bagged lunch.

They drove the remaining way in companionable silence, until about half an hour later when they turned off the highway and onto a dirt road that would take them to the camp where David would spend his summer.

~~~~

Rebecca woke up Monday morning with an emptiness in the pit of her stomach. She felt as though she was going to jump out of her skin. The realization that David was going to leave without so much as a goodbye had finally hit her. She honestly thought if she waited it out, he would reach out to her. And here she was, Monday morning with her pride intact but her heart shattered. Her mom always told her that she let her pride cause her more unhappiness than anything else and for once Rebecca understood what she meant. Yes, she could say she hadn't been the one to break their silence, but what had that earned her? Nothing but heartache.

She got up and finished packing for the cabin. She threw her toiletries and an extra couple of novels in and then zipped up her suitcase. Even with Ashley or Kim spending a couple of weeks in August, it was going to be a long summer at the lake, so she had best be prepared to kill some time. There were only so many times she could take the canoe out on the lake or walk down the beach. The cabin had been in her family for years and she felt as though she knew every nook and cranny of it. She knew the scratches some bored kid had made in the wood of the bunkbed in the kid's room. When going down to the beach, she was familiar enough to watch the third step of the cabin stairs where there was a soft spot. There were so many happy memories at the cabin, but this year, her last year living under her parent's roof, the summer seemed to stretch out in front of her forever.

Downstairs, she poured herself a cup of coffee and plunked herself down at the kitchen table. Her father looked up at her over the top of his paper, raising an eyebrow.

"My, you look excited about the summer start," he commented.

"I am. It's hard to believe I'm done with school; it felt like that would never happen."

"But? It's David, isn't it?"

Rebecca looked up in surprise. She didn't think her parents paid much attention to her relationship with David, other than to make sure she was in on curfew.

"Well, kinda."

"You two are still young. You'll have plenty of time together when you're at college," her father tried to reassure her.

"Don't you start too Dad! That's all Ashley and Kim have been telling me."

"Well, maybe if the people around you have all been telling you the same thing, it's because there's some truth there?"

Half of Rebecca's mouth pulled up in a tight bunch, and a feeling of frustration mixed with disbelief and disdain came over her.

"Yeah, yeah."

"Believe us or not, you have two months at the lake to relax and prepare to launch off into adulthood. The sooner you accept the situation, the better you'll be able to take advantage of your time."

Her father got on her nerves sometimes and for much the same reason as David. He was so often right. They were both calm and reasonable men who looked at things pragmatically. It could be so annoying when you were someone who went through life guided by your emotions.

"Hi!" her little sister Susanna came bounding into the room, full of energy and excitement. "Are we going yet?"

Susanna was the much-loved little sister who was referred to by her parents as the "late arrival." She had come along unexpectedly after years of infertility when her parents had finally resigned themselves to having an only child. Her attitude matched her conception and birth story. She always entered a room or a situation as though everyone had been waiting for her to arrive, saying "Here I am, let's get the party started!" While she could be annoying as were most little sisters, Rebecca loved her deeply and unconditionally. Seven years apart ensured there had never been any sibling rivalry.

"Your mom just ran to the store to pick up some last-minute things and then we'll be on the road," her dad told Susanna. "Are you all packed? Hairbrush? Bathing suit?... Toothbrush?"

"Yup, Yup, YUP!" Susanna had decided one year to conveniently forget her toothbrush at home. She was at a stage of her life where hygiene was a nuisance and she was quite dismayed to discover that toothbrushes could be bought almost anywhere. She had truly thought she had found a way to get out of two months of brushing her teeth. It was now a family joke when they went somewhere;

her dad always worked it in to ask Susanna if she remembered her toothbrush, even if they were on their way to see a movie.

Just then, they heard a thump at their back door and someone shouted, "Let me in!" Susanna jumped up and opened the door to let their mother in, two or three grocery bags hanging off each arm and panting. Her father jumped up and grabbed the bags. Her mother pushed an errant strand of her thin blonde hair out of her clear blue eyes. While she had the appearance of being a delicate woman who might blow over in the next gust of wind, she was as strong as an ox. "Daisy! I thought you said you had a couple of things to pick up? What is this, the whole store?" He shook his head in mock disbelief. In reality, Rebecca knew her father expected nothing less than chaos when her mother was trying to plan and organize something.

"Oh, you know, when you get there, you realize it would be nice to have a few more snacks," she turned towards her daughter and her voice became more like singing than talking. "One can never have enough watermelon and hotdogs at the lake, can one girls?"

Inwardly, Rebecca grimaced. She had great parents, but her mother had a habit of lumping her in with her sister, even though they were so far apart in age. Consequently, she was often spoken to as though she was a little girl.

"Oh, come on Becky, turn that frown upside down! You know how much you love it at the lake!" Her mother grabbed her daughter's head between her two hands, shaking her head slightly. "I know you're sad about David not coming but it'll still be fun, I promise! No, honey don't put those two together, you want to put all the frozen stuff together so they keep each other cold!" Her mother's flightiness was renowned in the family and while Rebecca was certainly used to it, it could still get on her nerves. She wasn't sure she could recall the last time she had had an uninterrupted conversation with her.

Chapter 17

The Past

The heat of midday was oppressive as the group of forestry workers cleared the underbrush. The day had started cool and fresh, and the crew chattered amongst themselves, sharing first names and where they lived. They had all arrived yesterday and were nervous and excited about their new jobs and being away from home. But as the morning wore on and the sun rose higher and higher in the sky, the sound of voices grew fainter as the group's energy level declined.

At noon the cook from the camp came by and handed out thick sandwiches, ice-cold drinks, and plates of cookies. The crew members searched for shade and leaned back to chug their drinks before tackling their lunch. It was slowly dawning on them that the summer was going to be more than just an opportunity to leave home and get away from nagging parents.

David's feet hurt in his new steel-toed boots, and he removed his hard hat, almost sighing out loud as the wind played through his sweaty hair. They had each been given a large water bottle when they left in the morning, and it was replenished as they ate. Those who hadn't drank their water were admonished by the cook and given a lecture on dehydration. Half an hour later, after a lineup at the porta-potty, they got back to work under the blazing sun.

Later that evening, a subdued group sat around the table in the dining tent. The clang of utensils against the plates made a symphony of noise made even more obvious by the lack of conversation. Dragging themselves back to their bunkhouse, they turned off the lights early. They followed this routine for the next few days until they had adjusted to the additional fresh air, sunshine, and hard labor.

On the fourth evening, the banter around the table was joking and full of life.

"I thought I was gonna pass out from that last root, it was in there tighter than a pickle jar lid!"

"You just gotta work on your technique a bit, Brad!"

"That's what she said!"

David smiled at the joking while shoveling food into his mouth. Just then Richard, one of his crewmates, and the boy who slept two bunks away nudged David with his elbow.

"Hey, you're kinda quiet."

"Just taking everything in," David responded.

"Some of us are going for a bit of a walk later for some, uh... fresh air, yah wanna come?"

"I think I've had enough fresh air today, but thanks," David smiled slightly, softening the blow of declining the invitation.

"It's not really for fresh air, we're going for a spliff."

"Yeah, I figured that, I'll pass but thanks."

Richard pursed his lips and reached for his glass, turning away from David. Unsure of what had just happened, David went back to eating. While he enjoyed some beer with his friends, weed had never been something he ever got into.

Later that night, David lay on his bunk and pulled out his paper and pen, as well as his favorite picture of Becky. He was starting to write a letter to his parents when he felt someone standing beside his bed, casting a shadow on his paper. He looked up to find Richard peering down at him.

"Nice picture, who is it?"

"My girlfriend."

"She put out?" Richard asked casually.

David pulled away from Richard in shock. "What?"

"You heard me. You two bump uglies? Play hide the wiener? Do the horizontal dance?"

"I'm not answering that," David couldn't believe this guy with his greasy black hair, and his squinty, close-set eyes. Why would he think David wanted to talk to him about his relationship with Becky? Hell, he didn't share that info with anyone except perhaps Chris.

"What's your problem Slater? Too good and hoity-toity to kiss and tell? Not interested in a small toke or two either, what do you do?"

David didn't have a chance to wonder how Richard knew his last name, although later he would assume that he had been talking to the other boys. He felt his heart begin to pound faster and he heard it rushing to his head. There wasn't much he could say to answer Richard without sounding stupid. It would be best if he just ignored him.

"Nothing, huh? That's what I thought," Richard guffawed and walked away.

David threw his pen down on his bed in frustration. He didn't want to make enemies and here he was, a mere few days in and he seemed to have attracted the attention of the resident bully. To make matters worse, he had been so exhausted from the new work that he hadn't had a chance to make any friends. He sighed and rested his chin in his hands. He hoped things would improve soon.

The days went by, and Richard continued to make snide comments and vulgar innuendos whenever he saw David. By now David had noticed there was a theme to the comments that revolved around David thinking he was better than Richard. He regretted not going for a toke when Richard asked him. He also wished he had kept Becky's picture to himself.

Soon they had a day off from the hard work of clearing the underbrush in the forest. One day didn't give them a chance to go home or do anything more than take a quick trip into town. Many of the crew stayed behind and slept, wrote letters home, and ate as much as the kitchen made available.

Later that evening, when they were all in the bunkhouse playing cards and chatting, Richard pushed in a trolly that had a TV on top. "Attention! Attention all! Tonight, we have some special entertainment, courtesy of yours truly!"

The boys began to clap loudly and egg him on, encouraging him to make an even bigger production.

"The lovely and generous Miss Crystal Love will work hard to keep us up and interested all evening. Rumor has it that she is a specialist in hoses and likes nothing better than to take on hoses of all sizes!" Richard wiggled his eyebrows up and down while he licked his lips. David couldn't help but think he looked like someone's lecherous backwoods cousin.

David felt like there was nowhere he could go to escape. If he got up and walked out, he would never live it down. While he had a collection of girlie magazines hidden under the mattress of his bed at home, he had never watched an actual dirty movie before. There was a section of the Blockbuster back home that was behind curtains that only those over 21 could go behind. The owner of Blockbuster was the father of one of his school friends and he watched the entry to it like a hawk. A guy at school had managed to get a hold of one of the VHS tapes when his older brother left it lying around, but on the night he and some of his friends had gathered in the basement to watch it, David had been in Philly for his gramma's funeral. Now here he was with a room full of guys he didn't know, about to watch his first porno, whether he wanted to or not.

"Pay attention Davie my boy, you might learn something you can try on that princess of yours," Richard said, throwing a pillow in his direction.

"In order to try something on her, he would have to have something bigger than his thumb to use," one of the guys shouted from across the bunkhouse.

The red slowly crept up David's neck as he took the comments in silence. He sat on the edge of his bed, looking at the floor.

"What's your girl's name, Davie?" Richard asked. "Come on, surely you can at least tell us that!"

"Rebecca," David spoke quietly.

"Rebecca? Becky? How sweet!"

Richard walked over until he was standing in front of David, he squatted and in a lowered voice, he asked "Is she a virgin Davie? She kinda looks it. If you're a really, really good little boy, does she let you in her white cotton panties?"

"Fuck off, Richard," David rolled over onto his side, his back facing his tormentor.

"What? Why so hostile? Do you have some pent-up frustration, Davie? Maybe the show will help you with that? And don't worry, we'll turn the lights off, so we won't see you wanking off."

He heard Richard turn on his heels and walk away from his bunk. What was it about him that provoked the other boy so much? David wasn't used to being the brunt of bullies. While he wasn't the most popular guy back home, he certainly held a certain level of respect, and he was left alone. He frowned and ran his hand through his hair. It was going to be a much longer summer than he had anticipated.

What was he supposed to do, lie here with his back to everyone? He didn't want to watch the movie, but the lights had been lowered so writing a letter was certainly out of the question. And if he didn't watch, it would only make him a bigger target for Richard. He flipped over onto his other side and looked around the room. Each boy was either lying on his stomach or sitting on his bed watching the TV.

"Hello, are you the vacuum repair man, er, I mean woman?"

"Why yes sir, I am, what seems to be the problem?"

"I don't know, my hose is plugged I think."

A hoot came up from the boys.

"I'd let her unplug my hose!"

"Show her your hose!"

The woman on the screen was dressed in a skimpy jean blouse with buttons which seemed to be restraining her breasts with difficulty. She had short cutoff jeans and a tool belt slung over her hips. Her platinum blonde hair fell in waves along her shoulders and David couldn't help but think about how fake it looked compared to Rebecca's beautiful cascades of blonde hair.

"I'm really good with hoses, let's take a look at yours," she said, batting her eyes at the camera and giggling.

The thin plot continued and so did the hoots and catcalls from the group. It was as though they were trying to one-up each other with their vulgar comments. It didn't take long, and through some miraculous twist in the plot both actors on the screen were soon naked and grappling on a couch.

David was watching the video with divided attention; the rest of his brain noted the looks on the faces of his bunkmates. Some were wiggling in their seats, their eyes shifting from the movie to the floor and back again in rapid succession. Others were nudging their friends and laughing. A couple were watching with wide eyes and slack jaws.

Suddenly, he heard Richard make a sound that imitated the moaning and grunting man on the TV screen. He was also making movements with his hand, as though trying to push something into his crotch.

"Oh Becky! Becky! Where'd you learn how to do that Becky? How's my hose, Becky?"

David felt his stomach clench and the right side of his top lip moved up in disgust. The voice in his head kept telling him it was only talk, that Becky was just a name and it meant nothing. But hearing her name come out of this idiot's mouth in such a grotesque way caused David's heart to pound and the veins in his temple to throb.

"Knock it off, Richard."

Richard's voice rose in pitch, "Oh, you have the best hose I've ever had gar...gar...glug...glug..."

Some of the others laughed as though it was the funniest thing they had ever seen or heard, while a smaller percentage looked around uneasily and avoided making eye contact with David or looking in Richard's direction.

Taking a deep breath, David worked hard to keep calm. Richard's words were blending with the sounds coming from the movie, creating an odd mixture of make-believe and the here and now. He knew the other boy was just trying to get to him, but it was working. The camp had a strict no-fighting policy and he had to keep himself under control. If he gave in and went at Richard with his fists flying, he would be the one sent packing, and then how would he help pay for college?

He lay down on his bunk, staring at the TV, unseeing. He kept talking to himself to keep his eye on the prize and not let Richard win. He thought about his dad, with his calm and steady demeanor; he wouldn't let something like this get to him. Then he thought about Becky. He regretted leaving things the way they had as it just made dealing with Richard that much more difficult. If they had parted well, he didn't think this would be having the same effect on him. It made him wonder what she was up to tonight and if she had decided that if he wasn't going to spend the summer with her, she might as well find someone else. He knew that made little sense, but being away from home and all that was familiar was getting to him.

Chapter 18

The Past

Rebecca couldn't believe only a week and a half of the summer had passed. Time seemed to crawl at a snail's pace. Every day she slept in until almost midday and then got up and helped her mother around the cabin. Then she would grab the blow-up air mattress and, following the trail that had been carved from years of family use, she made her way to the lake. She slathered herself in suntan lotion that had a 15 SPF, jumped on the bed, and began to float. She would begin by lying on her stomach and eventually flip over onto her back, struggling not to tip herself over and end up soaking wet.

Susanna and some friends she had made from neighboring cabins would be making castles in the dirty sand or chasing each other through the underbrush, pretending that one of them was the good guy and the others the bad guys. When one group managed to catch the other group, they would declare the game finished and start all over again. Rebecca had once tried to ask Susanna what the difference was between the good guys and the bad guys. She had simply looked at her as though she was incredibly obtuse, laughed, and walked off.

Rebecca used the sound of their voices as a gauge for whether she should open her eyes and paddle back, closer to the shore. One time she had drifted off to sleep and had woken with a start to realize she was almost halfway across the lake. In some ways, she felt as though she was floating through her holidays. She felt disconnected from her family as her mind was on more important things like college and David. She was in limbo between childhood and adulthood, with a foot in each part of her life but not entirely in either. The days began to drift by like the clouds she watched from the air mattress; her body languid from the heat of the sun beating down on her lithe body.

At night, after she had helped her mother clean up the kitchen and put away the dishes, she excused herself and went for a walk down the dirt road that joined the cabins together. She would stop and sit on a neighbor's swinging bench which was secured to a large thick branch. Tipping her head back, she gazed up at the stars, wondering if David was looking at them too.

Her quiet, introspective mood began to worry her parents as they watched their usually talkative and engaged daughter seem to sleepwalk through each day.

"Rebecca, why don't you come with us to the O'Brien's cabin tonight? We're playing some cards and the more the merrier?" her mother suggested one night after dinner.

"Oh, I don't think so," Rebecca answered with a faint smile.

"Why not? Moping around this cabin all summer isn't good for you."

"What do you mean? How am I moping?"

Her mother ignored her question and turned to her husband. "Frank, don't you think Rebecca should come with us to the O'Brien's tonight?"

"Sure, Daisy honey," her father responded automatically, his attention focused on

his fish filleting knife as he checked to see if he had done a good enough sharpening job on it.

"Can I come too?" Susanna piped in. "I wanna play cards too!"

"You aren't old enough to play cards with the adults honey," her mother responded.

"Why? Cards are just a game and games are for kids."

"Yes, but this is going to be a bunch of adults playing the card game."

"But if Rebecca goes then who will stay with me? I can't stay here by myself!"

"You're always telling us how you are old enough to be left home alone."

"Not at the cabin," Susanna had a panicked look on her face. "It's dark and creepy here, I can't stay alone."

"Don't worry Suzie-Q, I'll be here," Rebecca reassured her younger sister whose lower lip had begun to quiver.

"I didn't say she couldn't come with us if she doesn't want to stay alone, but she won't be able to keep up with the cards." It was obvious her mother felt like the situation was fast getting out of control. As much as she would like to see her eldest daughter come out of her shell, she hadn't thought this through.

"It's okay Mom," Rebecca patted her mother's shoulder. "You two go on and visit with your friends and have fun. Susanna and I will stay at the cabin and make some smores."

"Yeah!" Susanna yelled excitedly. "Smores are so good!"

~~~~

One day, when the weather forecast was expected to hit record highs, Rebecca was woken by the sound of laughter and slamming doors. Frowning, she sat up and swung her feet onto the floor. Just then, the door opened, and Ashley and Kim barreled into the room and flung themselves onto Rebecca's bed.

"Hey, girl! Want some company?"

"Ashley!! Kim! What are you guys doing here?"

"Miss me?" Ashley threw her arms around Rebecca and gave her a bear hug.

"Of course, I did, you goofball!" Rebecca squealed.

"Ashley and I decided to grab Chris and Terry, to come keep you company for the day!" Kim joined in on the hug. "So, get your suit on, let's make a lunch and head down to the water!"

Rebecca was grinning from ear to ear when she came out of her room. She had changed and pulled her hair up in a high ponytail. She was slathered in sunscreen and ready for the day.

The sound of laughter rang out as the teens raced from the cabin towards the lake. In the doorway watching them, stood Rebecca's mother with a large smile on her face. It was so nice to see her daughter acting more like herself. She had been worried by Rebecca's behavior since arriving at the lake; she had never seen her daughter so down for so long. Maybe this visit from her friends would be enough to jolt Rebecca out of the dark place she was in. Daisy turned to go into the cabin to make lunch for the kids.

~~~~

"This is the life," Terry said, lying on his back on an air mattress. The five teens had threaded a rope through their mattresses so they were able to float on the lake together.

"Mmmmm," one of the teens responded.

Ashley moved her hand back and forth, the water caressing her fingertips. The sun beat down on her skin, warming and lulling her as she drifted. Thoughts flitted through her mind, and she wished there was some way to freeze this moment in time.

"So, I wonder if David is as relaxed as we are right now?" Chris mused and the others began chuckling.

"From what he said about their working conditions, I somehow doubt it," Terry chimed in.

Rebecca remained quiet, staring up at the blue sky. She wanted to ask if Terry had heard from David, but pride kept her silent. She didn't want to know if they had heard from him when she hadn't. And she didn't want them to know she hadn't been talking to him either.

"I'm pretty sure he wishes he was here instead of breaking rocks under the hot sun with a bunch of stinky boys," Ashley piped up. She didn't want to dwell on David as she knew it was a touchy subject

for Rebecca, but she didn't want one of the boys to say something
tactless or ask Rebecca something that would spoil the laid-back
mood of the day.

Silence fell over the friends again, broken only by the sound of the
occasional boater going by. Every so often, when they had floated
out a bit too far, one of them would casually paddle them back.
Eventually, Chris reached out and tickled the bottom of Rebecca's
foot, causing her to squeal and jerk her foot away. The sudden
movement upended her air mattress and she rolled over into the
water. Splashing, she reached out and grabbed Chris's mattress,
pulling the corner under until the water began to cover it.

"Oh no you don't!" Chris laughed as he sat up, his legs dangling in
the water while still sitting on the raft. He began to splash water in
Rebecca's direction.

"Hey!" Terry protested, as he was caught in the crossfire. He
promptly sat up and splashed water on Kim and Ashley and they
soon joined in. Before long the idyllic, peaceful lake was filled with
screams and laughter.

"Hey! Guys!" they heard during a lull in their playing. They turned
to see Rebecca's mother on the shore, waving them in. The two boys
grabbed a corner of their mattresses and began to swim with the girls
hanging onto the back of a mattress, letting them do all the work.

"Serves them right for starting the water fight," Rebecca said to
Ashley and Kim. "Let them swim some of that energy off."

Before long they were in shallow water and had begun to walk
toward the shore.

"Well, it looks like you guys figured out how to entertain yourselves,"
Rebecca's mother Daisy commented with a smile on her face. "Dry
off and come up to the cabin for some lunch."

Later that afternoon, the teens lay stretched out on lawn chairs; the
boys were dozing while the girls read quietly.

"How are you doing?" Ashley asked quietly, looking at Rebecca.

"I'm much better now that you're here," Rebecca responded with a smile and reached out to grab her friend's hand. "Thank you for coming."

"I just wish I could stay longer but we're going to have to get back tonight before dark," Ashley sighed. "Terry has to get his parent's vehicle back."

"I figured as much, but damn I wish you could stay longer."

Ashley's voice became even quieter as she asked, "Have you heard from David yet?"

"No."

"Well, it's early days and he's probably still getting settled in," Ashley quickly reassured her.

"Yeah."

Rebecca picked up her novel and began reading. She didn't want to think about David right now. She wanted to relax and enjoy the time she had with her friends. She had spent enough time worrying about him, their relationship, and where it was headed. If her friend's visit had taught her anything, it was that it was time she started enjoying her summer.

Looking over the top of her novel, she surveyed her friends. Ashley, who was always thinking of her, putting up with her drama like the amazing best friend she had always been. Kim, her quiet and reflective friend who quietly supported and encouraged her. Her gaze fell on Chris, and she realized his eyes were open and he was staring at her. The corners of his mouth rose slightly as he acknowledged her eyes on him. It felt like an oddly intimate moment and the hairs on the back of Rebecca's neck rose. Her eyes dropped back to her book, and she stared at the page with unseeing eyes. There was something in the look that Chris had given her that she just couldn't put her finger on, but it made her uneasy.

She was saved from her ruminations when Terry spoke up.

"We have to leave in about an hour my friends," he said.

Ashley groaned and playfully tossed her novel in his direction.

"Hey, careful!" he protested, throwing the novel back at her. "You could take a guy's eye out with that thing."

"Oh right, what's going to happen? You think you'll get a papercut on your eyeball?" Ashley teased him. The five of them talked about their plans for the rest of the summer as they stood up, gathering their things and Rebecca asked if they would be able to visit her again.

"I'll definitely be back," Kim reassured her. "I'll find a ride somehow, and maybe this time it can be for more than a day?"

"That would be great, it gets a bit lonely here."

"Oh, I bet. Lazing around the lake and working on a tan can be emotionally taxing," Chris chimed in.

"Ha. Ha." Rebecca responded, pretending to throw her novel at him as Ashley had thrown hers at Terry.

"No, seriously, we'll try to get back again," Terry reassured her. "It's not a hardship to spend the day here."

"Thanks, guys. Don't get me wrong, it's nice and relaxing here but I miss my friends sometimes." Actually, she missed them all the time but there was a limit to how pathetic and whiny she wanted to sound, even in front of her lifelong friends.

"We miss you too!' Ashley cooed as she threw her arms around Rebecca while motioning for Kim and the two boys to join her. "Group hug!"

Rebecca giggled as they squeezed her against them, moving rapidly from side to side. She could always count on her friends to cheer her up.

Chapter 19

Present Day

"So, his closest friends were Chris, Terry, and Wade?" Rose sat at the kitchen table, writing on a yellow notepad.

"Yes, and Rebecca's best friends were Ashley and Kim," Jessie responded.

"And didn't you mention a Susannah?"

"That was Rebecca's younger sister."

Rose scribbled a note beside Susannah's name. "Do you remember anything about the place where David worked that summer?"

"No, but we can ask when we talk to him this afternoon," Jessie said. They had received a phone call from the lawyer this morning saying that David would be calling Rose's cell number early this afternoon. In addition to making a list of the people who might remember what was going on that summer, she was now also making a list of things she wanted to remember to talk to David about.

Jessie, who was sitting with a laptop in front of her was attempting to find contact information for each person on their list. She had started with a simple Google search and then went on to Facebook and LinkedIn to try and find out where they were located. So far, she had tracked down Terry and Wade and she was working on Ashley. Chris and Kim had proven a bit harder to find so she had set them aside for now.

"It seems like Terry and Ashley are still living in Meadowland," Jessie said. "Wade is nearby in Mapleton County."

"I'm not very familiar with the area so I'm having a hard time visualizing things. Would you be able to find a map of the area and send it to the printer? I'd like to mark things out on a paper version," Rose asked her sister-in-law.

A few minutes later, the two women were hunched over the map, circling the approximate area where David and Jessie grew up, Rebecca's house, and the lake where Rebecca had been staying with her family.

"So, we still need to figure out where the labor camp was located and where Rebecca was found," Rose stated.

"Until we get the camp information from David, I don't have much chance of finding out where the camp was set up but let me do some more digging around online and see if I can figure out where her body was found." Jessie bent her head back over the laptop and her fingers began to fly over its keys.

Staring at the map, Rose felt an acute sense of futility wash over her. Not only were they trying to figure out the truth of what happened more than 30 years ago, but it was also in a remote place. Although David had grown up a mere hour's drive from where they were living, it felt like another planet. It was small and rural and in all their years of marriage, they had never so much as driven through the area. David's parents were long gone and there just didn't seem to be a reason to. How on earth were they ever going to figure out what happened to Rebecca Evans?

"One step at a time Rose," Jessie stated, watching the emotions pass on Rose's face. "You look defeated, and you can't give in to that feeling. Remember, we just need to take one step at a time."

Rose was amazed at how Jessie could practically read her mind sometimes. Once again, she felt an immense amount of gratitude toward this woman who knew her so well. Just then, the doorbell rang, and Rose started in her seat.

"Don't be so jittery, it's just someone at the door," Jessie reassured her. "You didn't see the media swarming around here the other day though."

"I'll go get it then," Jessie got up and headed to the front door, with Rose close behind her. But she had nothing to worry about, it was only her next-door neighbor Trevor. He had been their neighbor for years, ever since she and David had moved in. Over the years, she had planned block parties with his wife Sheila, been invited over for barbeques and once, she had watched over their youngest while they had rushed their son to the emergency room after he fell out of a tree. "Hi, Trevor! How are you?" She greeted him with a warm smile.

"I'm okay, but I wanted to talk to you about someone trespassing through our yard," Trevor did not return her smile.

Taken aback by his cold demeanor, Rose was temporarily at a loss for words.

"Who trespassed through your yard and who are you?" Jessie stepped slightly to the left, coming between Trevor and Rose, as though to shield her.

"I'm her neighbor," Trevor told her coldly, "and someone cut through our yard late last night in order to get to this house."

"Who was it?" Rose asked, alarmed. "Did you call the police?"

"I don't know who it was and I didn't stop to ask their name. And no, I didn't call the police as there has been enough chaos on this street this week; we don't need any more," he told her. "I'm assuming it was more media trying to gain access to your place."

"Don't you think that, media or not, you should perhaps report stuff like that?" Jessie asked him crossly. He was rubbing her the wrong way, the pompous ass.

"It's okay Jessie," Rose cut her off. "I'm sorry about all of this Trevor. I'll see what I can do."

He nodded at her, turned on his heel and walked away.

"Wow, nice neighbors you got there," Jessie said, almost slamming the door behind him.

"There's been a lot of activity in front of our house, and it has obviously been hard on the other families on the block," Rose explained, sighing deeply. "We'll probably have to move after this is all over as we'll be pariahs."

Ignoring her comment, Jessie said "But seriously Rose, if the media are trespassing and creeping around at night, you really should let the police know. I would hate to see someone like Trevor decide to shoot first and ask questions later."

"How did you know he had a gun?" Rose asked, thinking of Trevor's collection.

"Just a good guess," Jessie smirked but then became more serious. "If it's been that bad around here, why don't we take a drive out to Meadowland and get a sense of things? Maybe I can even line us up to meet with Terry and Ashley."

"Oh, I don't know. David's going to call me, and I wouldn't want to miss it,"

"He's calling your cell, isn't he? You can talk to him just as easily there as here. Come on, I think a change of scenery will be good for you."

"Well, I guess I could. I'll just call Kayla and let her know where I'm going."

"She'll want to come along if you do that," Jessie pointed out. "Wouldn't it be more... relaxing if it was just the two of us?"

She was right, Kayla was so high-strung right now, that things would probably be more tense if she came along. She needed to get away from everything and everyone for a few hours.

Chapter 20

Present Day

Grabbing her bag and throwing her phone, notepad, and a spare pen in her bag, Rose headed toward the front door. Why was she feeling almost guilty for leaving? It would accomplish nothing just sitting around the house all day, waiting for the media to show up again. At the thought of the media, her mind went back to her neighbor. Why was the media slinking around in the middle of the night? She should have asked him what time it had happened; the idea of someone outside their home, while Jessie and she had been sitting at the kitchen table, made her skin crawl. The idea that someone might have been outside, looking in on them was frightening.

Once they were on the road, with Jessie behind the wheel as she was most familiar with the area, Rose began to relax. She fiddled with the Bluetooth in her car and connected Jessie's phone to it. The plan was for Rose to reach out to the people they wanted to talk to via Jessie's Facebook profile. Hopefully, they would be able to get a phone number and Jessie could connect with them and set up a time to meet. If they couldn't see anyone today, then it would at least end up being a sightseeing tour.

They had been on the road for about ten minutes and Rose had sent off Facebook messages when her phone rang. She answered it excitedly when she noticed where it was coming from.

"David!" she exclaimed after answering the call.

"This is the Vernon Ridge police station with a call for you from David Slater."

She felt silly for assuming she would be speaking to him immediately. "Hi Rose."

"Oh, it's so good to hear your voice honey!" she gushed. She didn't care that Jessie could hear her or the tone of her voice, which was beginning to tremble with emotion.

"It's good to hear you too, Rose."

"I have some questions for you that I don't want to forget but right now just hearing your voice..." she trailed off, unable to continue.

"I know babe, but you have to keep being strong. You can do this, you're my wife, and the Slaters are strong people and that means you too. How are the kids holding up?"

Taking a deep breath to steady herself, she tried to respond in a casual voice. "They're okay, worried of course, but you know how they are; Kayla is trying to tell everyone what needs to be done and Joshua is holding my hand," she laughed lightly as she drew a family picture that she knew her husband would understand.

"She has a whole bunch of lists and is considering signing up for law school, isn't she?" David chuckled. "But that is needed sometimes too, so you have both practical and emotional support."

"Speaking of support, I'm going to put you on speakerphone."

"Hi, big brother!" Jessie yelled out cheerfully. "What kind of trouble have you gotten yourself into this time, huh?"

"What are you doing here? Aren't you supposed to be in Timbuktu or something?"

"Yeah, but I decided you needed rescuing," she teased.

"All help is welcome," David responded, his voice serious. "But I don't have a whole lot of time before they are going to cut me off and take me back to my cell. What questions did you have?"

They went over a few housekeeping issues that Rose needed help with, from simple things like the password to their online insurance account to the location of the valve for the outdoor sprinklers. Then, Rose broached the subject of where he had been working that summer.

"It was for the forestry department. I'm sure the camp won't be there anymore, but it was on Old Dam Road about six miles from the intersection of Highway 261 and Guarder Road."

"And what was the address for Rebecca's family's lake cabin?" Jessie asked.

"Why do you want all this location information?" David sounded confused.

"We're taking a—" Rose began before Jessie interrupted her.

"We're taking ahold of things brother and we want to do some research on the important places from that summer," Jessie looked toward Rose and winked as though the two of them had a secret they weren't going to share with David.

"I don't know the address, but it was on Shareen Lake. I have to go now; they're waving at me to wrap it up. Were there any other questions?"

"No, I don't think so, but I'll probably remember something after we hang up," Rose joked. "Did you want to pass along your love to the kids and the twins?"

"Yes, of course, gotta go, bye," and the line went dead.

"Well, that should give us enough at least to find the area where his camp was located," Jessie said.

"Why didn't you want him to know we were doing a road trip to the camp?"

"I just don't want him to worry. It must be hard being in jail and unable to help or look out for your family," she explained.

They sat in silence as the miles began to unwind behind them. Rose must have been more worn out than she realized because she dozed off as she rested her head on the back of the seat, watching in the side mirror at the vehicles behind them. She woke up with a start about forty minutes later when Jessie hit a rough patch on the road. She looked around in confusion as the mists of sleep cleared her brain. She had been dead to the world.

"Sorry, I didn't realize I was that tired. Not very good company, am I?" Apologizing, Rose reached for her purse to grab her lipstick and freshen up.

"It's all good, you obviously needed to rest," Jessie smiled over at her. "We must be almost there?"

"Yup, just a couple more miles and we will be at my old stomping grounds," Jessie verified. "It's so strange to be going back after all these years."

She asked Rose to check and see if they had received any responses from Terry or Ashley about meeting up and Rose was pleased to see that both had answered. They decided to meet in an hour at a coffee shop called Blendz, in the center of town. Rose was about to type in a request for the address when Jessie stopped her to explain just how small of a town it was.

"Believe me, we'll have no problem finding it," she reassured Rose.

When they turned off the highway and headed toward Meadowland, Rose began to see what Jessie meant. The last mile into town was on a slight slope and from a mile away they could see the small town laid out before them. The road they were on led straight into what appeared to be the main street of the town, with smaller roads spreading out and crisscrossing over it.

She turned towards Jessie, a smile of understanding on her face. "I'm beginning to see what you mean about not needing an address." It appeared to be what her father would have called a one-horse town.

"We used to say we were small but mighty. There are quite a few small towns in this area, and they built the high school here and bussed all the surrounding kids in. We were the big city where other towns sent their kids for an edu-ma-cay-shun."

"I guess everything is relative, huh?"

"Yup," Jessie fell silent as they approached the entrance to the town. A small wooden sign with fading lettering on it welcomed them with the inscription "Meadowland! The Small Town with a Big City

Welcome!" A small gas station was on the right-hand side. "Oh look," Jessie pointed across the street from the station. "They tore down old man Harris's house!"

Raising both her eyebrows in her sister-in-law's direction, Rose realized Jessie was officially walking down memory lane. Her lips raised slightly in a smile; Jessie was looking around with a far-off look in her eyes.

"So, this is where you and David enjoyed your misspent youth," Rose looked around with only mild interest. The town looked like any other one you happened across in this state. It had a dusty almost sleepy feeling to it, and one couldn't help but wonder what the people who lived there did for a living. There were no factories nearby, no booming business in town, nothing.

Turning off onto a tree-lined street, Jessie leaned forward, her eyes taking in the houses.

"Everything looks so much smaller than I remember," she murmured. On the outskirts of town, a right-hand turn led them down a winding gravel driveway. At the end of the driveway stood a very large, modern-looking two-story with a wrap-around porch.

"Oh my, this is lovely," Rose exclaimed. "Is this where you grew up?"

'Yes and no," Jessie responded quietly. "I grew up on this land but not that house. It looks like ours was torn down."

"Oh," Rose wasn't sure what to say. Obviously, Jessie had expected to drive here and see her old family home, and disappointment was written all over her face.

Jessie looked around and with a smile pointed at an old tire swing hanging from a huge and very old tree. "That was my favorite spot, I used to spend hours out here, twisting and turning on that tire, lying back and watching the clouds, seeing what animals I could find in them."

Jessie's memories were interrupted by the sound of the front door of the house opening. A man came out, his arms crossed. Rose rolled down her window and gave a friendly wave as Jessie backed up so she could turn around. The man scowled at them, and Rose commented on how unfriendly he looked.

"Yeah, I think it's best if we get out of here," Jessie agreed, applying her foot to the gas pedal.

They retraced their steps and headed for the main street. Pulling into a diagonal parking spot in front of Blendz, Jessie sat still for a moment, as Rose reached for the door handle.

"What's wrong, Jess?"

"I don't know, but it suddenly struck me back there that we don't know what sort of reception to expect here. This might be a small town, but they get the news, and they will know David has been arrested. Rebecca was the town's daughter, bright and bubbly, a cheerleader and everything. The whole town was devastated that summer when she was killed."

Those exact concerns were in Rose's mind when they decided to come here. But she knew it was something they needed to do, for David's sake and yes, even for Rebecca's sake. Finding out the truth would honor the dead girl as well. But she knew she didn't have to explain that to Jessie, so she just sat beside her quietly while Jessie came to terms with what might be waiting in the coffee shop.

After a few seconds, Jessie grabbed her purse and opened her car door. "Well, whatever is waiting, sitting here isn't going to help things," she said.

When they entered the coffee shop, a bell tinkled overhead. While it wasn't a loud sound, it was enough for every head in the place to look up from their tables and towards the door. Not one person smiled at them. Jessie walked over to the counter and ordered two black coffees while Rose found a table to sit at that had enough room for them and their guests when they arrived.

They were just stirring the cream into their coffee, spoons clinking against the side of the glass mugs when the shop's door opened and a heavy-set woman in her late forties wearing a pair of tight jeans and a red plaid shirt walked in. She was cute in a way that was youthful and engaging but not in a way that would cause the men to stop and stare. She had an upturned button nose, and bright blue eyes and when she smiled in their direction, Rose detected dimples.

Jessie raised her mug in her direction as though to confirm she was who the woman was looking for and she came over to their table and grabbed one of the empty chairs.

"Well, I'll be, you have certainly grown into quite the swan Ms. Slater," she addressed Jessie. "My most vivid memory of you was as a scrawny kid with long legs who could run like the wind."

Jessie laughed, pleased at the way she was remembered. "I was a tomboy, wasn't I?"

"Tomboy? I don't know about that, but you always did exactly what you wanted to do, and damned what anyone else thought." She turned toward Rose and extended her hand. "My name's Ashley, and you must be David's wife."

"Yes, my name is Rose."

"Well, that's a pretty name!" While Rose couldn't quite put her finger on it, there was something about the way Ashley talked that seemed genuine and caring. It wasn't anything specific she had said, but something about the kindness around her eyes.

"Thank you for agreeing to meet with us Ashley," Jessie said, anxious to get to the issue at hand. "I know it must have been a bit unexpected."

"Yes and no," Ashley responded. "With everything about Rebecca and David in the news, you've been on my mind a lot. So, it didn't seem odd when I got your message."

"We're just trying to talk to people who might be able to tell us more about what was happening that summer," Jessie explained. "We reached out to you and Terry and Wade, but we haven't been able to connect with Chris or Kim yet."

"Well, I can certainly fill you in with what I know, but it was so long ago. Probably the most reliable information would be from the statements we gave the police back then. You know how memory plays tricks on you: sometimes, you over-romanticize some things and conveniently forget others?"

"That's okay, whatever you want to tell us we'll bear that in mind, and I think David's lawyer will be getting those statements at some point too," Rose explained. "What do you remember about that summer?"

"Gosh, I remember it being a very emotional time, even before we lost Rebecca. We were all heading our separate ways and we were excited to become adults but sad that we were leaving our childhood behind. And of course, the hormones didn't help," Ashley said with a laugh. "I know that there was a lot of what the kids today would call "drama" between Rebecca and David."

"Why was that?" Jessie leaned forward.

"Well, David was going to some kind of camp for the summer to earn money for college, and Rebecca was not happy that he wasn't going to be around," Ashley explained. "I loved Rebecca like a sister, but she was not known for being the most reasonable person."

"Why was she so upset?" Rose asked.

"Because she thought they should spend their last summer before college together. But David needed the money to go to school. Rebecca, may she rest in peace, came from a well-off family, and didn't quite get the whole "money" thing." Ashley used air quotes to emphasize the absurdity of not understanding the need to make money.

"So, they were fighting the summer she died?" Jessie had her chin resting in the palm of her hand, staring at Ashley's face.

"Well, they had sort of made up near the end. A truce I think is a more apt description. She knew enough not to push him and completely ruin their summer. I think she was still hoping he would show up one day. Whisk her off her feet, you know? She was like that, she lived in a world where she always got what she wanted. Until she didn't," Ashley ran a fingernail across the tabletop, a look of intense sadness crossing her face. "I don't mean to make her sound like she was a mean girl or something, she was nice to people and very sweet, but she did expect to get her way in most things."

"What do you think happened to her?" the words were out of Rose's mouth before she realized she was even going to ask the question.

Ashley looked up at her, a cloud crossing her eyes as she pressed her thin lips tight together. Sighing deeply, she weighed her words.

"Well," she finally said. "I don't for one minute pretend I know for sure what happened to her, or rather who did that to her, but I'm fairly certain of one thing and that is that something just isn't right with this whole DNA thing that the news is talking about."

"What do you mean?" Jess looked across the table at Ashley, her brows furrowed.

"They are saying they found David's DNA on Rebecca, but I don't believe it for one minute," Ashley said firmly.

Chapter 21

Present Day

The three women stared at each other across the table, Jessie and Rose waiting for Ashley to continue, Ashley was seemingly reluctant to finish what she had started. Just then, someone walked in the front door and up to their table. He immediately sat down and nodded at Jessie and Rose.

"Terry?" Jessie asked, sticking out her hand to shake his.

"The one and only," he responded. He was a nondescript man with hair that was past thinning and was firmly in the realm of balding. The hair that was left lined each side of his head and was an inky black.

"I'm Rose."

"I recognize you from the TV," Terry nodded in her direction. "You're David's wife."

"Yes, I am." She wasn't sure how he felt about her being David's wife. He gave no indication as to his thoughts.

"So, you decided to come for a spin out here in the boonies, huh Jess?" For the first time, a hint of a smile could be seen on Terry's face.

"We even drove down to the old house, but it was torn down," Jessie shook her head sadly. "Time can be a real bitch, can't it?"

"Oh girl, give it a few years," Ashley teased as she patted her hair and pretended to arrange herself.

The group laughed; the ice seemingly broken.

"The guy who lives there didn't seem very friendly," Jessie said.

"I'm not surprised; he's a decent sort of guy but the media have been coming down from the city and trespassing on his property. I don't know what they thought they were going to see, but it was a bit of a problem, especially last week." Ashley told them.

"That would explain our reception then," Jessie nodded. "He probably thought we were media. Has it been that bad? I know Rose and the kids have been dealing with the media too, but I didn't realize they were coming out here."

"Yeah, I overheard some overdone Barbie doll comment B roll to her cameraman," Terry said. "They were crawling the place for a few days."

"We were just chatting with Ashley about what it was like that summer Terry, what do you recall?" Jessie asked him.

"The only thing that stands out for me about that summer was Rebecca's murder, to be honest," Terry said. "I remember being excited to be moving out of my parent's place and going to school away from here, but other than that..." he shrugged his shoulders.

"After school was out, did you see David or Rebecca again?" Rose prompted his memory.

"I don't think so."

"Yes, you did Terry. Remember you, Kim, Chris, and I went to see Rebecca at her parents' cabin? We went for the day," Ashley nudged her old friend with her elbow.

"We did?" Terry looked confused. "I don't recall that."

"Yeah, remember, we spent the day floating on the lake and having water fights? It was really chill," Ashley tried to jar his memory. "It was the last time we ever saw Rebecca."

"Was that the summer she died? I remember being there and having a fun time, but I didn't realize that was the last summer we saw her," Terry shrugged. Ashley shook her head at the other two women as if to say, men: what can you do?

"Hey! It was like thirty years ago, give an old guy a break!" Terry protested, seeing the look she was exchanging with Jessie and Rose.

"So, what do you think happened to Rebecca?" Jessie looked first at Ashley and then at Terry, inviting Ashley to pick up where she had left off with them.

"Well, I hate to say it but if they got DNA, seems like they got David for it," Terry said, looking apologetically in Rose's direction. "I wouldn't have thought he had it in him, but the facts don't lie, right?"

"That's what I meant when I said there's something off about the DNA evidence," Ashley jumped in, anxious this time to add her thoughts. "Sure, they have DNA and that's pretty hard to argue, but I knew David and there's no way he could hurt Rebecca, no way."

Ashley sat back in her chair, her arms crossed and her attitude reminiscent of the man at Jessie's old land.

"That's just because you always saw David through rose-colored glasses Ash," Terry said. "You know you had a crush on him since sixth grade."

"Be that as it may, I knew him and he was a gentle person. There is no way he did those horrible things to Rebecca," Ashley remained firm in her conviction. "I'll be honest, I'm in the minority around here when it comes to that opinion, so I don't talk a lot about it, but there's very little you could tell me that would convince me he killed her."

Rose felt a weight lift from her shoulders. It wasn't just her wifely wishful thinking; David was a good man who would never commit such a heinous crime.

"But what about the DNA? It's hard to argue that," Jessie said. Rose looked at her sharply. Why was she trying to argue that David was guilty? Rose recalled Jessie's comment about finding out the truth, whatever it might be. Did she honestly think he might be guilty?

"I have no idea. Maybe there was a mistake or someone is trying to set him up, I don't know," Ashley said, throwing her hands up in the air. Rose felt deflated once more. Since David had been arrested, it felt as though every hour was a series of emotional ups and downs. She was thrilled Ashley thought her husband was innocent but discouraged that she didn't have a good explanation for the evidence they had on him.

She stared out at the street, her eyes glazing over as she wondered what David was doing right now. Was he bored, scared, upset? What was she doing here? What did she think she would accomplish that the police hadn't years ago? Maybe they were just kidding themselves in thinking this would help at all. A car slowly drove down the main street and Rose watched it pass, her mind occupied by random thoughts of the years ahead that she thought she and David would have together. What if that was all gone? Just then, the car that drove by reappeared and Rose realized it was a blue sedan, much like the one that had driven behind them on the way to Meadowland. Was it the same car?

Frowning, she tried to get a look at the driver, but the car sped up and was out of sight before she could see anything.

"Rose?" Jessie was prodding her with her elbow. "What's the matter?"

"What? Oh, nothing, I just thought I saw someone I recognized," she said, uneasy about telling them she thought they were being followed for fear they thought David had married a crazy woman.

Ashley and Terry were standing up and Rose realized they were saying goodbye. They all shook hands after they left the coffee shop and turned to leave. Jessie, remembering something turned around and called out to Ashley.

"Hey, do you know where I can find your friend Kim? We haven't been able to track her down so we can chat," She asked.

"Oh gosh, I haven't heard from Kim in a lot of years, she moved away right after high school and I think she went to college up north," Ashley responded. "But I can ask around and see if anyone else has any idea where she is?"

"That would be great, thanks a bunch," Jessie said. They were about to turn around and part ways again when Ashley threw her arms around Jessie and then Rose.

"I'm so sorry this is happening to you all," she said, sounding upset. "No one deserves this heartbreak."

Then she turned around and walked to her car.

Chapter 22

Present Day

Back in Rose's car, Jessie punched some information into the car's GPS and located Shareen Lake. They didn't have the exact address for Rebecca's family's cabin, but maybe they would get lucky and see someone who could tell them. They didn't need to see the cabin itself anyway, they were just trying to get a better idea of the distance between spots and what the layout was all those years ago.

"We'll drive out to the cabins and then we will try to find out the general area where the camp was located," Jessie outlined their itinerary. "This will just allow us to picture these areas in our mind when we get more information during the discovery process."

Rose was quiet as they drove out of town and towards Shareen Lake. The meeting with Ashley and Terry had unnerved her, although she wasn't sure why. They both had valid opinions and hadn't told Rose or Jessie anything they didn't know before, except that the teens had had a bit of a disagreement before they each went their separate ways for the summer. But that was nothing unusual. As Ashley said, teens were prone to drama.

"What's on your mind Sis?" Jessie used the back of her right hand to tap Rose's thigh and get her attention. "You're deep in thought."

"Do you think David's guilty?" Rose blurted out before she had a moment to consider whether she wanted a truthful answer.

A thick silence fell over them and Rose held her breath. Finally, Jessie spoke.

"To be honest Rose, I'm trying not to ask myself that question."

"What do you mean?"

"I don't want to try and come to an absolute decision on what I think," Jessie said, her voice quiet and tentative. "I envy people like you and Ashley, who have such faith in things."

"We don't have faith in things, we have faith in David," Rose explained, her brows pinched together in confusion. "You think David could do something like this? Did you even hear what happened to her? How awful it was! How could you, for one minute, think your brother was capable of that?"

"Oh Rose, I wish you hadn't asked me this outright. The fact is, I can't imagine David doing anything as awful as taking a young girl's life, never mind raping her and God knows what else, but they have DNA Rose, DNA!"

"But mistakes are made all the time, even with DNA Jessie!" They were practically shouting at each other.

"Don't you think I know that? That's why I'm trying not to think about whether he is guilty or not until we know all the facts for sure." Jessie explained.

"But you don't believe in your brother enough to have faith in him and who he is?"

"I have faith in facts, I have faith in what I can see and feel, hear and taste."

"But then that isn't faith, you're mixing up faith and proof Jessie. If you know it for a fact, you don't need faith!"

"Maybe I am, but I'm just not willing to say I believe my brother is 110 percent innocent until I get an explanation about the DNA," Jessie declared. "I'm sorry if that upsets you, but that's just how I feel." The two women sat in silence, stunned by their exchange. Rose felt shaken to her core, but her feelings were in turmoil and she was having trouble processing what she was feeling. Because although she was surprised that Jessie didn't believe her brother was innocent, what she was feeling was a betrayal. But she wasn't sure why. Why was Jessie allowed to have doubts? She was his sister; she was supposed to believe in him. Just like Rose was supposed to believe in him. Why was Jessie okay with not knowing?

They drove most of the way to the lake in silence. Neither woman was quite sure what to say to the other and the silence was fraught with tension and uncertainty.

Finally, Jessie broke the silence. "Can you check to see when the turn-off is?"

Rose picked up her cell and looked at the route they had outlined from Meadowland to Shareen Lake.

"It should be coming up in about two miles," she told Jessie.

A mile down the road, a sign notified them that they were to make the next right. Rose scrolled through her phone, looking at the different maps for the lake. Eventually, she found one that showed the cabins that encircled it.

"When you turn, I think you take a slight left onto a road called Hauden Lane; it should take us most of the way around the lake," she told Jessie.

"I'm just going to stop and top off the car first and see if anyone there knows anything about Evan's cabin."

After turning at the lake, she pulled into a small gas station and corner store. Pulling up to the pumps, she asked the attendant to top the car off and told him she would pay inside. As she headed toward the store, she gestured in disbelief toward Rose as neither of them had been at a full-service gas station in many years.

Rose took a deep breath, willing herself to relax and let go of the tension between her shoulder blades. She didn't want to be at odds with her sister-in-law right now. She needed all the friends and support she could muster. Whether Jessie believed in David or not, she was certainly being supportive.

~~~~

"I struck pay dirt!" Jessie declared when she returned to the car. "An old timer in the store talked my ear off and I came away with all the information we could possibly need."

"He knew where the cabin is?"

"Yes, and even better, I have directions to the cabin and where they found Rebecca!" Jessie pronounced with glee.

"Oh," Rose wasn't quite sure how she felt about going to the site where a young girl was brutalized and left dead.

"This means we only have to figure out approximately where David's camp was located," Jessie continued, seemingly unaware of Rose's lackluster response. "You were right, we head down Hauden Lane and take the fourth right which will take us to a small cul de sac of cabins. The Evans's cabin is the third one. Apparently, they still own it."

They drove down the winding road, with Rose counting off the turns.

"This one coming up," Rose gestured when they came upon the fourth turn. As they turned, she peered down the road and was surprised at how much darker it seemed. The trees lining the road had matured and leaned forward, acting like a canopy. The result was a darker and noticeably cooler area that was almost spooky.

Jessie turned onto the driveway of the last cabin, the potholes causing the car to jostle and forcing her to slow down. The cabin had a run-down air about it, as though the owners had given up trying to keep it neat and tidy. Maybe Rose was imagining it, but the cabin seemed to have a sad air about it. She mentally shook herself, trying to throw off the melancholy mood that had settled on her.

Jessie parked and they sat and stared at the cabin. It was obvious that it was currently uninhabited. Everything was put away and locked up. There were no lawn chairs or tables out, and there was no barbeque or even freshly cut wood lying on a pile. There was no indication that anyone had been there lately or had any plans to return.

"Well, now what?" Rose asked.

"I guess there isn't much we can do, but why don't we stretch our legs a bit and grab some fresh air," Jessie suggested.

They left the car and sauntered down the overgrown path and towards the lake. The dock was situated halfway up the rocky beach, and it was obvious that the water level of the lake had receded quite a bit since it was built. There was a thick patch of weeds beside the dock, and the water was as still as glass. This part of the property looked just as neglected as the cabin. They stood there for a few minutes, listening to the sound of the birds before deciding it was time to leave.

Pulling out of the driveway, Jessie shuddered a little.

"I know I'm being silly, but honestly that place gives me the creeps," she confessed.

"I thought it was just me!" Rose exclaimed, relief in her voice as she leaned back in the passenger seat. "I figured I had an overactive imagination today."

They broke into laughter as they realized they had both been questioning their sanity.

"Nope, I don't know if it's just because we know the family history, but it had a creepy, neglected vibe," Jessie reassured her.

"Where to next?" Rose asked.

Jessie simply turned and looked at her, raising both her eyebrows as though egging her on to guess.

"We're going to where she was murdered, aren't we? You thought the cabin wasn't creepy enough, now you want an actual murder scene full of ghosts, huh?" Rose teased her.

"Well, not to be contrary, but technically there would only be one ghost."

"Unless she brought friends!"

"That's true. Hey, you wanna grab my purse and pull that scrap of paper out of the side? Yeah, the blue piece. It has directions on how to get there. That old timer was more than pleased to give me detailed directions; he was so excited I half expected him to offer to drive with us," Jessie glanced at the slip of paper quickly before looking back at the road. She did this a couple of times and then seemed satisfied she knew where they were going.

Before they turned off the highway, Rose's phone buzzed and she looked to see it was Kayla calling. She answered and put it on speakerphone but before she could get a word out, her daughter's tearful voice began to wail in her ear.

"They're lying, they have to be lying!" she sobbed. "Why is this happening?"

"Whoa, whoa honey, slow down. Now take a deep breath and tell me what is going on?" Rose was alarmed at the sound of Kayla's voice.

Kayla responded by letting forth a torrent of words that were punctuated with sobs, gasps, and crying.

"I can't understand a word you are saying honey, you need to try and collect yourself? Is everyone okay? Is it Brandon or the kids?" Rose's fear was beginning to rise in her throat, threatening to choke her. She hadn't heard her daughter this upset in years.

"They... they announced that someone had come forward," she stammered.

"Who announced someone came forward?" Rose asked.

"The announcer, on the radio."

"Okay, who came forward?"

"They didn't give a name, they just said someone from Rutledge, where that girl was killed." Rose frowned and looked at Jessie. They needed to go through Rutledge to get to the murder site.

"So, someone came forward from Rutledge, and what did they say?" Rose was careful not to overwhelm her daughter with too many questions but was trying to find out what had upset her so badly one piece at a time. It seemed to be working, as Kayla was able to answer simple direct questions and that seemed to help calm her down as well.

"They said they saw Daddy with that girl!" Kayla broke into tears again, sobbing uncontrollably. Rose processed what she had told her while letting her daughter deal with it in her own way. Calling David Daddy was not lost on Rose, who knew Kayla hadn't called him that since middle school.

"When did they see him with Rebecca?" Rose asked. Kayla's constant referring to Rebecca as "that girl" was beginning to grate on Rose's nerves. She was a young lady who had a name and didn't ask to be brutally murdered. She hadn't done anything to their family, but Kayla made her sound like the other woman.

Kayla sniffled a few more times before she was able to pull herself together again. "They said they saw them together on the day she died, in Rutledge."

Rose bent over as if she had been sucker punched in the gut. David had told her and his lawyer that he had been cleared years ago because he had an alibi at the camp where he was working. All the blood seemed to leave her head and she thrust herself forward, so her head was between her knees. Jessie gasped and swerved over onto the side of the road and came to a quick stop. Rose's cell phone had gone flying and was resting at her feet, with Kayla's voice yelling out of it.

Jessie reached down and picked up the phone, telling Kayla they would call her back and hung up, just as Kayla began a barrage of questions. She sat and rubbed Rose's back comfortingly, unsure of what to say to her. After a few minutes, Rose slowly moved back into an upright sitting position. She stared straight ahead through the windshield, her eyes blank and unblinking. Jessie sat quietly, waiting for Rose to process what she had just heard.

"Maybe you were right not to be so sure of him," she finally said, in a flat monotone voice. "I guess I'm the fool."

"No Rose don't say that," Jessie protested. "There is no right or wrong in this situation and there are certainly no fools. There are still have so many unanswered questions and unknowns."

"Yeah? Like what?" Rose challenged her as she crossed her arms over her chest protectively.

"The so-called witness from Rutledge could just be someone who wants their five minutes of fame and is making this all up. They could have screwed up with the DNA, there is no motive and he has an alibi at the camp!" Jessie listed each item in rapid succession.

"Why are you trying to convince me of this? You don't believe it yourself!" Rose almost shouted.

"I don't know what I believe. I only know what we know for sure and that isn't a whole lot!"

"What am I supposed to do now?" Rose asked. "What am I supposed to say to my kids? Our kids!"

"Well, I don't know about you, but this doesn't change anything for me. I'm going to keep on with what we have been doing. We'll get familiar with the case, where things happened, and what those who were around have to say about that summer. I'm not going to obsess over whether he is guilty or not. I'm going on a fact-finding mission and hopefully that will lead us to clarity." Jessie finished her speech, turned on the car, and pulled off the side of the road and back onto the highway.

They drove in silence, each woman wrapped up in her own thoughts. Eventually, Jessie made a turn onto a secondary highway and Rose realized she had left Kayla hanging. She didn't have the emotional energy to phone her right now, but she sent a text saying everything was okay and that she would call her later.

Chapter 23

Present Day

They turned off the highway and onto a road that ran parallel to the town of Rutledge. About a mile out, they turned left. After a while, they slowed down, looking for the trail that was marked on the map. "There it is!" Rose almost shouted as they drove past an opening. Jessie slowed down and backed up to the trail. They turned onto the trail and slowly made their way forward. The trail was overgrown to the point of being barely visible. As they wound deeper and deeper toward the treed area, Rose found she was holding her breath, as though expecting to see Rebecca after the next bump.

The car slowed down when a small cross on the left-hand side came into view. It looked freshly painted and well cared for with the foliage around its base cleared away. Jessie turned onto the pathway that ran parallel to the cross, the car rocking back and forth as she carefully made her way down the narrow path.

They came to an opening in the trees that was just big enough to fit the car with a few feet on each side. The area had been trampled down, either by vehicles or people walking over it repeatedly. Looking around, Jessie turned off the car engine.

"Not much to see," she commented quietly.

"Nope."

Opening the passenger car door, Rose slipped out and looked around. She began to walk slowly around the cleared spot, deep in thought. Was this where her husband became someone she didn't know? Did there exist in this space a memory of David that she knew nothing about? A hand came down on her shoulder and she jumped nervously.

"Sorry, didn't mean to scare you," Jessie said. "I think I'm going to walk out to the road and take a look at the cross. I have no idea what I might see, but I just feel like I should. Wanna come?"

"No, you go, I'll stay. I feel like..." She let the words trail off, unsure of how to explain what she was feeling. Jessie patted her shoulder in understanding and left her standing there, absorbed in her thoughts. What had happened here so many years ago? She looked around, taking in the trees that seemed to be hovering, as though they wanted to absorb the open space within their limbs. Taking a deep breath, she inhaled the scent of the underbrush, the dead vegetation mixed with the smell of live plants.

A twig sounded to her left and her head swung in that direction. Why would Jessie be over there? The trees were thick and would be very difficult to get through. The pathway to the road was behind her, not in that direction. The hair on the back of her arms rose and met the fabric of her shirt.

"Jessie?"

Nothing but a thick blanket of silence confronted her as she peered through the darkness in the direction of the sound. Fighting the urge to run, she stood rooted to the spot, willing her ears to listen carefully. A moment later, a rustling noise occurred, almost directly across from her. She gave a start as the sound of a flock of squawking birds took off in flight. Taking a step backward, her calves met the front of her car and she felt herself falling backward. To stop the backward fall, she flung herself forward at the waist and then her arms flailed as she lost her balance and fell on the ground, the palms of her hands breaking her fall.

"Damn!" she exclaimed as she felt the sting of prickles on her palms. Lying on her stomach, she lifted her hands off the ground to inspect them. Suddenly, she felt eyes on her. Her breath caught. Her heart raced, thrumming in her ears. But she felt an overwhelming urge to stay very still. She didn't want to look up and see who or what was watching her. It was only when she caught a movement out of the corner of her eye that her adrenaline kicked in and she shot to her feet, turned around, and ran toward the pathway that had led them there. She ran as though the hounds of hell were on her heels, her breath ragged. Halfway down the pathway, as she was frantically looking over her shoulder, her foot caught in a hole, and she went down with a thud. Tears came to her eyes, and she cried out in pain. Disorientated, she heard a sound in the distance; the sound of someone running. Were they running to her or away from her? She began to sob in fear and frustration as she realized the sound was becoming louder, as well as closer to her.

"What happened!?" Jessie cried out as she ran up to Rose. She dropped to her knees beside Rose and looked her up and down, trying to determine if she was hurt or to get some idea of why she was crying.

"Someone... someone was there..." Rose managed to say. "I think they were following me!"

"Who was following you?" Jessie was incredulous as she frantically looked around, as though to find evidence of who was following her sister-in-law.

"I don't know; I was looking around and I heard something in the trees, but then I fell and then they were right there and I ran and my hands hurt and I fell in the hole and I thought someone was going to get me but it was you," the explanation rushed out of Rose in a flow of words.

"Have you hurt your foot badly? Did you break an ankle or something? Do you think you can walk?" Jessie asked. "Can you walk back to the car with me?"

"I don't want to go back there!"

"Okay, I can go and bring the car out and you'll get door-to-door service," Jessie tried to make light of the situation, hoping to calm Rose down.

"No! Don't leave me alone!" she almost shouted.

"Well, we have to do one or the other Rose, we can't just sit here forever."

"I know, I know. Just give me a minute to see if I can stand up."

"Okay, there's no rush. We can just sit here for a few minutes," Jessie smiled at Rose, trying to reassure her with her presence, much like a mother in the dark of night trying to calm down a child who has had a nightmare. "I think you probably heard some animals. There is no way in here that I can see except for this pathway. There are no vehicles on the road and no one else is around. Someone would have to walk in from quite a distance."

"I know what I heard and what I..." she shuddered slightly, "...felt."

Jessie reached down to look at Rose's foot. She asked her to move it and Rose was able to gingerly move it from side to side.

"Maybe I scared myself more than I did any real damage," Rose suggested reluctantly. At the time she fell, she was convinced she was going to suffer permanent damage, either from broken bones or because whoever was following her was going to get her. Now that she was able to take some calming breaths and the adrenaline had an opportunity to stop pumping, she realized she was probably okay.

Helping her stand up, Jessie encouraged Rose to lean on her while she tentatively placed some weight on her foot. When it was evident she was able to stand, Rose let go of Jessie. Feeling a bit bashful, she had a hard time looking Jessie in the face. She must think she was crazy, running around in the forest like a wild woman.

"I'm okay now, why don't we walk back to the car?" she suggested.

"Are you sure?"

"Yes, I'm fine. I'll just watch and make sure I don't step in another hole and twist it further," Rose said.

The two women slowly made their way back in the direction of the car. The deeper into the trees they progressed, the more Rose had to fight for control of her emotions. She silently reassured herself that Jessie was with her, that no one was in the forest, and that they would be alright. Jessie walked slowly and carefully, keeping her eye on the terrain, and pointing out uneven areas as they approached them. When they came into the clearing where the car was, they stopped and looked around. Rose half expected there to be someone there, waiting to jump out at them. Her eyes darted around, taking in the trees, the car, and the trampled-down clearing.

"See, everything is just as it's supposed to be," Jessie said. "Let's jump in the car and get out of here."

Approaching from the back of the car, Jessie headed for the driver's door and Rose for the passenger side. Rose was about to open the door when she stopped abruptly. She stared straight ahead and felt the blood in her veins go cold. Directly in front of the car, where she had fallen, the brush was trampled back about two feet past where she had lain. A small piece of white material was snagged on the brambles.

"Jessie!" she yelled.

Popping out of the seat that she had just sat down in, Jessie asked "What?"

Rose was pointing a shaky hand towards what she had seen, and Jessie moved to the front of the car. Unsure what she was supposed to be looking at, she glanced at Rose, shrugging her shoulders in confusion.

"The ground, all the brush here is trampled down, way back past where it was, and something is hanging there!" Rose raised her hand to show Jessie where the cloth was located.

Jessie squatted in the bushes to inspect the ground and then stood up. She was looking at it intently when she suddenly spoke up, almost shouting at Rose to get in the car. Not needing to be told twice, Rose jumped in the car and locked her door. Jessie had run and jumped in and locked her door too. She started the car and put it in reverse. She made a tight turn in the clearing by cranking the steering wheel, backing up as far as she could in the clearing, and then moving forward, cranking the wheel again and backing up again. She did this a couple of times until the car was pointed down the pathway leading away from the spot. Once again, they jostled down the pathway and as soon as they emerged, Jessie made a quick right turn onto the gravel road and hit the gas.

"What did you see?" Rose finally managed to ask.

Jessie looked shaken as she looked in her rear-view mirror, as though expecting to see someone in hot pursuit. Running her hands through her hair, she gave a shaky laugh.

"I'm not sure, but I think I saw a man."

"You're not sure?"

"Well, I looked up and I saw someone moving through the trees. Not towards us or away from us, but more parallel. I think it was a man, but I just caught a glimpse," Jessie explained.

The women sat in silence, each of them trying to covertly keep their eye on the mirror on the side of their car door. No one was behind them, but they felt as though they were being pursued. Once they hit the main highway, they both let out a sigh of relief.

"What the hell," Jessie said, as she expelled a huge gush of air she had been holding.

Chapter 24

Present Day

"Are you still up to try and find David's work camp from that summer?" Jessie asked. "I'll understand if you just want to go straight home."

The thought of home was certainly welcoming for Rose at that moment. But they had visited every other location, it would be a shame not to do this one as well.

"Let's see what we can find, but this time neither one of us gets out of the car," Rose said.

"You'll get no argument from me," Jessie let out a shaky laugh.

Rose's mind was going a mile a minute as she tried to understand what had just happened. Was it a local person who was just out wandering in the forest? But if so, why wouldn't they have either said "Hi" or moved on? But who else could it have been? No one knew they were there today, so they couldn't have been in the trees because of them. Then she remembered the car. The blue sedan she had seen behind them as they were heading out. The one she thought she saw in Meadowland. Was someone following her? Again, she looked in the mirror to make sure no one was following them.

"Um, Jessie?"

"Yes?"

"On our way out here, I noticed a blue sedan behind us for quite a while. I think I saw the same car while we were sitting in the cafe in Meadowland."

"Really? Why didn't you tell me?"

"I didn't think it was important. I mean, I noticed it but brushed it off. Who would be following us, and why? I thought I was just imagining things," Rose said.

"I don't know, but you have to tell me when something out of the ordinary or creepy happens Rose! Stop worrying that I'll think you're crazy or something," Jessie blurted out in an angry voice.

"I'm sorry, Jessie. It wouldn't be inconceivable, with all that's going on, for me to be feeling a little paranoid," Rose felt herself become defensive.

"Maybe so, and I guess hindsight is 20/20. You had no way of knowing what would happen in the clearing," Jessie conceded. They were close to the area where the forestry camp was located thirty years ago, but this time there was no gravel road or pathway for them to follow. There was a big sign on the highway that steered them toward something called the Junior Forestry Camp and onto a well-maintained road. David had made it sound as though the camp was stuck out in the middle of nowhere, but it appeared that a lot had changed. As they traveled down the road toward the camp, they could see in the distance rows of shack-like cabins and a large brick building that appeared to be the hub of activity. Pulling into the camp, they parked in a large, expansive parking lot and sat looking around.

"So, what are we hoping to accomplish here Jessie?"

"I mainly wanted to get a sense of the distance between Meadowland, Shareen Lake, the place where Rebecca was killed, and the camp. I don't know that there is much else to be learned, do you?"

"I don't think so either. The staff will have changed in thirty years, the camp is just a camp. Now that we have a good idea of where everything is located..." They continued to look around uncertainly.

Finally, Jessie spoke up. "Well, we did say we didn't want to get out of the car, didn't we?" She started up the car and backed out of the parking lot and away from the camp.

Rose sighed with relief. The day was taking its toll on her and she just wanted to get back home to take a hot bath and then get to bed early. "We need to contact the lawyer tomorrow and find out what is up with this so-called witness," Jessie suddenly said. "Do you know how late he works?"

"No, I don't," Rose said as she rummaged through her purse for her cell phone. Before she could call Barry, she noticed there was a notification that she had a voice message waiting. Her phone must have rung while they were in the forest. She hadn't checked it since getting back into the vehicle. The message was from Barry. Rose tapped the speaker button so Jessie could hear what he had to say as well. His voice was calm and soothing as though to reassure the listener that he had things well under control. Nothing seemed to throw him.

"Hi Rose, it's Barry here. Listen, something has come up and you may hear about it on the news. It's not a big deal, but I wanted to make sure you heard it from me first. Someone has come forward to say they saw Rebecca and David leaving in her car the day she was killed. Now, I don't have much information other than that, but we'll be receiving more information when discovery starts. Give me a call if you have any questions."

"Doesn't sound like there is much point giving him a call by the sounds of it," Jessie commented. "This whole legal process is frustratingly slow, isn't it?"

"That's what I'm discovering."

They sat in silence as the highway rolled away underneath the car, a ribbon stretching miles and miles behind them. The day had been so long and emotionally demanding. Yes, they had covered quite a few miles, but it was visiting the past that seemed to suck all the energy out of Rose. Talking to Ashley and Terry about the past, as well as their differing opinions on what had happened was difficult to hear, but it was the cabin and the place where Rebecca was killed that had left her disturbed and shaken to her core.

"Can you grab my phone and open up Facebook Messenger? I want to try and connect with Wade. He is in Mapleton County, but I'm done driving around today—maybe we can just chat with him on the phone?" Jessie pointed at her purse where her cell phone was kept.

After scrolling through the phone, Rose found Wade's name and sent him a message asking if Jessie could call him, and if so, which number she should use? Looking out the car window, Rose wondered if they were just wasting their time and if the only positive result of all of this was just to help them feel as if they were doing something. Maybe it was just something to keep them busy. As much as the family teased Kayla about her need to take charge and do things, Rose knew she came by it honestly and that she had a hard time not feeling useful. The day had passed quickly and it had allowed her to get out of the house and away from prying eyes. Her mind briefly went to the blue sedan, but she mentally brushed it off. She felt the phone vibrate in her hand and looking down, she saw that Wade had responded to her request already. He said that he would love to chat with her again and he gave his number. Whilst Rose knew she was only doing the typing for Jessie, she felt as though she was almost catfishing him.

"Wade gave me a number so I'll call him and put him on speaker, okay?" she asked Jessie.

"Great, that was fast!"

The phone only rang a few times before it was answered by a man with a deep, gravelly voice.

"Well, Jessie, long time no talk!" Wade boomed before Jessie could even get out a greeting.

"Hi Wade, how are you doing?" Jess laughed, pleased that Wade remembered her so easily. "I'm driving so I'm on speaker and my sister-in-law is in the car with me. David's wife Rose."

"Oh, yeah," Wade's voice was much quieter now and a lot less jovial. "I was so sorry to hear about things with David."

"Yeah, it's been quite the bomb going off in the middle of our lives," Jessie agreed.

"And I'm sure sorry we have to meet under these circumstances, Rose."

"Yes, I'm sorry too Wade," Rose responded.

"As you can probably guess, Wade, I wanted to talk to you about that summer when Rebecca died," said Jessie. "I was so young that there is a lot I'm sure I have either forgotten or that I didn't even know about, and I was hoping you might be able to fill in some gaps."

"Well gee Jessie, I can sure try, but to be honest, I had a lot going on myself that summer and I don't know how much I can add to things. I was moving away from home and starting my first adult job. The rest of the crew was either working at summer jobs or enjoying their last summer of freedom before college," Wade explained. "And you know teenage boys, they're pretty self-absorbed and I wasn't paying much attention to what was going on around me."

"Oh, come on Wade, I seem to remember you were a pretty sensitive young man," Jessie teased and Rose looked at her sister-in-law with a smile, and both her eyebrows raised. She had never seen Jessie flirt so blatantly before. Jessie turned a light shade of pink but kept her eyes looking forward and on the road.

"Ha! Don't confuse sensitive with awkward, Jessie!" Wade chuckled. "But seriously, once school was out, I was on my way to a new life in a different town. I was working at my new job when I heard about Rebecca. It was gut-wrenching for everyone. She was such a lovely young lady and had so much promise and life ahead of her."

"I'm going to cut to the chase, Wade," Rose interjected. "We've talked to Ashley and Terry, and they have their thoughts as to what happened to Rebecca. What do you think happened?"

There was silence at the other end of the phone as Wade seemed uncertain about what to say.

"Don't worry about the fact that David is my husband," Rose reassured him. "I want your honest opinion."

"Well, I'm not sure what I think. David and Rebecca were so tight, and everyone thought they would go to college and then get married and have a couple of kids and a dog, you know what I mean? But they were fighting a lot near the end of our senior year. It was as though the closer they got to graduating, the more tense things became. By the time summer arrived, they weren't a whole lot of fun to be around as a couple because there was always something happening, you know?"

"Uh-huh," Rose didn't want to interrupt the man as he delved into his memories for something helpful.

"It was almost as though Rebecca was trying to hold on to him and he was slipping away. The more she clung to him, the more he pulled away. He was a good kid, you know? But he was young, and he had a lot of living to do so he wasn't, shall we say, as faithful as she would have liked."

"I didn't know that!" Jessie exclaimed, surprised to hear about this side of her brother.

"It was just a kid thing; a bunch of us went out one night and Rebecca was busy and couldn't join us. David ended up drinking too much and necking with some girl who was visiting her cousin. Of course, it's a small town, and word got back to Rebecca. She went ballistic, and all hell broke loose. To tell you the truth, it was a bit tiring. There was always something."

"Was it normal teenager stuff do you think?" Jessie asked. She had looked over towards Rose, wondering if the mention of David's youthful indiscretion would upset her.

"Looking back, I think so. At the time it was all high drama, and seemed very serious but yeah, it was teenage stuff," Wade said.

"Do you think David killed Rebecca?" Rose was tired of beating around the bush, waiting for him to give some indication of what he thought.

"Oh man, I really don't know," he sounded almost agonized by the thought of having to form an opinion. "Part of me can't ever imagine David doing something like that, no matter how mad he got at her, but then I hear they got fresh evidence and I wonder, like, do we ever really know someone, you know?"

"Yeah," Rose sat back in her seat, letting go of a breath she hadn't realized she was holding.

"But you should talk to Chris. He and David were tight and if anyone would have a good idea, it would be him," Wade suggested, sounding like he couldn't wait to pass the potato of speculation on David's innocence on to someone else.

"Do you know where I could find him?" Jessie asked. "I tried different social media platforms, but I couldn't seem to find him and nothing came up with an online search."

"Chris didn't really keep in touch, but I can ask around and see if I can find a number for him or something," Wade offered.

"That would be great Wade, I kinda hit a dead-end there."

There was silence as though each of them was unsure where to take the conversation. Then Wade turned the tables on them and asked what no one else had been brave enough to ask before.

"What about you two? What do you think?" Wade asked. "Did David kill Rebecca?"

"I honestly don't know Wade," Jessie answered, looking quickly at Rose, as though to apologize for her response.

"That's fair enough," he was silent as he waited for Rose to answer.

"I feel in my heart that he isn't capable of such violence," she finally said. Looking out the passenger window, she felt her eyes well up with tears. The feeling of certainty was slipping through her fingers and the absolute conviction she held yesterday was on shaky ground.

Grief overwhelmed her as she knew she had lost something today, something that had helped keep the ground beneath her firm for so many years. Using the back of her hand, she wiped a tear that had made its way down her cheek.

"Well, Wade, I appreciate you being honest with us and telling us what you remember from that time," Jessie said. "If you think of anything else, please reach out."

"No problem at all Jessie. I'm sorry I couldn't be more help," Wade hung up and Jessie reached over and patted Rose's leg.

Chapter 25

Present Day

The next day, Jessie and Rose were nursing cups of coffee around the kitchen table when Stacey rang the doorbell.

"Hi hon!" she brushed by Jessie to give Rose a firm hug. "So, tell me what you found out yesterday, bring me up to speed on things!"

Pouring another cup of coffee, Rose and Jessie filled Stacey in on their busy day. When it came to the two women fleeing the scene of Rebecca's murder, Stacey's eyes grew wide.

"You could have been killed Rose!" she exclaimed. "What on earth were you two thinking?"

The sisters-in-law shrugged simultaneously and continued with their story. They weren't interested in re-living the fear of the forest and wanted to put it behind them. They explained about the forestry camp and their conversation with Wade, including his comment about David's teenage indiscretions.

"So, David was a cheater back then, was he?" Stacey sipped her coffee, her eyes glancing over the top of the coffee mug in Rose's direction. Jessie glanced from one woman to the other and looked like she wanted to say something but thought better of it.

"My goal today is to try and track down his friend Chris," Jessie said instead. "And Rose is going to see if she can get to visit with her husband."

"What do you need me to do, Rose?" Stacey took hold of Rose's hand and squeezed it gently. "Cooking, cleaning, shopping? You name it and I can give you a hand."

"Thanks, hon. The only thing I need are a few groceries – I haven't had a chance to go out in days." Rose grabbed a pad of paper off the counter and began to write down a few items on a list. "Just some milk, coffee, that kind of thing."

"I can do that!" Stacey smiled broadly as though trying to lighten the mood in the kitchen. "Promise me that If you think of anything else, you'll let me know?"

"I will, thank you."

The three of them sat around the table, the silence stretching and becoming awkward. Stacey began to look pointedly at Jessie, as though to encourage her to leave. Draining her mug, Jessie sighed deeply and stood up.

"I'm going to go poke around online and see if I have better luck finding Chris this time," she said.

"Bye Jessie, nice seeing you again," Stacey said, her voice just as cheerful as before. She was silent until Jessie left the kitchen and walked down the hallway.

"Okay, what is really up Rose? You look so defeated today. What happened yesterday?"

Rose was surprised by the earnestness in Stacey's voice. "Of course, I feel defeated. My husband is in jail accused of murder!"

"Yes, and before you went out yesterday, you were in the same situation," Stacey pointed out. "But what happened that made you look so defeated?"

"I don't know; it was a busy day and I definitely had some scary moments, but other than that, I don't know..."

"I think you should try and relax today. Go visit David, maybe go and get your nails done or something and just take it easy."

"Why?"

"Look, we both know Jessie can go at things like a bull in a china shop. She doesn't always consider those around her, and I think it may have been a bit too much for you." Stacey and Jessie had never been close and sometimes Rose had even noticed the tension between the two women, but this was the first time that Stacey had spoken negatively about her.

"She's just trying to help and anyway, I want to get to the bottom of things. Talking to the people who knew David back then might make things clearer."

"But at what cost, Rose? Let the police and David's lawyer do their jobs, you don't have to be the PIs, out looking for clues," Stacey argued. "You need to take care of yourself and your family."

"Well, I'm doing that too," Rose's brows furrowed as she tried to figure out what her friend was so concerned about. "I had a good night's sleep last night and I'm here for my kids. What am I not taking care of?"

Stacey looked her straight in the eye, her face lined with worry. "I'm just concerned about you, that's all hon."

"You don't need to be I'm okay," Rose smiled at her friend, hoping to ease her anxiety.

"I found him!" Jessie bound into the kitchen, a huge grin on her face. "He's a sneaky little devil but he was no match for me!"

"Chris?" Rose asked.

"Yes, I think I spelled his last name wrong before; this time I found him on LinkedIn."

"That's awesome, Jessie, are you going to call him?"

"Yes, he listed the name of his current employer, which just happens to be in town. Isn't it a bit strange that he was David's best friend in high school and now they live in the same town and have absolutely nothing to do with each other?" Jessie asked.

"It is odd. David has never even mentioned his name before," Rose said. "Maybe he didn't realize they lived so close?"

"Maybe, but once we connect with him, Kim is the only one we need to find," Jessie said as she scrolled through her phone to find the phone number of Chris's employer. Tapping on the number, it rang on the other end. "Hi, is Chris available?"

"Chris Athorn? Yes, my name is Jessie Slater."

The women were silent as she waited to connect with Chris.

"Hi, yes, uh huh, did he say why? Okay, goodbye," Jessie stood looking at her phone, her jaw slack, and her face shocked.

"What is it, Jessie?" Rose asked.

"He won't talk to me," Jessie responded.

"What do you mean he won't talk to you?" Stacey chimed in.

"She said that he didn't want to talk to me, and he told her to tell me not to call him again."

"What?" Rose was shocked. What possible reason could he have for refusing to talk to the sister of an old friend of his?

Jessie stood in the middle of the kitchen floor, looking at her cell phone. Rose could tell her mind was going a mile a minute. Over the years, Rose had seen that look on Jessie's face whenever she didn't get her way and was trying to turn things around.

"Stacey, you call and ask to speak to Chris. Use your cell phone and give your name. The receptionist won't recognize the phone number if it comes up and he won't recognize your name," Jessie explained.

Reaching into her purse, Stacey reluctantly pulled out her phone. "I don't know Jessie. If he doesn't want to talk to you, he doesn't want to talk to you. Maybe he heard something on the news about David and doesn't want to get involved."

"Then he can tell me that himself," Jessie insisted, showing Stacey her phone so she could copy the phone number for David's office.

Stacey dialed and put it on speaker so they could all listen in. Then, she asked to speak to Chris. After giving her name, they waited a moment and then someone came on the line.

"Hello?" a male voice said.

Jessie grabbed the phone from Stacey's hand and spoke into the receiver.

"Chris, this is Jessie. What the hell is going on? Why won't you talk to me?"

"Jessie! I asked you not to call me, I can't talk to you."

"Why not?"

"You know why not, so quit harassing me or I will be talking to my lawyer," Chris said decisively and then the line went dead.

Chapter 26

Present Day

"Why would your friend Chris behave like that?" Rose asked David. She was sitting on the other side of a plexiglass partition, a phone in her hand. Her husband sat on the other side, looking across at her.

"I have no idea," he answered, a faraway, preoccupied look on his face. "Maybe he just didn't want to get involved."

"But it sounds like you two were such good friends. And how come you've never mentioned him before?"

"I don't know, it just never came up."

Rose looked at her husband closely. He was looking tired and drawn, with dark circles under his eyes. She instantly felt like a heel for bugging him with questions he had no reasonable way of answering. He had a lot bigger issues on his mind than why his friend from thirty years ago didn't want to talk about him.

"The kids send their love," Rose changed the subject, hoping to cheer him up. "Kayla is anxious to see you and I had to put my foot down with her that she didn't have seniority over me when it came to visiting."

They smiled at each other knowingly. Barry had told them that David could have one visitor, besides his lawyer, every day. That meant they would have to take turns seeing him. However, they did manage to obtain a concession that Kayla and her husband could visit together as well as Joshua and Sarah.

"How is Joshua holding up?" David asked.

"Oh, you know Joshua, he is a rock. He is quiet and strong and reasonable." Rose and David had often been amazed over the years at just how different their two children were. The same parents, the same upbringing, and two opposite ways of approaching life.

"What did Jerry say? How are things going at work?" David looked at her hopefully when he mentioned his boss's name.

"He said they can hold your job for now, but he couldn't promise they could do so indefinitely. He said they would wait and see how long this drags out." Rose hadn't wanted to share this news with him but she couldn't very well lie to him.

"That's nice of him," David responded. "They don't have to do that."

"Of course, they do! You have been loyal to that company for years and you have worked hard and helped them become the company they are today!" Rose was indignant that her husband was so grateful to the company that she felt had turned their back on him. But she couldn't dwell on it and risk being negative during this precious time with David.

"I've been meaning to ask you hon, when we were waiting for the judge to decide on your bail, you said something about if it was more than $100,000 that I should talk to Barry about getting banking information. What did you mean by that?"

David looked a bit taken aback by her question, as though he had completely forgotten about saying anything.

"Oh, I just meant that we would have to make other arrangements if it was more than we anticipated, that's all," he said. "But that wasn't an issue at all, now, was it?"

Rose quickly changed the subject. It seemed as though she was walking through a minefield trying to keep their time together positive.

"Jessie mentioned she talked to you and told you everything about our trip down your memory lane?"

"Yeah, I wish you two wouldn't do stuff like that. I don't want you guys gallivanting around, stirring up the past," David frowned, moving around anxiously in his seat, frustrated that he was stuck in jail and unable to control what was happening in her world.

They sat quietly, each of them uncertain of what to say next. Feeling like anything she said upset her husband, Rose waited for him to speak.

"Barry told me that he is beginning to get some documents through the discovery process. He is going to let me know what evidence they have, as soon as he has the time to go through everything but there are boxes of information," David finally spoke up.

"Well, that is good. At least we will have an idea of what we are up against and how they made this mistake," Rose said. "Does he have any more information on the person who says they saw you in town with her that day?"

"Not yet," David ran his hand through his hair and Rose had an uncontrollable yearning to be able to touch him. While it felt wonderful to be sitting across from him and hearing his voice, it was also a double-edged sword that just fed her hunger for him. She felt tears pricking behind her eyes and she blinked rapidly, trying to stop them from falling.

"Is there anything I can bring you? Maybe something to read? Or some cigarettes? Soap?" She smiled teasingly at him, but his lips barely moved.

"Maybe some newspapers or magazines; I don't know if I have enough focus to read a book."

"Fair enough." She glanced at the clock hanging high on the wall behind him. Their time was fast coming to an end. "David, I want you to know that I love you and everything is going to work out. We have been through a lot over the years, and we didn't make it through just to be taken down by some horrible mistake."

"I know," he said quietly. "No matter what happens in life, I can always count on you, can't I Rose? You'll always believe in the best in me and stay by my side."

"Damn straight I will," she smiled sadly, wishing she could offer him more solace than just words.

~~~~

Later that night, their kids and Jessie joined Rose for dinner: pizza and pop loaded up on the kitchen table. The grandchildren had finished eating and had gone upstairs to play. Rose and Jessie were telling everyone what they had learned while on their road trip the day before and Jessie was regaling them with a comical interpretation of their mother running from the car and down the pathway with her arms flailing and landing on her butt. Everyone was laughing when Jessie looked up from the table and her eyes met Rose's as she brought napkins to the table. They exchanged an understanding look; there was no need to tell the kids just how spooked they had been and how convinced they still were that someone had been out there in that forest.

Kayla was excited to be able to finally see her dad the next day and was peppering Rose with questions on what she could expect during her visit.

"Tell her Mom, tell her how they will have to strip search her and then take her across the prison and past all those cells of violent criminals who will be shaking their cages, tell her Mom!" Joshua smirked at his sister and in return she lobbed a piece of pepperoni in his direction.

"It's a jail, not a prison or San Quentin, Josh," Rose shook her head at their antics. Nothing warmed her heart more or made her so convinced everything was going to turn out than being surrounded by her children. They were laughing at Brandon's rendition of an incident involving the twins when Jessie popped up from the kitchen table, holding her cell phone in one hand and looking down at it in disbelief.

"Well, shit!" she exclaimed.

Everyone stopped talking and stared at her. She flipped her phone around as though everyone would be able to see exactly what caused her outburst. All they could see was that she was reading a newspaper article.

"What Jessie?" Rose asked, annoyance in her voice.

"They are reporting on the eyewitness who said they saw David with Rebecca Evans on the day she died!"

Everyone continued to stare at her, waiting for her to say more.

"Richard Drees!" Shock and disbelief played across Jessie's face as she spat out his name.

~~~~

"Who?" Sarah asked, her brows furrowed in confusion.

"Yeah, who's Richard Drees?" Rose asked.

"I don't know, but how is this information public?" Jessie asked. "David's lawyer didn't know when we talked to him, so how did the media find out?"

"I don't know how, but I'm going to find out," Rose grabbed the phone and punched in Barry's number. She walked out of the kitchen and into the living room so she could have some quiet.

She barely allowed him to say anything more than hello before bombarding him with questions. "What is going on Barry? Why are we hearing on the news that the eyewitness is Richard Drees? How did they know the witness's name before we did?"

"I'm sorry Rose, they got the information before I was able to tell you—"

"Well, the news stations had the information long enough to put together a clip and air it," Rose pointed out.

"Yes, I know, but I have protocols I need to follow before I can contact you with updates," Barry explained.

"How long can it take to make a phone call, Barry?" she was becoming annoyed.

"Not long, Rose." She heard him sigh on the other end of the phone and she was reminded that this was way past office hours for him. "But I have to make arrangements to talk to David and that can take a bit of time, depending on what is happening at the jail."

"Well, you can call me while you're waiting to talk to David and then I can at least pass the information along to my kids so they are prepared," Rose explained, trying not to sound just as frustrated. There was silence at the other end and Rose waited for him to say something.

"I'm afraid I can't do that Rose," he finally admitted.

"Why not?"

"Because technically, David is my client."

"Well yes, but I'm his wife."

"Listen Rose, you will have to talk to David about that, I'm just following protocol. I'm David's lawyer and so I have to pass things through him first."

"I understand that, Barry, but it isn't like David cares. He would want us to know what is going on." She was growing increasingly annoyed by Barry's insistence on following the letter of the law. She waited again to hear what he had to say, but there was a deafening silence on the other end of the line. Rose felt her stomach lurch as the reality of what he was saying suddenly hit her.

"Did David direct you to speak to him first before he allowed you to tell us anything?"

"It's best if you talk to David directly about this. I don't want to get involved in family matters any more than is necessary," Barry said. "I'm sorry Rose, but I have to go. Once I talk to David tomorrow morning, I will call you and we can talk about where things stand with the case."

She hung up and stood looking at the phone in her hand. Her insides felt hollowed out and her face was flushed. What the hell was going on with David? Why was he acting like the gatekeeper for information on the case? Her mind shot back to the conversation she had with him about what she was to do if the bail was higher than they had anticipated. He had told her to get information from Barry. Information she obviously didn't have. What wasn't he telling her?

"Gramma, look at what I made!" Bethany came bounding down the stairs, her hand held high, waving a piece of paper.

"It's a stupid picture!" Jonathon shouted as he ran down the stairs behind her. "A stupid girl picture!"

"Jonathon, don't talk to your sister that way!" Rose regretted opening her mouth the moment she finished speaking. The words themselves weren't wrong, but her tone was angry and scathing. Jonathon looked at her with wide eyes, unsure how he had managed to upset her so badly. Rose softened her voice and spoke again.

"It isn't nice to say things like that to your sister. Jonathon. Why this is a lovely picture, Bethany." In an attempt to lighten the mood, she ruffled the hair on the tops of both her grandchildren's heads. "Why don't we go and grab some ice cream in the kitchen."

In the kitchen, Jessie looked up, her eyebrows raised and a question on her face. Rose made a slight shake of her to indicate it wasn't a good idea to discuss her phone conversation with Barry in front of the children.

Once the kids had eaten their ice cream, argued over who had the bigger share, and then hugged their Uncle Joshua and Auntie Sarah goodnight, their parents said their goodbyes and the house fell silent. When Rose told her son and his fiancée and Jessie about her phone conversation with Barry, she could barely meet their eyes. She felt shame and an overwhelming feeling of not being good enough; it simmered and rolled in her gut. She had been married to this man for so many years and today she didn't know who he was. He was a man who didn't trust her. She had thought they were partners for life but it turned out he thought it was every man for himself. What kind of fool had she been?

"But why would Dad do that?" Joshua shocked them all by almost shouting. The man who was always their rock, who was always calm and collected sounded like he was on the edge of losing control. "What is happening?"

No one even attempted an answer. It was the question burning deep within each of them.

Chapter 27

Present Day

"Kayla? Can you call Joshua and let him know we are meeting with the lawyer at one this afternoon? I just heard from him, and he wants to go over some of the discovery information." Rose was on the phone talking to her daughter. The call from Barry had come early this morning, just as she was waking up and trying to decide what the day held for her.

"No, it has to be at 1 pm because he said the judge has set the preliminary trial date for next week. He wants us to know what will come out in the trial and he still has a lot of work to do to prepare," Rose grabbed mugs from the cupboard and handed them to Jessie while using her chin to point at the coffee pot that was sitting on the counter. "If you can't find a sitter, then maybe just one of you can come? Or I can let you know what he said when I get back."

Jessie poured them each a cup of coffee and then leaned against the counter, listening as Rose finished her conversation with Kayla.

"Lord save me," Rose declared as she hung up. "I think she was hinting that I should babysit the kids so she could be the one to meet with the lawyer."

"Well, at least she knew enough not to ask outright," Jessie laughed. "So, they've set a date for the preliminary hearing? When next week?"

"Wednesday morning."

"I'm anxious to hear how Barry plans on handling it. I hope he can quash this somehow before it goes any further," Jessie said.

Rose looked at her sister-in-law, both of her eyebrows raising questioningly.

"What?" Jessie responded.

"I thought the evidence had convinced you that David is guilty?"

"That is not what I said. I said I believe in evidence and I trust my feelings a whole lot less. I don't see how David could have done anything to Rebecca, but I have to allow for the facts, given the evidence."

"That makes sense. I'll be honest, I'm not sure what I'm feeling right now," Rose confided. "Just days ago, I was absolutely convinced of his innocence; in fact, I couldn't even entertain the possibility that he could be guilty. But..." Rose's voice trailed off.

"I know. And the way he has been acting isn't helping much either, is it?" Jessie said.

"Nope."

The house was silent except for the occasional sound as the women sipped hot coffee. They discussed what else they could do to find out more about what had happened that summer, but they both lacked solid ideas. It seemed as if their enthusiasm for discovering the truth had seeped out of them.

"You know what?" Jessie suddenly pushed herself away from the counter and placed her half-finished coffee in the sink. "I think we need to take a break from all of this. We need to go and do some shopping!"

Rose laughed at Jessie's suggestion. She wasn't sure that the benefits of retail therapy extended to taking your mind off your husband's upcoming trial.

"I'm serious. There is nothing we can do right now and it has been a hellish few days. We both deserve to just relax a bit. We'll pop by the mall and then afterward we'll grab some lunch before heading to the lawyer's office."

"Sure, why not?" Rose was smiling as the women grabbed their purses and headed out the front door. While Rose enjoyed shopping just as much as most people, she wasn't sure if her heart was in it this time.

Jessie declared that she had to find a more formal outfit for court as she wouldn't be taken seriously if she showed up in her usual work outfit of torn jeans and a stained T-shirt.

The larger, more upscale mall in town was located about eight blocks east of Barry's law offices so they decided to go there rather than the smaller one near Rose's house.

Rose insisted on driving as Jessie had played chauffeur the day before and she slipped behind the wheel of her car and pulled out of the driveway. They had seen very little evidence of local news reporters around lately and Rose was grateful for that; it was hard enough to live through all of this chaos without having to do it under the watchful eyes of strangers.

They were driving along, chatting about what style of clothing Jessie was looking for, when Rose grew quiet, her eyes darting back and forth between the road and her rear-view window.

"What's the matter? Do you think someone is following us again?" Jessie twisted in her seat to look behind them just as Rose swerved over to the side of the road and came to a screeching halt. They had not been going overly fast as there was some traffic on the quiet residential roads, but her fast maneuver caused a couple of cars behind her to honk their horns as she opened the car door and went flying out of her car and strode towards the blue sedan behind them. She was approaching the sedan that had pulled over several car lengths behind her when it suddenly backed up and away from her. It then pulled back onto the road and swerved around her, its tires screeching. Rose leaped out of the way to make sure the car didn't clip her as it passed by. She peered into the car, trying to get a look at the driver but to no avail. The driver was wearing a hat that was pulled low over their eyes and the windows were tinted enough that she could see very little.

Rose ran back to her car and jumped in the driver's seat. She thrust her car into drive and took off.

"What are you doing?" Jessie screamed. "You can't chase them in the middle of town, in a residential area!"

The adrenaline coursed through Rose's body, causing her hands to sweat as they gripped the steering wheel. She eased up on the gas pedal and let out a breath. Jessie was right, chasing this person, whoever they were, was not the answer. She had reacted instinctively, feeling as if she could just talk to whoever it was that was following them, she would have the answers they sought. She didn't know why she was so convinced of it; after all, it could just as easily be a reporter trying to get photos or a different angle on the story.

"Damn it!" Rose pounded her palms on the steering wheel, frustration in her voice. "What the hell is going on?"

"I don't know Hon but getting you and possibly others killed chasing whoever that was, is not going to help. Or for that matter ending up in the newspaper as the crazy wife of accused murderer David Slater, found careening through residential streets in pursuit of a phantom blue sedan. I can see the headlines even now," Jessie waved her hand across the windshield in front of her, mimicking a newspaper headline.

Rose laughed weakly, knowing that Jessie was right. But when she saw that sedan again, she felt a white-hot rage flow through her. For a brief moment, it represented everything that was happening in her life and to her family. She wanted to pull whoever was behind the wheel of the blue sedan out and onto the road. In her mind, she could see herself shaking the person and pounding their head up and down on the pavement. The shock she felt at her violent reaction was sobering and she realized she was going to have to work hard at not letting this nightmare get to her and change who she was at her core. She had pulled over to the side of the road and now she looked down at her hands, trembling as she laid them on her lap.

"Do you mind driving, Jessie?" she asked quietly. Without a word, the other woman got out of the passenger side and opened the driver's side to let Rose out. When Rose stood, she wrapped her arms around Jessie, buried her face in her shoulder, and began to sob uncontrollably. Jessie held her tightly and rubbed her hand up and down her sister-in-law's back while making hushing sounds.

"It's going to be okay Rose, it's going to be okay," Jessie reassured Rose while looking off into the distance, wishing she felt as certain as she sounded.

Chapter 28

The Past

"Have you asked anyone to the prom yet, Jimmy?" Alicia asked, turning in her desk in front of him so she could see him easier.

"Please call me James." He had decided when he entered high school that he preferred to be called a more adult name, one that sounded sophisticated and far from this dinky town. Unfortunately, many people still insisted on calling him Jimmy.

"Of course, I'm so sorry... James," she smiled prettily at him and he was taken aback by her beautiful blue eyes. He had always admired her trim figure and silky blonde hair, but he had never noticed her eyes before today.

"So? Have you?"

"Um, no, not yet," he stammered slightly, unused to having someone from the 'in' crowd speak to him without jeering or laughing.

"Well, you'd better hurry before everyone is taken," she smiled shyly at him. "I'm sure whoever you ask will be a lucky girl."

He watched as she grabbed her algebra textbook and made her way to the classroom door. When she arrived at the door, she looked back at him for a moment, dazzling him with another smile. What on earth was that all about? Was she hinting that she wanted him to ask her to the prom? No, that wasn't possible She was Alicia. The Alicia. The Alicia that all the boys drooled after and talked about in the locker room at gym time. A few of them said they had screwed her, but he had a sneaking suspicion that it was just wishful boasting for most of them. Except maybe Matt Broder. He had dated Alicia until just recently and they had been an item for several months. He would often smack her ass when he said goodbye to her in the hallway and she would squeal and tell him to knock it off. But he didn't. It was as though he knew she liked it.

James wasn't clear why they had broken up, but it had been the subject of much speculation in the high school. And with prom coming up, there was a lot of talk about who everyone was taking as a date. He had overheard some of the cheerleaders arguing over who Matt would be inviting and he had noticed more than one of them preening and sticking out their boobs when he came around. James had no idea what they saw in him. He was dumb and tended to fall asleep in class. He didn't seem to do any studying and he never paid attention in class. He knew he would be able to go on to college because of his football career. Unlike James, he had his whole life laid out for him and he didn't even have to work for it.

He would be given whatever he wanted or needed.

When he arrived home after school, he went straight to his room before his parents arrived. They usually arrived home from work about half an hour after him, but he wanted to take no chances that he might run into them before supper. In the last few years, they had laid off him quite a bit. Ever since that day when his dad tried to lay a beating on him and James had grabbed him by his arm and twisted it behind his back. Whispering in his father's ear he had said "Don't. Ever. Try. That. Again." He had grown to be about two inches taller than his father and about 25 pounds heavier. Add the speed of youth to those dimensions and James could easily have stopped his father in his tracks if he had ever tried anything again.

Of course, that didn't stop the verbal abuse from both his father and his mother, so he tried his best to avoid them. He stayed in his room until it was time to eat and then he left the house until they were in bed. It was a pain in the ass to have to be away from his own home that much, but he considered it a small price to pay to get away from them. As the years went by, they had only grown more miserable and bitter. They were convinced that life had dealt them a bad hand and the world owed them something that it hadn't bothered to deliver on. And they often used James as a prime example. Here they had wanted a proper baby and had ended up with a dud. The scrawny-looking thing that cried non-stop had grown into a snot-nosed dunce that didn't have a lick of sense. No wonder his mother didn't want him; no one in their right mind would want to be saddled with him.

This line of beratement had been a steady hum in the background of his life, always there but he had learned to tune it out. Whenever their abuse became too much to bear, he would run away and hide in the trees behind their house. He would wander aimlessly until it got dark and then he would find a sheltered area, near a large rock or under some shrubs where he could rest for the night. When he returned to the house, usually the next day after school, his parents would have calmed down and forgotten all about the day before. They never mentioned that he had been gone all night or asked him where he had been. It took years for James to realize that they simply hadn't noticed he had left. Once they had taken their frustrations at life out on him, he had ceased to be useful and therefore he went unnoticed.

He spent the next few days mulling over what to do about the prom. He could ask someone to go with him, even Alicia, but what would he wear? How could he afford to buy a corsage or rent a limo like everyone else?

He figured out the answer to the limo question when he went to school and saw that everyone was abuzz. The parent-teacher association had decided to rent a couple of limos for the prom to ensure that no one made the mistake of driving and drinking. They knew there was a high possibility that some of the students would imbibe, and they didn't want anyone to get hurt. The limos would act as a sort of taxi service for the night, escorting students to and from prom.

After spending more time trying to figure out what to do, and after sitting in Algebra class and noticing Alicia looking over her shoulder at him several times, he decided to throw caution to the wind. He wasn't sure how he would get the proper clothes, or money for a corsage, but if he asked Alicia to the prom and she said yes, then he would figure it out. If she said no, then it wouldn't matter.

He waited until after class one day and as she was walking towards the door to leave, he reached out and gently grabbed her elbow to hold her back. She flinched slightly but then looked at him and relaxed. The other students filed out of the room, talking excitedly about the weekend.

"Um, I was just wondering if, um..." he stammered, looking at the floor. Alicia reached out, cupped his chin, and raised his head so he was looking directly at her.

"What is it, James?" she asked quietly. "What are you wondering?"

He took courage from the look on her face. It was gentle and understanding, as though she knew he was having a hard time, and she didn't blame him.

"Do you have a date for the prom?" he finally blurted out.

"I haven't said yes to anyone yet," she answered. He frowned slightly. What on earth did that mean? Either she had a date or she didn't.

"I've been asked by a couple of nice boys but the one I really want to ask me hasn't yet," she said as she licked her lips. He was mesmerized by her tongue as it darted in and out delicately.

"Oh, I see," he said.

"What did you want to ask me James?" she encouraged him.

"Um, I wanted to know if you, ah, if you wanted to ah, you know, go to the prom with me," he finally managed to get the words out. It was amazing he was even able to talk as his lips and mouth were so dry, he could barely swallow.

"I would love to go with you James," she answered. "Thank you for asking me."

He was stunned. She hadn't told him no. She hadn't even told him she would think about it as she must have told the other boys. Could it be that he was the one she had been waiting to ask her?

"Now pick your jaw up off the floor Mr. Daniels," she laughed gently as she turned away and walked out the door.

He walked home from school in a daze. The only thought that he could keep straight in his head was that she had said yes. She had said yes. She wanted to be his date for the prom. She said yes. By the next morning, he had convinced himself there had to be a misunderstanding or some kind of a joke. This couldn't be happening to him. These kinds of things just didn't happen to people like him.

He was watchful at school that day, looking for a sign that people were looking at him or laughing behind his back. In the class he had with Alicia, he watched for some indication that she had changed her mind or hadn't been serious when she accepted his invitation. She smiled at him when she took her seat and said goodbye to him afterward. Was it possible that this was real?

A week went by, and James began to plan how he would find the appropriate clothes for the prom. He considered stealing his father's bank card, but even if he managed to get it out of his wallet, he didn't know the code for it. He went around to his neighbors and managed to find the odd job mowing lawns or helping with some painting or jobs around the house. But it wasn't near enough. He didn't have anything worthwhile to sell and he certainly couldn't ask his parents for the money. The very thought of that made him shake his head and almost laugh out loud.

He decided to stop by Rocky's, the diner that served French fries, burgers, and plates of nachos to local kids during the day and the teenagers on Friday or Saturday nights. He knew they wouldn't hire him to wait on tables, but maybe they needed something done in the back, like hauling garbage or something.

He was sitting in the diner's office, waiting for Murray the owner. The office was the size of a closet and smelled of old oil. Murray had greeted him when he came in and then promptly disappeared when the cook appeared waving a ladle and talking rapidly in a language James couldn't place.

The few words he had managed to say to Murray seemed to be well received and James took it as a positive sign that he wanted to continue the conversation.

As he sat waiting for Murray to return, he looked at the opposite wall, which was about six feet from the tip of his nose. There was a picture of a farmer's wife tending to some livestock. In the background was a run-down barn and rolling wheat fields. James felt an odd sense of déjà vu that left in its wake a queasy feeling in his stomach.

He heard some female voices coming from the front of the diner and they made their way toward the back where the washrooms were located. He could tell they were teenagers by the overly excited sound of their voices, punctuated by annoying giggles.

"Why do you think it'll work, Alicia?" James stiffened in his seat as he heard Alicia's name mentioned. Suddenly, he was paying complete attention.

"Because he's insanely jealous and when he finds out I'm going with Piggy Boy, he's going to freak," he heard Alicia say.

"But what if he has moved on and he doesn't get jealous?"

"Then... Some. One. Is going to have to tell him that I said Piggy Boy was much 'better' than he was," Alicia said with a laugh. "Believe me, he might think he is interested in that little slut but as soon as he sees me with him, he won't be able to help himself. I will suddenly look very, very interesting and he will drop her like a hot potato."

Just then he heard one of the girls rattle the doorknob to the washroom.

"Come on, some of us have gotta go!"

There was a shuffle of activity near the door and then it went silent. James sat in the chair, his eyes still on the painting. A minute later, he got up from the desk and walked out of the office.

~~~~

James lay on his bed, listening to the music coming from his portable disc player. It was turned up louder than usual because he wanted to drown out the sound of his thoughts. There was a burning rage simmering in his veins, as though the circulating blood consisted of rivers of fire. He should have known; he had been right all along. As he stared at the ceiling, he heard his parents come home and begin banging around downstairs. His father would be getting a beer out of the refrigerator and his mother would be pouring herself two fingers of vodka. What a happy domestic scene James thought, and he snorted.

Nothing ever changes. Life sucks and it just keeps going on. He would always be the loser and he was getting tired of it.

He jumped up off the bed and flung open his bedroom door. In the kitchen, he opened a box of cereal and filled up a bowl. Then he poured milk all over it. He was tired of hiding out from these two old people. He was tired of them ruining his life.

"What the hell are you doing?" his mother's voice came from behind him.

"Eating," he said.

"Lookie here Charles, we got us a smartass today," she yelled over her shoulder, in the direction of the living room. James continued to slurp up the cereal as his father came and joined them in the kitchen. "Apparently there is something wrong with my cooking; it's not good enough for him anymore," she said as she reached into the cupboard pulled out a frying pan and turned on the gas stove.

"I didn't say that, I'm just hungry," James said evenly. "I wanted something before dinner."

"What?" his father roared. "You want two meals? I don't think so—you want your cereal, then you've picked what you want. Do you think money grows on trees? We can't afford to be feeding you two suppers!"

James looked at his father. For the first time, James felt as though he was really seeing him. He was a tall man, but thin. The parts of his head that were not bald had thin patches of greying hair. He had a hooked nose and eyes sunken into his head. This was the man who had terrified him his whole life. This pathetic man.

When his parents stood beside each other, they looked comical. His father was 6'2" tall which was exactly one foot taller than his wife. He was tall and thin, and she was short and, for the first time, James noticed she appeared frail.

"Don't you think it's high time you got a job? School isn't going to last forever, and you need to be ready to move out," his mother joined in. "Don't be thinking you can just stick around here forever leeching off us!"

James was always amazed at their skewed way of looking at life and he shook his head. According to them, they had plied him with riches and given him everything. They had ignored the number of times he had gone hungry because of some imagined wrong. They forgot his thrift store clothes that he had to beg and plead to buy. The holes in his knees and socks that had caused the kids at school to mock him. In their world, he had been showered with money. They were so sick, and their sickness was like a foul stench that clung to him. He had spent a lifetime wondering what was wrong with him. Today, as he looked around the kitchen at his father, lighting his cigarette and blowing smoke rings up to the ceiling, and his mother who was pouring old bacon grease into the pan to begin supper, he realized there was nothing wrong with him. They were the wrong ones. They were the source of everything bad in his life. As this realization sunk in, he felt the fire in his veins cool and he became very still. This was something he could fix.

Chapter 29

Present Day

"The purpose of this preliminary hearing is to determine if there is enough evidence to move forward with a trial," Barry was talking to Rose, Jessie, and Kayla in his law office conference room. Joshua hadn't been able to get the time off work and was counting on the women in his family to be his ears. Brandon had taken some time off work to be with the kids so Kayla could be present.

"They will present all the evidence they feel necessary to show they have enough to at least put before a jury. The evidence they bring forward is not necessarily the same evidence that will come out at trial because in a prelim, no motions to suppress evidence are made yet."

"So even if it isn't good evidence, if there is something wrong with it, like it isn't true, they can still present it?" Kayla was incredulous.

"Yes, they can. We will have an opportunity before the trial to put forward motions asking the judge to not allow some of the evidence. That is part of the work I will be doing between now and the actual trial."

"You're talking like it's a done deal, that we will lose this hearing," Jessie pointed out.

"Just as with the bail, I want to be upfront with you about our chances. The truth is, I think they have enough evidence here to convince a judge," Barry stated bluntly. "Of course, I will do everything in my power to fight it, but realistically, if I were you, I would prepare to have to go to trial."

"How does the judge decide if there is enough evidence?" Kayla asked.

"The prosecution has a much lower burden of proof than in the trial. They only have to show the judge that there is enough evidence to have what we call probable cause to believe he could have done it and that the state should be given the chance to prove it before a jury."

Barry looked around the table, allowing a minute for what he had said to sink in.

"This brings us to the evidence. The state has sent over a lot of files, boxes full in fact. This is a thirty-year-old case so a lot of information in the files is old. They were written before the county's files were computerized. But the main pieces of evidence they have are the following," Barry lifted his left hand and indicated the number one by lifting his index finger. "The most important evidence is the DNA match. It is what is called familial DNA. That means they have DNA that was found on Rebecca Evans at the time of her autopsy. When it was originally found thirty years ago, there were no databases available to match with a suspect. In 1998 CODIS or the Combined DNA Index System was set up and eventually, the DNA was run through that database. Nothing came up. The weakness of that system is that it only contains the names of people who already have a criminal record. However, in the early 2000s, they began to use what is called familial DNA to find suspects."

Rose leaned forward in her seat, listening intently. This was the evidence that could change her life and the lives of her family. She needed to understand.

"The simplest explanation is that instead of only using CODIS to find a DNA match, they broaden the search and use other private databases. They match the sample DNA they have to various samples on the database and try and find someone who is a close relative to the person who left the sample DNA on the victim. In David's case, they found someone who was a cousin. Once they realized how closely connected that person was to David, the next step was to see if there was a match to David's DNA."

"When will they do that?" Kayla asked. "That would definitely show that it isn't the same DNA!"

"Before they arrested your father, they had him under surveillance," Barry explained, his voice becoming gentler. "They found a discarded cup your father had drank out of and they used that. They have already matched it to the sample DNA."

"No," Kayla whispered, her temporary excitement gone. "That's not possible."

"I'm afraid it is," Barry said. "Once they had the matching DNA, they obtained the warrant to arrest him."

It was so hard for them all to grasp that the day the police had come to their door, all of this had already happened. They had been going about their lives, oblivious to what had been set in motion and was careening directly toward them.

"The second piece of evidence is twofold," Barry continued. "We have Richard Drees who has come forward and said he recalls seeing David and Rebecca together the day she was murdered."

"But what about his alibi? He was working at the forestry camp," Jessie pointed out.

"That is the second part of this evidence. They have found someone who worked with David who says they had the afternoon off that day and all went to town to see a movie. He also says David left for quite a while during the movie."

Barry's words hung in the air and the women sat in stunned silence. Kayla stood up and slowly walked out of the conference room. For the first time in her life, Rose felt truly unable to put her feelings aside and comfort her daughter. She felt lightheaded and realized she had been holding her breath. Pushing her chair out, she bent over at the waist and put her head between her legs.

"I'm sorry to have to tell you all this," Barry said quietly. "But you have to know what we're facing going into this preliminary trial."

Chapter 30

The Past

A week before Prom, a double funeral was held for Charles and Nancy Daniels at the Baptist People's Church. Townspeople showed up, ostensibly to pay their respects, but in reality, to catch up on the latest gossip and see how that strange son of Charles and Nancy was holding up. They were disappointed when he only stayed for the formal part and didn't hang around for the food and refreshments afterward. They wanted to talk to him and get all the details of the fire that had razed his family home to the ground, while extending their condolences and wishing him well of course. But after the pastor had finished speaking, James walked down the aisle of the church and out the front doors. The last they saw of him was his back as he walked down the side of the road that led out of town, the smoke from his Marlboro lingering around him before floating away.

Chapter 31

The Past

The days began to blur into each other and soon became weeks. The blisters on David's hands hardened into callouses, despite the thick work gloves he wore. The crew had become hardier, and no longer simply fell into bed after dinner. The areas where their skin was exposed had tanned either to a deep brown or a constant red. There was a rhythm to their days now and they knew if it was Tuesday they would be having a chicken dinner. Sundays were for beef roasts and pasta night was on Thursdays.

The boys had gradually switched bunks as they learned which ones snored, which ones called out in their sleep, and which crew member they wanted to spend time talking to. Their aching muscles grew strong and accustomed to the repetitive nature of their labor.

"Hey, Davie!" David's stomach clenched as he heard Richard call him. He was walking to the dining room for dinner after cleaning up and changing out of his work clothes. He looked over his shoulder and saw Richard coming up behind him.

"Yes, Richard?"

"You heading home to see your girl on the long weekend?"

"Yes, I am," David answered, providing no more information than necessary. While he had settled into life at the camp, he still wasn't used to Richard and his obnoxious personality.

"I bet you can't wait to get your hands on her. Been a long time, hasn't it?" Richard laughed as he caught up to him and clapped David on the back hard enough that David stumbled forward. Rather than responding to the question, he gave a small smile in Richard's direction.

"Me, I'm gonna find me some little fillies and give them a taste of the big Richard," drawing out the word "big," he grabbed at his crotch as he pulled up ahead of David and turned to face him while walking backward.

"So, you mean you're going to give them some Dick?" The words were hardly out of David's mouth before he had a chance to think about what he was saying. He knew that Richard was very clear when someone made the mistake of asking if he shortened his name to Dick that it was not a name he would ever answer to.

Richard stopped so abruptly, they almost collided. They stood face to face for what felt like an eternity to David. Richard looked down at him with a shocked expression as though he couldn't believe what he had heard. Suddenly, he reached out, grabbed David's shoulders, and began to shake him. He threw his head back and for a moment David braced himself, squeezing his eyes shut, preparing to be headbutted by the camp bully. But what the heck was that sound? His eyes flew open at the chortling that almost sounded as if someone was choking. To his shock, it was Richard. And he was laughing.

"Well, what do you know? The boy has some spunk in him after all!" He let go of David and then threw his arm around his shoulders, dragging him along the last few feet to the dining room. "Who knew you had it in you?"

Scratching his head in bemusement, David walked toward the food lineup and grabbed a tray. Richard began to tell the guy in front of them about the hilarious thing that David had just said. He slapped David on the back, guffawing as though it was the funniest thing he had ever heard. After adding two helpings of chicken to his dinner tray, Richard headed off, chuckling to himself.

David mentally shook his head, uncertain of the strange shift that had just happened in their relationship. Dare he hope that maybe Richard would leave him alone? Richard had been the only real downside to his summer job. Even worse than the black flies that were large enough to carry away the apple pie the cook made them every Saturday night. After that fateful evening of porn, Richard hadn't missed an opportunity to make gross comments to David about Becky, hoses, and various bodily functions. It had gotten to the point where David would cringe whenever he saw him coming towards him. He had even gone so far as to ask the supervisor who scheduled their crews if he could please not put him with Richard. The supervisor had tried to accommodate him but occasionally the schedule inevitably put them together. Those days were excruciating for David. He tried hard to ignore Richard and pretend what he was saying wasn't getting to him when all he wanted to do was punch him squarely in the nose.

Later that evening, David noticed he had mail. When the mail arrived at the camp, one of the helpers from the kitchen would go through the bags and separate it out and put it on each worker's bed. He was excited to realize two letters were sitting at the foot of his bed. Flipping through them, he noted that one was from his parents, or rather from his mother, the other one had a return address he didn't recognize. He lay on his bed and read his mother's letter first, letting the anticipation of reading the second letter rise in him. Being around the same people day in and day out made him hungry for contact with someone new.

He scanned through his mother's letter and then reached for the second envelope. Carefully pulling back the flap, he unfolded the paper and began to read. Soon, he was scowling and he sat up on the edge of his bed. He could barely understand what the letter was saying as it made no sense. It was the ramblings of what sounded like the delusional thoughts of a drunk person. What the hell? He lay back down on his bed, tossing the two letters to the side. He hadn't realized how much he had hoped it was from Becky until he began reading it.

He wrote to his parents once every week or so but he still hadn't
been able to write to Becky. He knew he should, but his pride just
wouldn't let him. He hadn't received anything from her, and he
rationalized that it wasn't up to him to write first—that was on her.
She was the one who had been unreasonable and ruined their last
few weeks at home and he was dammed if he was going to be the one
to break down and reach out. He knew he was being childish, but he
couldn't help it. He was also aware that the longer they went without
contacting each other, the more difficult and awkward it would be
when they finally saw each other. Maybe he should ask his dad if
they could swing by the cabin on the way back to camp after the
long weekend. Maybe he could spend the day with Becky, they could
go for a long walk and get back on track. It wasn't ideal, but it beat
trying to write a letter that explained what he was feeling.

~~~~

The next Saturday, the area experienced record temperatures. The
boys drank so much water, that their bellies felt bloated, and their
bladders were full. It was about an hour after lunchtime and the sun
was at its peak. They moved sluggishly, barely going through the
motions as the energy seemed to seep from them and into the hot
dirt at their feet. Suddenly, the whistle to end the day went off and
everyone looked up, startled. They weren't due to quit for another
couple of hours. The man in charge motioned for them to gather
around him.

"This weather isn't good for anyone, how about we shut it down for
the day?"

A cheer went up around him as the boys managed to find enough
energy left to show their enthusiasm.

"You can either go back to the camp until dinner time or you can
get washed up and come with me into town. You might even have

enough time to catch a matinee in the air-conditioned movie theatre."

There was almost a stampede as they clambered over each other to get into the bus that had brought them here a few hours ago. There was an excited hum in the bus as it pulled away and headed back to the camp. After weeks of hard work with only a few days off, they were excited at this unexpected treat. Rutledge was a small town that consisted of a post office, movie theatre, grocery store, gas station, and a school. While the population of the town was only a few hundred, it served as the hub for a large number of farmers, villages, and even lake communities. Most of the folk in these rural areas bussed their children into Rutledge's school, grabbed their mail at its post office, and took their wives out for dinner at Arlie's Steakhouse. For the camp teenagers who had seen no one else but their supervisors and each other for the last few weeks, a trip into town seemed almost too good to imagine. Until now, they had assumed they would have to wait for the July long weekend and the middle of their camp time, to have a chance to visit or see anyone else. And it wasn't lost on David as they pulled into town that he was now about half an hour closer to home. It seemed like another lifetime ago when he and his dad had passed through Rutledge on their way to the camp.

The boys split into groups when they were dropped off at the center of town with strict instructions to meet back at exactly 4:30 sharp, or the bus would leave without them. Some of the groups headed for the corner store, intent on finding something to snack on that was loaded with sugar and additives. Other groups began to stroll casually down the sidewalk, looking around at the people curiously. David was with a group who headed directly to the movie theatre. They reasoned that they could find it all there: good snacks, girl-watching, and air conditioning.

At the last minute, Richard stepped forward and declared he was up for a movie too. With an inward groan, David realized it was too late to back out without it seeming to be a direct result of Richard joining them. Which it would have been.

"Hey, this one looks interesting," one of the boys declared as he looked over the Now Showing movie posters. "Isn't that the "Ted" guy?"

They gathered around the poster and peered at the starring actor's face.

"Yeah! That's the guy from Bill and Ted's Excellent Adventure," Richard said, "but does the movie have any women in it? I'm tired of looking at homely dudes."

"Someone by the name of Sandra Bullock. Sheesh, what kind of name is Bullock anyway?" said Doug.

"Good thing she's pretty," David said with a smile. "It starts in ten minutes, why don't we check it out?"

The group went up to the cashier and requested five tickets for the movie Speed.

"I sure hope this is good."

"To be honest, I don't even care 'cause it's cool in here, I got a soda and I don't have to smell John's pits!" Doug said, elbowing John with a laugh.

"You're one to talk – when you take off your boots at the end of the day all the ants in the dining room bail out the door," John lobbed back at him.

The group made their way toward the theaters, jostling each other and laughing as they went. It wasn't a large theatre complex, only two screens in total, and it was close to being empty. The attendant took their ticket pointed them towards the far door and said in a monotone voice, as though they had said it a million times already today.

"Speed is playing in theatre two, second on your left."

They watched the trailers, rating them each on a scale of one to five as to how much they wanted to see the movie being promoted. While they were split on the best upcoming movie, with some voting for Waterworld and others for the next Diehard, the one they did agree would be a bomb would be the movie about toys.

"Who but little kids are going to want to watch a whole movie about a wooden cowboy?" they chuckled amongst each other.

The rolling sound of the drums that heralded the 20th Century Fox's logo blared into the theatre and the boys sunk deeper down into their seats, digging into their popcorn with their eyes glued to the screen. They had spent about half an hour that way, enthralled by the non-stop action on the screen when suddenly David shuffled his way past his friends.

"'Scuse me, 'scuse me," he whispered.

"You're going to miss this, David!"

"I know, I'm sorry, it's my stomach," he rushed down the steps and disappeared into the dark.

The rest of the movie flew by in a series of explosions, laughs, and sudden gasps from the audience. It was only as the lights came up that the boys realized that David still hadn't returned.

"Wow, what a time to get the squirts; that was a hella good movie!" John exclaimed.

They were still talking about the adrenaline-filled movie as they stepped out into the lobby, looking around for the washrooms. Just then, David came through the front doors of the theatre.

"Yo! I thought the movie was over and you had left me here," he said, slightly out of breath.

"Nah, it just ended. You missed the best movie ever, man!" Doug shook his head at David. "You feeling okay? You were gone a long time."

"I'm better now. Man, I don't know what I ate today or maybe it was the sun and heat but it just came over me like pow!"

"Pow like explosive?" Richard guffawed. "Get it? Explosive? Explosive diarrhea?"

"Yes Richard, we got what you meant," Doug rolled his eyes. "But seriously dude, you gonna be okay to walk back to grab the bus? We gotta be there in the next half an hour or so."

"Yeah, I'll be fine, I think I... er... got it out of my system," David explained, looking embarrassed and giving the boys a sheepish smile.

~~~~

As the lights dimmed in the bunkhouse that night, David lay on his bed, trying to relax. His stomach was still unsettled, and he rolled over, hoping that in the morning he would feel better. It had been an eventful day and he just wanted it to be over. Not having to work the whole day was a pleasant surprise and he was grateful to get out of the hot sun and into the coolness of the air-conditioned theatre, but he hadn't been able to shake the uneasiness rolling around within him.

Chapter 32

Present Day

They dropped Kayla off at her house and then swung by the grocery store to pick up something to cook for dinner. There had been little conversation in the car from the time they left the lawyer's office and the very air around them seemed to press down with an unbearable weight.

Rose's mind was going a mile a minute, and she seemed unable to make sense of everything. The evidence the prosecutors had against her husband was substantial and if it was all a horrible mistake, Rose couldn't see where the error had been made. Jessie was also caught up in her thoughts. She had been trying to keep an open mind and she thought she was doing a good job until the hard evidence was laid out in front of her. Every fiber of her being screamed out that this couldn't possibly be true. Sure, her brother wasn't perfect, but a murderer?

They kept their thoughts to themselves, uncertain of what they could say that would help each other. Rose turned on her classical music playlist and they made their dinner to the soothing sounds of Chopin's Nocturne No. 20. The music soothed her thoughts and helped calm her racing mind.

"What was it like growing up with David?" Rose asked as they sat down to dinner.

Jessie reached for the bottle of red wine she had just opened and poured them each a glass.

"I don't know, it was pretty normal, I guess. Of course, the six-year age difference meant that David and I didn't have a whole lot to do with each other," Jessie said.

"Yeah, that's what David always said. He felt like he didn't know you much as a kid; you were only 12 years old that summer, huh?"

"I was 12 and convinced I was mature and old enough. I recall thinking that by the time you became a teenager you were practically an adult, and I was so close that it counted. I also recall thinking that David was so old, and I was surprised that Mom seemed so upset when he was getting ready to head off to college."

"Was it just about her eldest going off to college that was bothering her, or David in particular?"

Jessie put a forkful of chicken on her plate and paused to think. "I'm not sure; Mom always seemed a bit sad and anxious when it came to David."

"Just David? Not you?"

"Well, they do say parents often don't worry as much about the youngest after having gone through milestones with the oldest," Jessie shrugged.

"I suppose," Rose looked thoughtful. "But given that you were a girl, I would have thought she would have had a whole different set of milestones and things to worry about."

"I really wouldn't know, being the happily childless woman that I am," Jessie proclaimed. Holding her wine glass high, she clinked it against Rose's glass and gave a toast to her life choices.

"Was David the same when he was a boy? I mean, has he changed much over the years?"

"I'm not sure, although I do remember overhearing Mom telling a neighbor that it was as though he had grown up overnight when Rebecca died. But I guess that was to be expected."

"It's so hard to know how to interpret things now," Rose commented. "You could say it makes sense that if a young man's girlfriend is brutally murdered, that it would be a loss of innocence."

"Yes."

"But you could also interpret it as being that he changed because he knew he had done something awful," Rose continued.

"I know what you mean. There is so much about my childhood I'm looking back on now and seeing as if through a different lens."

"Like what?"

"I've always thought David was adopted," Jessie said.

"Really? Why would you think that?"

"Once when I was little, probably around eight or ten, I was rummaging around in our attic and I found a birth certificate with a name I didn't recognize. I asked my mom about it, but she brushed it off and said it was a cousin's or something. I got the impression that I had upset her, so I never pushed it, but the strangest thing was that..." Jessie trailed off as she gazed off into space.

"What? What was the strangest thing?"

"It had David's birthdate. I don't know any cousins that share David's birthday."

The two sat quietly at the kitchen table, their empty dinner plates pushed away. Lost in thought, they wondered if this memory of Jessie's had any relevance today.

"Is it possible that if David was adopted, that the whole DNA thing could be a mistake?" Rose looked confused and uncertain.

"That doesn't make any sense. They originally found him through one of our cousins who had entered their DNA into a private database. It was only when the police had narrowed it down to a cousin that they realized that the murder victim's boyfriend was a cousin of the person who was such a close match. If David was adopted, his DNA would not match at all, would it?"

"But remember, they said that was what originally made them reconsider David as a suspect. But then they matched his DNA to the sample they had from the autopsy," Rose pointed out.

"So, David would have to be related in some way to that cousin at the very least?"

"I'm not sure how that works, but either way, David's DNA matches the sample so it doesn't even matter," Rose explained. "Maybe he had a twin?"

"That my parents didn't know about but had the birth certificate of? That makes no sense. If he had a twin, where is he? And why wasn't he raised with us?" The women sat looking at each other in frustration.

"My head hurts; I think I'm too tired to be trying to figure anything out tonight. It's been a long, exhausting day," Jessie slumped forward, her chin resting on the palm of her hand.

"I'll second that," Rose agreed.

"Do you mind if I go and pour myself a hot bath and then crawl into bed with a book? I love you dearly, but I think I need some downtime," Jessie asked.

"Of course, I don't mind. You go and relax a bit. I'm going to clean up here and then maybe go and spend some time cleaning out my email inbox and watching cat videos on Facebook," Rose encouraged Jessie with a wave of her hand.

~~~~

As much as she enjoyed Jessie's company, she was happy to be by herself, even if it was just tidying up the kitchen, setting the dishwasher, and going to sit in front of her computer. Just having some space to be quiet and think things through felt like a luxury. Scrolling through her social media, she realized that a journalist or someone in the media had been trying to contact her there. She quickly pressed delete and got rid of them, saving any messages from people she knew. Most of the messages expressed their concern over how she was doing and made thinly veiled attempts to pump her for more information. She sent a thank you message to every one of her friends and family who had reached out and ignored any probing questions.

After dealing with her messages, she wondered if she dared to search David's case. She quickly decided it would only upset her and that she probably had more information than the average reporter anyway. Reading what the press had written would only upset her, as she was sure they were already convinced of his guilt. But could she blame them? How many times had she heard that someone had been arrested for a crime and assumed they were guilty? After all, the police wouldn't charge someone if they weren't able to prove it, would they?

She leaned back in her office chair and looked out the window. The sky had grown a dusky color and she marveled at how the world kept turning, no matter what happened in one's life. The sun continued to rise and set every day, regardless of what was happening. Tonight, she felt a sense of stability from the realization. There were some things she could count on, no matter what.

As she sat there, basking in the silence and warm comfort of her home, she caught a movement out of the corner of her eye. She swung her head back to look at her computer screen and inhaled sharply. The cursor was moving independently across her screen. She grabbed her mouse, rapidly moving it across the desk. The cursor did not respond. She clicked on her mouse, trying to connect it to the cursor. Nothing happened.

The cursor clicked on a new tab in her internet browser and words began to appear in the address bar. She felt the blood in her limbs turn cold as she realized what was being typed.

"rebeccaevansautopsy"

"Jessie!" she croaked, her throat seeming to constrict around her voice.

The cursor continued to move around the screen, clicking on link after link until it suddenly stopped.

"Jessie, come here!" she managed to scream.

The cursor landed on the address bar and typed out two more words.

"Jessie! Please!"

She was looking at the autopsy report for Rebecca Evans. She had no idea how she had gotten to this page; she didn't even know these types of things were online. Her eyes skipped over the page, her eyes landing on a word and then hurriedly moving to another. Asphyxiation, penetration, contusions, livor mortis, the words were accompanied by photos of a young, broken girl, her body splayed obscenely. Blood rushed to her ears, pounding with every beat of her heart. She gasped, struggling to draw oxygen into her lungs as her vision narrowed, darkness crowding her vision. The world was spinning around her as she felt herself slip down and off the chair, hitting her head on the cold hardwood floor.

When she opened her eyes, her head was resting on a cushion from the living room and Jessie was bending over her, a worried look on her face. She cried out in relief when she realized Rose was awake.

"God, Rose, you gave me a fright; what happened to you?"

"I... I must have fainted..." She looked around her office, her eyes settling on her computer. "The computer..."

Jessie placed her hands gently on Rose as she tried to sit up.

"Slow down girl, take a minute to make sure you aren't still feeling faint."

"But the computer..." Rose protested.

"It will wait, it isn't going anywhere."

Rose laid back again, resting her throbbing head on the cushion. "I was sending some messages and then something took over my computer," she tried to explain.

"Took over your computer?"

"Yes, the cursor was moving by itself, even when I tried to take overusing the mouse," Rose said. "It... it..."

Overcome by the memory of the autopsy images, she began to sob. Jessie put her arms around her and drew her close, letting her cry.

After a few moments, when the tears had slowed, Rose raised her head off Jessie's shoulder.

"I'm sorry," she sniffed. Jessie stood up and grabbed a couple of tissues out of the box on Rose's desk.

"Please don't apologize, Rose, you have been through an incredible amount of stress, it's a wonder you haven't broken down before this."

"It was just too much—who would do that? Why did they do that?" Rose cried out, lowering her head again.

"Take a deep breath and tell me what happened. You said that the cursor was moving by itself?"

Taking a deep breath to steady herself, Rose continued. "Yes, the cursor started moving by itself and it opened up a page online, and it... it had her autopsy!"

"Hers? You mean Rebecca's?" Jessie asked, incredulous. "Why would it be online?"

"I don't know, and it... it had pictures Jessie!" Rose shuddered, a wave of revulsion causing her to feel nauseous. "Why would someone do that?"

"I don't know, but it sounds like someone hacked your computer to show you those." Jessie left Rose on the floor and sat down at the office chair. She looked at the desktop and then moved the mouse. When the cursor moved, she navigated around the computer and opened an internet browser, and then clicked on the history button. The list was empty.

"Whoever it was cleared your history so you can't go back to that page."

"Good! I don't want to," Rose said adamantly.

"Unfortunately, I think it means we'll have a harder time finding out who did this to you."

By now, Rose had sat up, her back against the wall. "I guess it doesn't matter who sent it, probably some sicko who was watching the news and had too much time and computer knowledge. What is wrong with people?"

"I don't know," Jessie said, looking distracted. "Look, I'm going to call a techy friend of mine and see if he knows how or if we can figure out who did this."

Rose eased herself into a standing position, gingerly rubbing the back of her head. A knot was starting to form.

"Are you okay? Should we call an ambulance or go and get you checked out?" Jessie suddenly noticed that Rose was moving.

Rose rolled her neck from the left to the right, then she rotated her shoulders forward to make sure everything felt the way it should.

"No, I'll be okay. Nothing a good night's rest won't cure."

Going up to her bedroom after saying goodnight, Rose was left with an unsettled feeling in the pit of her stomach. Having someone take over her computer like that had left her feeling exposed and somehow invaded; as though someone had been in her home. She knew logically it was probably someone who had nothing better to do with their time than try to terrorize someone whose face had been in the news. But where had they gotten access to Rebecca Evans's autopsy report and photos?

Chapter 33

The Past

"Rebecca! Rebecca!" Daisy yelled out, her voice growing louder. Where was that girl? The last week or so, Rebecca had been disappearing for hours at a time and Daisy would have to go and search for her daughter. Inevitably she would be found far down the beach, sitting on a log or a large stone and gazing out at the water. Daisy would have begun to worry about her daughter's mental health if it wasn't for the fact that Rebecca's mood had shown improved significantly after her friends had come for a visit. She laughed more, smiled often, and spent far less time just lying in bed. She talked about Ashley coming to spend a couple of days with them and Daisy was happy for her.

"I'll go find her!" Susannah yelled as she took off down the beach. Rebecca's younger sister would use any excuse to spend more time with her idol. Their age difference meant there was little sibling rivalry and ensured Susannah's undying devotion to her big sister. Daisy wasn't sure how her youngest was going to handle things once Rebecca was at college and spending even less time with the family than she was now.

Daisy went back into the cabin and pulled the potato salad she had made last night out of the refrigerator and set it down in the middle of the table. She tossed a salad and heated the leftover hotdogs in the microwave. By the time she had finished stirring a new jug of juice, the girls walked into the kitchen.

"Just in time, lunch is served" Daisy gestured dramatically at the spread on the table.

"I'm going to have to go away to school just to go on a diet," Rebecca laughed. "The people who talk about the freshmen five don't know my mom!"

Daisy smiled, pleased with the appreciation her daughter always showed for her cooking. It was so nice to see this side of her again instead of the moping, depressed girl she had been for the first part of the summer.

"You must be excited about Kim's visit," she said.

"I am, we're going to have so much fun!"

After her friends had visited her, Rebecca had bugged both Ashley and Kim to come and visit her again. Ashley wasn't able to make it, but Kim and Rebecca couldn't wait to spend time chatting and getting caught up with each other and tanning on the lake.

"Is Dad back yet?" Susannah asked. Their father had taken to getting up early in the morning to go fishing with a couple of the men in the neighboring cabins. Afterward, they cleaned their catch and sat around chatting before he ambled back to the cabin in time to have some lunch and an afternoon nap. After his nap, he would inevitably arise with a stretch, commenting that "this is the life" before grabbing a beer out of the fridge and sitting out on the deck.

"I'm right here," Susannah's father came up behind her and answered her question while tickling her midsection. Soon she was squealing and giggling, protesting her father's onslaught.

"Okay you two, enough," Daisy said while rolling her eyes. "Wash up and let's have some lunch, we wouldn't want you to be late for your nap, Frank."

Sitting at the table, they all loaded up their plates and dug in. There was a contented silence in the cabin and Daisy looked around the table at her family. A sense of deep contentment spread over her, and she felt as though she was wrapped in a giant hug. She had everything she could ever want in life; a husband who adored her and two beautiful, healthy children. How had she gotten so lucky?

Immediately she was struck by guilt and dread as her mother's voice echoed in her head, reminding her not to tempt fate by getting too comfortable. Her mother was a harsh woman who, although she would never have used this word, was a big believer in karma and was highly superstitious. She would say that what goes around comes around and that speaking or thinking thoughts like the one Daisy just had was asking for trouble. While she knew her mother was an intensely unhappy woman who blamed every situation on anything or anyone except her poor life decisions, shaking her mother's voice from her head was something she had never quite been able to do.

"So, Dad, are you going into town today?" Rebecca spoke up.

"We have to go and pick up your friend, don't we?"

"Well, yeah... about that," Rebecca looked shyly at her father and lowered her eyes innocently. "I was thinking I could go and pick her up. I want to get a couple of magazines and maybe a Slurpee and Kim and I were thinking about maybe a movie. I know you don't like hanging around town, especially on these nice days. They're saying on the radio it's supposed to break heat records today."

"It's already awful hot," Daisy commented as she wiped perspiration off her brow. "Frank, why don't you let her go into town herself and maybe she can pick up some Doritos for tonight's card game?"

Frank looked over at his eldest daughter. She looked back at him, her eyes wide and guileless. She had never taken the car by herself before and they both knew it would be a big deal if she was allowed to go.

"You think you can handle the responsibility?" he asked her seriously.

"Dad, I'm practically a college girl already. If I'm not ready now, when will I ever be?"

When you're married off and a mother yourself was Frank's unspoken answer to her question. Yes, she was heading off to college, but that didn't mean she wasn't still his little girl. He slowly reached down into his front pocket pulled out the car keys and extended them in her direction.

"Thanks, Dad!" Rebecca said, reaching for the keys just as her father pulled them away.

"Wait just a minute: what are the rules of the road again?"

"Never drive drunk, never pick up hitchhikers, I change my own flat tires and never go under a quarter tank of gas," Rebecca recited the rules her father had taught her.

"Okay then," he passed her the keys. "And don't be gone all afternoon; your mother doesn't want to have to worry about you."

"Of course not Dad, I wouldn't want Mom to worry." Smiling, Rebecca got up and gave her father a quick hug, knowing full well her father was more apt to worry than her mother.

After helping her mother clean up the kitchen, Rebecca changed her clothes and ran a brush through her hair. Her heart raced in anticipation of her upcoming adventure. She knew it was silly and that it was only a trip into town, but it was a chance to change her surroundings and do something different.

She practically skipped out the front door and down the steps to the car. Slinging her purse on the passenger seat, she waved to her dad who was still sitting on the deck. After driving out of sight of her father, she reached over and turned on the radio, letting the music fill the car as though giving her a reassuring hug and reminding her that there was a whole life waiting for her.

Singing along to a Sheryl Crow track on the radio, Rebecca drove down the road, window down and with the wind playing through her hair. The drive to town was about thirty minutes from the cabin. The first half of the trip was spent on a gravel road that was packed down from the heavy traffic of lake country visitors and cabin owners. The sides of the road however were loose gravel that could snare the tires of unsuspecting drivers and quickly pull them into the ditch.

Rebecca was determined to make sure there were no mishaps during her first trip into town on her own, so she drove cautiously over the gravel roads. By the time she turned onto the paved highway she felt more confident, and pressing harder on the gas pedal she slowly increased her speed. Just outside of town, as she passed the Welcome to Rutledge sign, the speed limit dropped, and she began to look around with interest. From the many trips she had made to the town with her family over the years, she knew it wasn't large, but she had an idea of where the main stores were located and where she wanted to shop.

She would start at the grocery store and pick up the Doritos for her parents and see if she could find a couple of magazines she hadn't read yet there as well. Once she had those, she would be free to just cruise around town and spend time checking things out as Kim's parents wouldn't be dropping her off for at least another forty-five minutes.

Chapter 34

Present Day

Today was her day to visit David, and Rose was surprised to find herself feeling a bit torn. She hadn't seen David for a couple of days, and she missed him, but she wasn't looking forward to the process she had to go through to see him. And seeing him from the other side of a plexiglass window was difficult. She didn't want to think about how she was going to handle her conversation with him if it turned to the evidence that was to be presented against him at the preliminary hearing. She had decided she wasn't going to bring up the fact that she knew Barry had been instructed not to tell her anything without going through him first. She just wasn't ready to have that conversation.

She ran her brush through her hair and leaned forward to inspect the lines on her face. She was developing dark circles under her eyes and her skin hung loosely. The idea of facing another day of uncertainty made the weariness she was feeling sink even deeper into her body.

"One day at a time, one day at a time," she murmured to her reflection.

The doorbell ringing downstairs caused her to jump with surprise. She heard Jessie's footsteps walking across the floor and the sound of the door opening. Walking to the top of the stairs, she looked down and saw Jessie closing the front door, a box in her hands.

"You have a delivery," Jessie said, as she looked up and saw Rose standing there.

"Who's it from?"

"Don't know." Handing her the box, Jessie sipped from the coffee mug she held in her other hand.

"Well, let's see what we have here," Rose walked into the kitchen. "Shall we take bets on whether it's a condolence gift or hate mail?"

"I'm not making any bets on anything anymore," Jessie was emphatic in her position.

Rose laughed lightheartedly as she slipped her finger under the tape that secured the edge of the rectangular box. She lifted the lid off the box and stared at its contents.

"Well, I guess the answer is it's neither; looks like it's from an admirer," Jessie looked over Rose's shoulder and at the flowers in the box. "Oh my God, what are those?"

There were roses nestled amongst paper in the box. The outer tips of the roses were jet black, fading to a burgundy red the closer the petal was to the center of the flower. A scent of decay wafted up from the flowers and Rose dropped the box on the kitchen table, pressed the back of her hand to her nose, and backed away.

"What the hell?"

Jessie leaned over and grabbed a spatula out of a container sitting on the counter, then moved slowly toward the table. She poked at the box with the utensil and looked confused. Tilting her head to the side, she squinted as though trying to see better.

"Oh my God," she gagged and backed away quickly.

"What is it?" Rose demanded, her voice shrill. Jessie shook her head and continued to grimace. Determined to find out what was in the box, Rose walked up to it and looked down.

At first glance, they had thought it was just a box of black roses, but after staring at it for a minute, Rose realized that there was movement deep within the flowers. Maggots. The flowers were teeming with crawling maggots. Confusion filled Rose as she struggled to comprehend what she was seeing. Since when were maggots found on flowers? They were usually only found on... Rose gasped.

She grabbed the lid and threw it on top of the box. She snatched a dishtowel from the stove and used it to protect her hands as she picked up the box and quickly walked to the front door. Setting the box on the front step, she backed up.

"Jessie!"

"What? No need to yell," Jessie was standing right behind her.

"Call the police and Barry. I don't know what's in that box, but maggots like dead meat and I'm not going to find out why they are in that box," Rose said shakily.

For a minute Rose contemplated the idea of calling 911 and reporting that a box had been delivered to her home with maggots in it, but she quickly decided to call Barry first. He told her to leave it on the steps and that he would send someone for it.

"This is getting out of hand," Jessie shook her head from side to side. "Even if this is just some sicko with nothing better to do, this has got to stop."

Rose sat in the house on the second last step of the stairs and placed her chin in the palms of her hands. Jessie was right, she couldn't keep living like this, a new ugly surprise around each corner. Maybe she should go and spend some time with Kayla or Joshua, just to get out of the house and out of whoever's attention she seemed to have attracted. But would that just mean they would turn their attention to the kids? She certainly couldn't have that happen.

She grabbed her phone and called Kayla. The call was quick and to the point. There was going to be a family Zoom meeting tonight and it was a command performance—someone from their family had to attend. Then she made the same call to Joshua. While they tried to find out what was on the agenda, she just told them it was important that they talked.

She ended her call with Joshua and looked up to find Jessie's eyes on her.

"My kids need to know that they have to be careful out there. We don't know who this is or what their intentions are. If they decide to harass the kids as well they need to be prepared," Rose explained.

"That makes sense. I guess." Jessie frowned and placed her hands on her hips. She looked uncertain of what she should be doing next.

"I'm going to call Stacey and see if there is any chance that she and Roger have room for us for a couple of nights."

"Don't worry about me. I have friends in town, or I can stay at a motel," Jessie said quickly and Rose gave her a small smile.

"I honestly don't know what you and Stacey have against each other," she shook her head at the thought of the relationship between her sister-in-law and her best friend.

"I don't have anything against her. She just isn't my type of person, that's all," Jessie tried to explain.

"Uh-huh," Rose said as she listened to the sound of Stacey's phone ringing. When she didn't answer she left a voice message. "Hi Stacey, Rose here. I'm wondering if you and Roger are up for a sleepover—at your place. Give me a call and I'll fill you in."

"Would you mind listening for Barry while I jump in the shower? If he comes while I'm busy, just fill him in on what happened, okay?"

"Can do," Jessie agreed.

~~~~

Sitting in front of a plexiglass window, Rose waited for her husband to be brought into the cement room. The fluorescent lights hung from the ceiling and cast a bright glare across the room. She could have sworn she turned green the moment she was under them. When David walked in, he looked remarkably rested and almost happy.

"Hi Hon," he greeted her as soon as he picked up the phone.

"Well hello to you too," she said with a smile. Maybe seeing David was exactly what she needed to set her doubts aside. "You're looking pretty good!"

"Well, you know, there are some perks to being in jail," he laughed, and she raised her eyebrows and tilted her chin down in questioning disbelief.

"I don't have to worry about taking out the garbage, making sure the bills are paid, making that meeting with an important client..."

"Well, just don't get too used to the easy life!" she retorted. Of course, it was hard to continue feeling happy for him when she considered all the tasks and duties she had had to pick up since he was brought here.

"Are you ready for the prelim?" She decided to switch the topic entirely.

"As ready as I'll ever be. From what Barry says it will probably be pretty anti-climactic. Although at least I'll have the chance to face Richard Drees and look into his lying face," David shook his head as though still unable to believe that his former friend was testifying for the prosecution.

"Yeah, someone coming forward was a bit of a shock." Rose said. "Do you know who he is?"

"Yeah, he was this asshole that was at the camp I worked at that summer," David responded.

Rose wondered if David would say anything about the delay in the family discovering the identity of the eyewitness.

She didn't have to wonder long as he soon brought up her unwanted delivery. "I hear you had some roses delivered this morning," he said.

"I'm afraid so; they were disgusting, and all covered in maggots," Rose shivered involuntarily at the memory.

"Roses and maggots are bad enough without adding the dead animal and the note," David said with a grimace of disgust.

"What?"

"Didn't Barry tell you?"

"No, I haven't talked to him since he picked the box up this morning," Rose said, looking at her husband in alarm. "What kind of animal and what did the note say?"

"Oh shit, Rose, I shouldn't have said anything," David ran his hand through his hair in frustration.

"Whether you should have or not doesn't matter, just tell me about it," Rose prodded.

"Apparently under the roses, there were a few dead birds, and tucked into the side was a note that said, 'almost time,' "David told her reluctantly. "I'm sure it means nothing except someone has a sick mind and was bored."

"Why do we think that is an acceptable alternative? Everyone is saying it's probably some sicko, but that doesn't make me feel any better!" Rose blurted out. "The idea of some crazy person taking the time to kill animals and send me dead black roses crawling with maggots does not make me feel okay!" she was almost yelling.

"I know, I know," David said, his voice low and calm. After years of marriage, he knew that she needed him to remain the quiet, soothing partner when she lost it.

They sat there for a few minutes, each of them silent. Rose put one of her hands up against the plexiglass and David matched hers on the other side. She looked at their hands and then shook her head.

"Look at us, we're like two actors in a bad gangster movie."

"That's us, Bonnie and Clyde," he said.

"I'm sorry, I hope I haven't killed your good mood, David. It's just been hard without you," she didn't want to sound whiny, but she couldn't help it. She wanted him home where he belonged.

"It's okay, you're a strong woman, and we'll get through this," David reassured her.

"You're right," she sat up straighter and smiled at him slightly. "Oh, I wanted to let you know that neither of the kids is going to be able to come visit tomorrow. Are you going to be okay without company for a day or should I plan to come?"

"No, I'll be fine, I think Barry wanted to go over some things for the preliminary hearing anyway so that'll work just fine."

They said their goodbyes and Rose left reluctantly. Every time she had to leave him behind, it got harder and harder. What must it feel like to be stuck in jail while the rest of the world and your family kept living life away from you? She couldn't imagine how difficult it must be.

She had heard back from Stacey, and they planned for her to go and spend the night. Stacey insisted it was no problem and that it would be fun. Rose picked up a bottle of her friend's favorite red wine and then went to the house to pack a bag. She didn't intend to stay more than a night—just to keep whoever was harassing them uncertain of her movements. She might go and stay another night later in the week as well. Stacey had reassured her that she was welcome to crash there any time she wanted as she was concerned about what was happening. When Rose had told her about her hacked computer and the roses, she had almost come directly to pluck Rose out of her house. It took all her debating skills to convince Stacey that she would be okay, that Jessie was there until later, and anyway, she was going to visit David.

Both Stacey and Roger met her at the front door when she pulled up to their home. As soon as she walked up the walkway carrying her overnight bag, Rose was engulfed in Stacey's arms and Roger jumped up and down around her knees.

"Well, this is quite the greeting!" Rose laughed.

"Of course! Come in, come in."

Rose handed her the bottle of wine, and she automatically went to the kitchen for a corkscrew and two wine glasses.

"It's not even five yet!" Rose protested.

"And your point?"

"Well, no point I guess," Rose laughed. "Although I don't want more than one glass until after I chat with the kids. You did say I can use your computer, right?"

"Absolutely: mi computer, su computer."

"Good to know!"

"I've decided that once your call is over, we're going to take the whole sleepover thing to the nth degree and forgo cooking. We're going to order pizza and curl up on the couch and watch some Netflix."

"That sounds like an excellent idea, Stacey!"

~~~~

Sitting at the dining room table, Rose logged onto the laptop and into the video conferencing software. A few minutes later, Kayla and Joshua had signed on as well. They were curious as to why she was calling an online family meeting.

"The truth is, I wanted to keep some distance between us all," Rose began. "There have been some concerning things happening and I don't want you two dragged into it."

"What concerning things? What are you talking about?" Kayla asked.

She explained to them about the blue sedan following them, her computer being hacked, the autopsy report and photos as well as the most recent flower delivery.

"I don't know who is doing these things, but I don't want you two to get caught in the crosshairs, if at all possible," she explained. "It could be someone who is just wanting to terrorize us for no apparent reason, or..."

"Or what?" Joshua asked. "Or maybe it's that girl's murderer? The one who wouldn't be afraid to kill again?"

"I don't know, but there is no logical reason for that person to come after us. They got off on the murder and now your father is facing their consequences. They should be staying as far away as possible but

I just don't want to take any chances that whoever it is sees you two and decides to harass you as well."

"But this is insane Mom," Kayla said. "We need each other more than anything right now. If it is some crazy person, if they know how to get to you, they probably know about us already."

"I know, and that is why I wanted to talk to you guys. You need to make sure you keep your eyes and ears open and be on the lookout for anything suspicious," Rose said. "You don't have to be paranoid but just keep in mind that right now, we have to be extra careful."

"What about you Mom?" Joshua asked. "How are you keeping safe?"

"I'm going to stay here at Stacey's for the night and your Aunt Jessie is at a friend's place. I figure by shaking things up every few days that whoever this is will not be able to keep tabs on me as easily."

"That doesn't sound like much of a deterrent, does it Josh?" Kayla addressed the question to her brother.

"I'm also not staying alone, I will always have someone with me, either Stacey or Jessie," Rose continued her explanation. "It is all I can do right now. I spoke with the lawyer, but he said there isn't much they can do at this point."

They discussed the situation for a while longer, with her kids asking her to make sure she didn't go heading off into any forests alone for a while. As they were saying their goodbyes Rose spoke quietly one last time.

"And Kayla, please keep an extra eye on those beautiful grandkids of mine, okay? Promise?"

Chapter 35

Present Day

Rose threw her head back, laughing out loud. They had decided to watch a stand-up comedian's special on Netflix and it was exactly what Rose needed. She had heard somewhere that laughter released endorphins and produced a sense of well-being and tonight she would be willing to testify to the truth of that. She was the most relaxed she had been since before David was arrested. Of course, her sense of well-being could also have to do with the wine they had consumed.

She hadn't realized how much she needed to relax until she felt her body let go of some of the stress she had been carrying. Being at Stacey's place, curled up on the couch with Roger had brought a sense of relief and escape that she understood now had been sorely needed.

"Thank you for letting me stay here, Stacey," she looked over and addressed her friend who was on the other end of the couch. "This has been good for me."

"Of course, you know you are welcome here any time."

"Unfortunately, I can't hide out here forever, I need to face the world at some point," Rose's lips twisted ruefully. "Jessie mentioned something about seeing a document in her parents' papers that made her think that maybe David was adopted. I was thinking I might go through some of the stuff that David has stored away and see if I can find anything."

"How is that connected to David's case?" Stacey asked, her eyebrows furrowing.

"Oh, sorry, I didn't mean to imply there was, I just need to get my mind off things for a bit. I've been meaning to go through the stuff David has stored in the basement but just haven't had the time. When Jessie mentioned seeing papers in her parent's attic, it reminded me of the boxes David has of theirs."

Rose yawned and stretched her body out straight as an arrow. The movement startled Roger and he abruptly jumped off the couch.

"Sorry there, fella," Rose murmured.

"It's okay, he needs to go out for his final bathroom break before bedtime," Stacey said, making a motion to get up off the couch.

"I'll let him out," Rose motioned for her to stay on the couch. She went to the back door and opened it for Roger. Stacey had a cute little backyard set up for Roger that included a lawn chair lounger that matched hers, a cement fire hydrant for him to use, and a small agility course for him to practice on.

Roger stood stock still beside her at the door and looked outside. A low growl rose in his throat and Rose looked down at him in shock. She had never known Roger to growl at anything or anyone, and she had certainly never seen him not leap at the chance to go outside. A chill ran up her spine and she looked out of the house and into the dark night.

"What's wrong?" Stacey was suddenly standing behind her and Rose jumped. "Sorry, didn't mean to frighten you, but I heard Roger growling."

"Yes, he doesn't seem to want to go outside."

Stacey reached around Rose and pushed the door shut. "Then I guess he stays inside; I'm not going to make him, and we are not going out there," she insisted. "Let's lock up and go to bed. Things will look much less creepy in the morning."

~~~~

After a fitful night's sleep, Rose finally got out of bed shortly after the sun rose. The night had been punctuated by periods of staring at the ceiling and hearing every creak in a house that wasn't hers. When she did doze off her dreams were filled with unfathomable but disturbing images, as though she were watching clips from different horror movies. She went downstairs and put on a pot of coffee so it would be hot and fresh when Stacey woke up. When it was ready, she poured herself a cup and sat on the rocking chair on the front stoop. While there was a full patio set out back, after last night's eerie encounter with Roger and the dark, she decided she was more comfortable where she was in full view of the neighbors.

She was rocking back and forth, sipping her coffee, and watching the neighborhood come awake when she heard Roger scratch on the front door behind her. She let him out so he could do his business on the lawn and come and stretch out beside her. While scratching his ears, Rose wondered again if someone had been in the backyard last night. Maybe having an unpredictable schedule for where she was sleeping wouldn't be so helpful. Whether it was a member of the press or a sicko, they seemed intent on following her around. She would have to let Barry know again today that she was becoming concerned about it. It would also probably be a good idea to contact a security company today and upgrade their system. They had a system that was about ten years old, and it had been a basic model even then.

"Well, well, here you two are," Stacey spoke through the screen door. "I woke up and the whole house was empty."

"We decided to make sure the neighborhood was still standing," Rose said with a smile at her friend. "It's a beautiful morning."

"That it is," she agreed as she opened the door and sat on the top stair with her coffee. "What are your plans for the day?"

"Well, I'm going to talk to the lawyer about my stalker; call and have a better security system installed at home; and then maybe go through those papers of David's," Rose told her. "What about you?"

"Nothing near as exciting, just some errands to run. Are you going to stay here again tonight? You are more than welcome to."

"No, I don't think so but thank you. I'm going to stay at my place tonight as I'm not sure the whole keeping the stalker on their toes bit is working," Rose said with a rueful smile.

"Surely there's got to be something the police can do about this?"

"Not without some idea of who is doing it," Rose said. "Unfortunately, except for the delivery, there isn't any proof that anyone has been harassing me. It's just been seeing something in the forest, having a blue sedan behind me a few times and Roger being creeped out at the back door."

"Do you think that neighbor who said they saw someone crawling around your place might have seen this person?"

"I honestly don't know what to think," Rose shrugged.

~~~~

Spending the day marking things off on her to-do list made Rose feel productive and in control and she hadn't felt that way in what felt like forever. Jessie had decided to spend one more night visiting her friend and Rose was determined to enjoy her time alone in the house. Ever since David had been charged, there had been people coming and going through the house almost constantly and she had had no time to spend by herself just recharging.

She made herself an omelet and some hashbrowns for dinner and sat in front of the TV and watched a show on Netflix while eating. Afterward, she drudged down the basement stairs to look for the old family papers David had kept. She knew they were in a plastic box about the size of two shoe boxes, but she couldn't remember exactly where they had been stashed. Beginning under the stairs, she ducked to avoid a nasty bump to the head and peered around. Old luggage, a metal bedframe, spare ceramic floor tiles, and a Christmas wreath were pushed to one end of the area and a stack of boxes was on the other.

"Here we go!" she exclaimed as she spied the box she was looking for. It was about halfway down the pile, but she managed to extract it gingerly, like a block in a game of Jenga. As she backed out of the small, enclosed area, she shivered as she felt her ear brush a cobweb. "Yuck, yuck!"

Just then, she heard a creaking noise come from above her. Without thinking, she jerked her head up to try and locate the sound and banged her head against the stairs. Stars exploded in front of her eyes and a sharp slice of pain shot through the back of her head. Groaning, she dropped the box and grabbed her head.

"Damn it! Oh damn, it!" she cried out.

After the pain subsided enough for her to pick up the box and move out from under the stairs, she stood still listening to see if she could hear anything else. All was quiet. Upstairs, she sat the box on the dining room table and then cautiously checked the rooms to make sure she was alone. She wandered from room to room holding her phone, ready to call 911 if she found someone. When she was convinced she was alone, she returned to the box and opened it.

There were some small photo albums containing black and white pictures, the kind that used to be produced when film was developed by an agency. There were a couple of yearbooks that Rose remembered looking at with David shortly after they were married. She opened them up now and flipped to the page where David's photo was. He looked so young and so earnest. He had long hair that hung over his eyes in a style that she remembered swooning over when the boys in her class had it cut that way; it was so reminiscent of the boy bands of the mid-90s that she had to chuckle. She flipped through a few more pages until she found a photo of Rebecca Evans.

A pretty girl with blonde hair, piercing blue eyes, and a pert, upturned nose, Rose was taken by how innocent and young she looked. She had to remind herself that this was thirty years ago when they were all so much younger. Under her name, the quote said, "Let's take on the world!" and Rose felt an ache of sadness realizing that this sweet young life never had a chance to take on much of anything before it was so brutally snuffed out.

Once she was done with the yearbooks, she began going through the other papers that were in the box. There were birth certificates and death certificates for both of David's parents, a receipt from the cemetery where they were buried, and various insurance documents. She found a childish picture of a stick animal with the words "Mommy" and "David "written in barely legible chicken scratches along the side. She smiled, recognizing the picture because it was very similar to the ones she had from her children. If she tried hard enough, she could almost imagine a proud and happy young David presenting the picture to his mommy as a gift offering, confident of its irreplaceable value.

She had almost reached the bottom when she noticed a small piece of paper caught along the seam of the box. The paper and box were yellowed to an almost identical shade, and it would have been easy to miss it if she hadn't been looking carefully. After a couple of attempts, Rose managed to slip her finger under the paper. She carefully pulled it away from the box, not wanting to tear whatever it was. When it was safely in her hands, she flipped it over and saw a birth certificate. Yellowed around the edges, the paper had a stiffness that came from a paper that was thicker than usual. It bore a seal of the state where David had been born.

Michael John Cordell was born on September 3, 1974. It was a short-form birth certificate and had no other real information on it other than the date it was issued, place of birth, and that he was male. There was no mother or father's name. While Rose knew what state he was born in, she wasn't sure she had ever heard of where he was born. She had always assumed it was near Meadowland. Whoever this certificate belonged to, they shared David's birthdate, and they were both born in Frederickson County.

She sat holding the birth certificate in her hand, absently waving it up and down. Whose birth certificate was this and why was it mixed in with papers that had originally belonged to David's parents? Did David know about this birth certificate and who this person was? The more she thought about it, the more confused she became. Finally, she threw the certificate back in the box and closed the lid. The next time she spoke with David, she would ask him about it and see what he knew. Although it was a bit of a mystery, as far as she could tell it had nothing to do with David's arrest.

It had accomplished something though, and that was to take her mind off David and the murder. It had been nice to focus on something that had nothing to do with murder for a change. Deciding that she should get a photocopy of the birth certificate to show David, she retrieved it from the box and went into his office. As she placed it face down on the scanner and hit copy, she looked around the office, making a mental note that she needed to find a minute to run a rag over everything. David was usually in and out of his office, but it had sat untouched since he was arrested and there was a thin layer of dust beginning to form. A surge of resolve ran through her and she left the office to get a rag and some furniture polish from the hallway cupboard. No time like the present.

She moved everything off his credenza and wiped down the top, putting things back in neat piles. She turned and began doing the same thing to his desk. She took a pen and a couple of paperclips that were on his desk and opened the pencil drawer to put them away. As she was closing the drawer, her other hand already reaching for his stapler, she caught sight of something out of the corner of her eye. Opening the pencil drawer wider rather than closing it, she saw a credit card-sized swipe card. Picking it up, she flipped it over and saw the Marriott Hotel's logo. Why would David have a hotel key from the Marriott Hotel in his desk drawer? She couldn't remember the last time they had stayed in a hotel, never mind a Marriott. Frowning, she moved the contents of the drawer around, looking at what else was there. Pens, markers, binder clips, paperclips, and a couple of scrunched-up receipts.

Unfolding the receipts and flattening them on his desk, Rose peered at them. One was a receipt for two nights at the Marriott Hotel in Denver. It was dated almost exactly two months ago. She racked her memory trying to remember why he would have been in Denver. On business? He wasn't doing near the amount of traveling now as he had done before the COVID pandemic as people seemed to realize that a lot of business could be done virtually and save a lot of money. The only recent trip she could recall was when he had gone with a colleague from work to a conference. But that wasn't in Denver. She picked up the second receipt and looked at it as well. It was a receipt for dinner charged to a room at the Marriott. The receipt was itemized, and Rose felt her breathing grow shallow. He had paid for two meals and four drinks: a steak, a salad, two old-fashioned, and two glasses of white wine.

Oh God, no. She stood at his desk, her eyes closed, clutching the last receipt. She felt anger rise from deep within her. Not now, not amidst everything else. She couldn't deal with this. Not again.

Chapter 36

The Past

She was walking back to her car, her purchases in a bag when she looked up and abruptly stopped in her tracks. Across the street, she caught a glimpse of a familiar face. A face that was framed by blond hair. A face that she would recognize anywhere.

"David! David!" she yelled out. She couldn't believe it; David was here in Rutledge. Could he have decided to take time off from his work at the camp to come and see her? "David!"

He didn't seem to hear her as he kept walking and turned the corner at the end of the block. She ran to her car and jumped in. He had probably stopped here in town to pick something up before heading out to see her at the cabin. He had no way of knowing she would be in town on this precise day and time. If she could catch up with him before he went to the cabin, they could have some time together just the two of them, without her younger sister tagging along and her parents keeping an eye on them.

She drove in the direction he was headed and soon saw him as he passed in front of the post office. She lowered the driver's side window and leaned out.

"Wow, they'll let anyone visit this town, won't they?" she grinned at him. He seemed surprised to see her, but then again, he wouldn't be expecting her to be here and surprise him. She pulled over into one of the free parking spots and leaned over to open the passenger door for him.

"Hop in!" she encouraged when he lingered on the sidewalk, an uncertain look crossing his face for a brief second before he slid in. She threw her arms around his neck and pressed her lips against his.

Feeling his lips against hers for the first time in weeks sent a tingle of excitement down her spine and she slipped her tongue into his mouth. Within seconds, his uncertainty melted away and his arms wrapped around her, drawing her close.

"Oh David, I've missed you so, so much," she murmured, her forehead pressed against his. "I'm so sorry, I was such a bitch to you."

"It's okay," he said, his voice so low she barely caught what he said. "I've missed you too."

"I can't believe you're here—pinch me in case I'm sleeping!" she exclaimed, pulling away slightly. "I feel like any minute now my mom is going to be calling me for breakfast 'Rebecca, get out of bed already!'" She giggled at the thought and rushed on, her words almost tripping over each other. "Were you trying to surprise me? Were you going to show up at the cabin unannounced?"

"Umm... I think we should talk," he said as he pulled her back towards him. She giggled as he nuzzled her neck and ran his hands up and down her back.

"Yes, we can talk, let's go somewhere and talk," she purred in his ear.

"Really? What did you have in mind?" he asked her, raising his eyebrows up and down rapidly.

"Oh, just wait and see!" she threw her car into reverse and backed out of the parking spot.

They drove around the town for a couple of minutes before finding a trail that led off the road and toward a stand of trees that was about the width of a football field.

"Where does this go?" David asked.

"I don't know but wherever it is, there will be more privacy than in town," Her grin stretched from ear to ear as she looked over at him and he couldn't help but chuckle. The trail took them around the back of the trees and then directly into the center of them. Once the trees had swallowed them and their car up, it was obvious that this was a location known to others. There was an old firepit and debris of all kinds lying around. Looking around Rebecca noticed how the trees were so thick that the sunlight that made its way through cast thin, distinctive rays of light all around. If she hadn't been with the love of her life, she would have found the place a little creepy.

Before she had a chance to think about the spot any further, David reached forward and pulled her towards him.

Chapter 37

Present Day

James was sitting at a roadside truck stop, reading a newspaper, and taking a much-needed break to fill his rig and grab a shower. As much as he loved driving trucks, sometimes it felt as though the world was going on without him. He drove in his own little world, up and down highways, and outside the windows, people lived their lives. His only real connection to the world was when he stopped to read the newspaper. Sure, he could listen to the radio in his truck, but he preferred to listen to music and some podcasts that the mainstream media would never air on their stations.

He unfolded his newspaper and glanced down at the front-page article. He frowned and bent his head closer. He couldn't believe what he was seeing. It was him. The man he thought he would never meet. He skimmed the article and discovered where he lived. It was that simple; after years of wondering, the information just dropped into his lap, just like that.

Chapter 38

Present Day

Her knuckles were white as they gripped the steering wheel of her car. She was on her way to the jail to talk to David. She was going to get some answers out of him one way or another. She had forgiven his infidelity once because she reasoned that everyone makes mistakes, and he was a good man. It had been hard at first, but she had almost gotten to the point where she didn't think about it very often. Except when Stacey or Jessie brought it up. She sometimes thought she had forgiven him faster than his sister or her friend. They had been so upset at him that she had often wished she hadn't confided in them. But she knew she would never have gotten through those dark days if she hadn't had someone to talk to; someone who she could open with and not put on a brave face and pretend her life was perfect. But now they brought it up periodically and she was afraid it had colored the way they thought about him. And now this.

She knew without a shadow of a doubt that he had been in Denver with another woman. There was no other explanation. The colleague that he told her he was going to the conference with was not a salad-eating, white wine-drinking man. He leaned more towards lots of beer and a big plate of greasy nachos.

She pulled into the parking lot and stomped into the building. She told the front desk who she was there to see and tapped her fingers impatiently waiting for them to wave her through. David wasn't expecting her or the kids today and had told her that he was going to catch up on some reading. He would probably be alarmed and wonder why she had arrived unannounced. So be it, she wasn't overly concerned with his feelings at the moment.

"I'm sorry, I can't let you through," the guard told her. "He already has a visitor."

"Is his lawyer here?" Rose asked. "Barry Lorman."

"I'm sorry, I can't tell you that Ma'am."

"Well, can I wait here and see if there is still time after his visitor leaves? I'm his wife," Visiting hours would be over in an hour and she was hopeful that whoever was visiting him wouldn't stay the whole time.

"Your time," the guard shrugged, indicating the waiting area with its out-of-date magazines and sticky coffee table. Rose sat down with her purse on her lap, staring at the wall across from her. She had no interest in trying to find something interesting to read in one of the magazines and there was no way she could concentrate if she tried to scroll through her phone. She just kept thinking: I can't believe I am here again. I'm such an idiot, I'm here again. Stacey had tried to warn her, she brought it up from time to time and even when this whole thing with the arrest happened, she as much as told Rose to take the blinders off. But Rose didn't want to hear it. She was a loyal wife who stood by her man. She was an idiot. Her head flopped back against the wall behind her, and she sighed deeply, staring up at the ceiling. She began to count the number of tiles going left to right. She lost count several times and had to start over whenever the door would open, and someone left the visiting area of the jail.

Rather than the counting helping to relax her, she only grew more tense. Finally, she stood up and headed towards the washroom that was located next to the reception. She pushed open the ladies' room door and barely made it into the first stall before she brought up everything that was in her stomach. Shaking, she turned on the cold water tap and cupped her hands to scoop water in her mouth. Swishing the water around in her mouth, she made the mistake of raising her eyes to the mirror; her eyes looked hollow and haunted against her pale white face.

"Get a grip, Rose."

~~~~

Sitting across from her husband, Rose noticed that some of the hair near his temples had turned grey. When had that happened? She couldn't help but look at him with new eyes. He was an attractive man who, like many men, seemed to grow more attractive with age. A burning began in her middle that spread to her limbs. She needed to keep it together until she was at home. She could break down then.

"I thought you weren't coming today hon, is everything okay?" he looked concerned to see her.

"Surprised to see me?" she asked, her eyebrows rising along with the left corner of her mouth.

"Is something wrong?"

"Wrong? No, I just have some questions for you."

"They must be pretty important to bring you down here today. What sort of questions?"

"Do you know who the birth certificate in your parent 's old box of papers belongs to?" Without thinking it through, she decided to open with the easier, less emotional question.

"Birth certificate? I don't recall any birth certificate," he tipped his head to the side and frowned at her, as though he suspected this wasn't the reason for her visit.

"There is a birth certificate in the box that has your birthdate but with the name Michael John Cordell. Is it possible you were adopted?" she probed.

"I don't know whose birth certificate that is, but it isn't mine; there's no way I was adopted," David insisted.

"How can you be so sure?"

"Because I would know, my parents would have told me. Mom always talked about her pregnancy with me and how much harder it was than with Jessie. That would mean they would not only have kept it from me, but actively lied about it," he explained. "Nope, that would make absolutely no sense."

"Okay," she decided there was no use pushing the subject any further. "Now, why did you come here Rose?"

She leaned back in her chair, crossing her left arm across her stomach, with her right elbow tight against her body as though to protect herself. She cradled the phone in her right hand, pressed up against her ear. She looked through the glass at her husband. An overwhelming sense of sadness washed over her at where their life had brought them. This wasn't the way it was supposed to be. When she had taken her wedding vows, she envisioned years of laughter and happiness, punctuated with rough patches when money was tight or when one of the kids had trouble in school. But this? This was so far outside of how she thought her life would turn out.

"I know, David," she said quietly.

"Know what?"

"I know about Denver and the Marriott."

The color drained from David's face as he stared at the face of his broken-hearted wife.

They sat in their chairs, looking at each other, neither one saying a word. David slumped forward slightly, as though the weight of the world was suddenly just too much to bear. He rubbed his hand over his face and his day-old stubble.

"Oh Rose," was all he managed to say when he finally spoke.

It was only then that Rose realized she had been holding her breath. It was only as it left her that she realized she had still been holding on to hope. She wiped away the tears that were rolling down her cheeks as she stood up and replaced the receiver on the wall. She heard him calling her name as she disconnected the call and turned and walked out of the room.

Chapter 39

Present Day

Her mind was whirling with unprocessed thoughts and her body sat stiffly in the driver's seat of her car, unable to relax for fear she would fall apart. When she found out last summer that David had cheated on her while on a business trip, she felt as though her world would crumble. But they had worked through it and with time and a liberal amount of counseling, she had felt they were in a good place. She had renewed her dedication to her marriage and her husband. They had both grown complacent over the years and his mistake, as she had taken to thinking of it, had made them realize they needed to tend to their marriage so that it would continue to grow and thrive. She was able to deal with his infidelity because she knew it was an accident, a mistake he had made one time. It was a fluke, an abnormality.

But what could she do now? How could she reason it away this time? She felt as though the discovery that he was having an affair was a tangible thing that she needed to handle. Where could she put it? How could she continue to hold it when it hurt so much? She wanted to kick it like a football and watch it fly far, far away from her. Her mind simply couldn't grasp the idea that her husband had been deceiving her. For how long? When did this start?

Rose was only halfway back to her house when she couldn't hold herself together any longer and pulled into an empty parking lot. She leaned forward, her forehead touching the steering wheel, her shoulders shaking uncontrollably as she sobbed. The sick, aching feeling in the pit of her stomach eased a bit as she let go of her pain. After about five minutes, she reached over and opened her glove compartment to search for something to wipe her tears. Rummaging through the pile of random papers she located a travel package of tissues. Rose wiped her face and blew her nose. When she looked in the rear-view mirror, she realized her eyes were puffy and red and her face was splotchy.

She grabbed her purse off the passenger side of the car and opened her door. Maybe some fresh air would help clear her mind a bit. The parking lot was attached to a small mall that also had a gas station. She walked over to the station and purchased a bottle of water, careful to keep her eyes down so she didn't have to face the curious and inquiring eyes of the clerk.

Back at the car, she leaned up against the driver's door and sipped her water, the whole time wondering what she was going to do when she got home. She could carry on as though nothing had happened. She could continue to meet with Barry and report any news to the kids. She could traipse around with Jessie, looking for information on what happened that summer. But she could also leave. She could book a flight to somewhere warm and exotic. She could drown her sorrows with cheap drinks, hot sand, and a cool pool. She could pretend none of this was happening. What was stopping her?

The kids. Their worlds had been turned upside down enough. They may be adults but they were still her children and she couldn't add to their pain and confusion by pulling a disappearing act. She mused how when your children are born, you somehow think that they will be your responsibility until they are adults. But the truth is, you always have a sense of responsibility towards them. You never get to the point of being carefree like you were before you had them. Thinking of her kids, she reached for her phone in her purse to see if they had been trying to get ahold of her in the last few hours. With the bottle of water in one hand, she reached into her purse with her other, searching around with her fingers for her phone. As she grabbed it and pulled it out, it slipped from her fingers and fell on the ground, bounced once, and landed under her car.

"Shit!" she exclaimed. "Just what I need." Close to tears, she put her water bottle in her car and then got down on her hands and knees to retrieve her phone. "Oh, for God's sake," she mumbled, struggling to reach the phone which had slid about a foot under her vehicle. As she scrabbled under the car her fingertips found the phone and she managed to slowly pull it toward her. Once it had moved a couple of inches, she grasped the phone to pull it out. As she did, she glanced up and saw a black disc attached to the underside of her car. Peering at the disc, which was about an inch and a half in diameter, she saw that there was an impression of a star in the plastic. While she would never consider herself an expert in cars, she knew enough to realize the disc was not an integral part of the car.

Sliding out from under her car, she stood up and backed away. Her hands were shaking as she called Jessie's cell.

"Hi Rose, what's up?"

"There's something under my car!"

"What?"

"Under my car, someone has attached something under my car," Rose managed to say.

"Slow down, what do you mean something is attached under your car?"

"My phone fell under my car and when I managed to get it, I noticed something attached to the underside of my car; it's round and I'm positive it doesn't belong there," Rose blurted out. "I don't know if it's a tracking device or a bomb!"

"Where are you?"

Rose told her which parking lot she had pulled into, and Jessie gave her instructions to stand back from her car and wait. She paced nervously up and down the parking lot, keeping her distance from her car. As her heart gradually slowed down, she began to feel a bit silly and wondered if she was overreacting. What if it was just a part of her car that she had never noticed before? She looked at her phone to see how long it had been since she spoke with Jessie. Maybe it wasn't too late to call her back and tell her to not come. After, all what could she do anyway?

"Shit." She was too late. Jessie was in the passenger seat of a red SUV that was pulling into the parking lot. The SUV joined her by parking on the other side of the parking lot and Jessie jumped out and ran to Rose.

"Where is it?" Jessie asked. Rose pointed to her car's driver-side door. "It's under the driver's door, near the front tire."

The man who was driving the SUV had gotten out of the vehicle and walked around the front to join them.

"Rose, this is my friend Collier; he's the friend I've been visiting and he's really into technology. I think he might be able to help us," Jessie said.

"Technology?" Rose asked, a bit confused.

"Well, I figure it is either a bomb or a tracking device. If Collier doesn't recognize it as a tracking device, we call the police," Jessie said.

"Just stay here and I'll go take a peek," Collier said as he strode towards the car.

Rose instinctively took a step back, as though being an extra foot or two away would help her if her car exploded.

Jessie reached over and grabbed Rose's hand. "Don't worry, Collier and I were talking on the way over here and the chances of it being a bomb are slim."

"Why do you say that?"

"If it was a bomb, why hasn't it exploded yet?" Jessie asked. Rose thought that the fact that nothing had exploded yet didn't rule out the fact that it could still be an explosive device.

Before Rose could respond, Collier moved out from underneath the car and walked towards them, a relaxed look on his face.

"Not a bomb I take it?" Jessie asked, and Rose couldn't help but notice that despite her conviction that it wasn't a bomb, Jessie had a definite look of relief on her face.

"Nope, it's a GPS tracking device," Collier said.

"Tracking device?" Rose sounded incredulous. "Why would anyone want to track me?"

He reached for his phone and began to tap away. Rose looked at Jessie, frowning slightly, a question on her face. Jessie shrugged to show she had no idea what he was doing either.

Collier passed his phone first to Rose and she looked down to see he had typed a message for her in his note's app: "It also has a sound recorder in it that is activated by noise. Someone may be listening to us right now."

Rose gasped and looked up at him, her eyes wide.

"What?" Jessie asked, looking quickly between Collier and Rose, trying to find out what was happening.

Rose passed the phone to Jessie for her to see the message.

"Oh my God," Jessie muttered.

Collier motioned for them to follow him to the SUV, and they all hopped in.

"I don't know what the range on it is for picking up the sound so I thought we should play it safe," Collier said. "So, what do you want to do about this?"

"Do? What can I do? Is there any way I can find out who put it there?" Rose asked.

"We can try, but it depends on what kind it is," Collier said. "If it's a real-time GPS, we may luck out and be able to use the serial number to track it to an account. But if it's passive, you're probably out of luck."

"So, if someone is listening to me at the same time I'm talking, I might be able to find out who planted it, but if they're recording, no?"

"Basically, but even if it is real-time, it'll be hit and miss if we can figure it out—it will be a case of relying on the kindness of strangers, or in this case, customer service agents," Collier explained.

Feeling overwhelmed by this latest discovery, Rose slumped forward in defeat. One thing after another kept coming at her; sometimes before she even had a chance to digest one surprise, another blindsided her. When would she be able to catch her breath?

"Collier, is there any way of deactivating it?" Jessie stepped in and took over as she realized Rose was in no condition to make decisions.

"Sure, I can do that," he replied.

"Okay, why don't you take the tracker and I'll jump in the car with Rose? We'll go to her place and hunker down for the rest of the day," Jessie rubbed her sister-in-law's back. "We can decide on what to do with it later."

"You don't have to come with me Jessie, I'm okay," Rose protested.

Jessie frowned in response, letting her know that she was not going to argue about it with her. There was no way in hell Rose was going to go home without her.

~~~~

Curled up on her living room sofa, Rose nursed the hot cup of tea Jessie had brought her. Dark and swirling, hot steam rose from the cup. She stared at it with glazed, almost unseeing eyes but her calm, almost detached exterior hid a mass of bubbling fear and uncertainty. What had happened to her life? To her family? Who was tracking her and why? When had the affair started and why wasn't she enough? A lone tear fell down her cheek and landed on the hand that was gripping the teacup.

"Talk to me," Jessie said in a low, calm voice. She had never seen Rose look so defeated before and it scared her. "What are you thinking?"

Raising her eyes to look at Jessie, one side of Rose's mouth lifted, and she slowly shook her head. "I wouldn't know where to begin."

"Let's start with how you are feeling, right this moment," Jessie prodded.

"So many different emotions. I'm feeling sad, scared, angry, betrayed, and overwhelmed," she said. "I'm not even sure which emotion is the strongest."

"Maybe it's time to get angry. Whoever it is that is messing with you has a lot of gall."

Startled, Rose looked at Jessie questioningly for a second before she realized that she hadn't told her about David's infidelity.

"And why do you feel betrayed? Where does that come from?" Jessie went on.

Rose inhaled deeply and then slowly breathed out. She could try and keep it from Jessie, but to what end? To salvage her pride? No, she felt as though she hadn't had any pride since the police knocked on her door. Concern that Jessie would take David's side and turn against her? No, that wasn't Jessie's style.

"Earlier today I found out my husband has been having an affair," Rose said with a resigned note in her voice as she traced the rim of her teacup with her index finger.

The silence in the room was heavy. and after a minute Rose looked up to see her sister-in-law wiping a tear from her eye.

"Why are you crying?" Rose asked.

"Because I'm human and I have compassion?" Jessie looked annoyed at her question. "And he's my brother and I can't help but feel sad for how he has turned out."

"Oh."

"And I also cry when I'm angry," Jessie went on to explain. "If he wasn't in a prison cell right now, I swear I would strangle him."

"Well, you may have to get in line," Rose said with a faint chuckle.

"How did you find out? Did he tell you?"

"Hell no, I don't know if he would ever have told me. I found a couple of receipts on David's desk," Rose shook her head, still in disbelief that her husband could have betrayed her again.

"Honestly, I don't know what to focus on right now: David's betrayal, trying to decide if he is guilty or not, or figuring out who is following me. And why!"

Chapter 40

Present Day

Rose was sitting on the couch, deep in thought when she realized she had been staring at her phone, which she was holding in her right hand. She almost dropped it when it rang.

"Hello?"

"Hi Mom," said Kayla, "I'm picking the kids up and then we're going to head over to your place to visit. Do you want me to pick up something for dinner or do you have something yummy planned?"

"No," Rose was shaking her head as though she thought her daughter might be able to see her.

"No, you don't have anything yummy planned or no, you don't want us to pick something up?"

"Neither. This isn't a good time for me hon, maybe another night," Rose found herself saying. There was silence at the other end of the phone, as though Kayla had to take a moment to digest what her mother had just said.

"You don't want us to come over tonight?" she finally asked. "Is everything okay?"

"It's just not a good time for me, I need some time to rest." How could she explain to her daughter that her entire world was crumbling around her? How could she tell her what her father had done?

"Do you want me to leave the kids with Brandon and come over?" Kayla suggested.

"No, no you go and spend a nice evening with your family," Rose realized that she couldn't recall a time ever telling her daughter and her family that they couldn't come over for a visit. No wonder she sounded confused and concerned.

"Okay, but if you need anything, you'll let me know, won't you?"

"Of course, sweetheart," Rose tried to make her voice sound as light and carefree as possible.

"Wow, that must have been hard for Kayla," Jessie said after Rose had hung up.

"Hard? No, she was a bit confused, but hard?"

"Well, she is used to just popping in and I think she takes it for granted that you will always be there for her," she explained.

"I suppose," Rose sounded doubtful. She knew Kayla was used to her being available whenever she called, but that was how she wanted it. Her family was very important to her, and she cherished the time they spent together and how closely knit they were.

"Anyway, I think you did the right thing. You need to focus on yourself right now," Jessie continued. "Decide how you are going to handle things going forward."

"Handle things?"

"Well yeah—are you going to stick by David despite him being a colossal idiot? Or are you going to file for divorce and let him figure his own life out?"

"I honestly haven't even given it any thought. I feel like my life is happening around and to me, and I don't have control over anything," Rose's voice broke.

"Well then, it's time you took back some of that control and I think saying no to your daughter was a good start," Jessie said.

"I suppose," Rose agreed weakly. But it didn't seem as though she had much say in the matter right now and couldn't see where she could possibly take any control.

"You are responsible for what you do in these situations Rose," Jessie began, as though she had read Rose's mind. "You can sit back and wait for something else to happen, or you can make some decisions and move forward."

"I want to leave him," Rose blurted out before she even thought about what she was going to say.

"Okay then," Jessie said.

"But then people will think I don't believe he is innocent of murdering that poor girl," Rose protested.

"And how is that your problem?"

"Well, it's not but..." Rose began. She stopped speaking when she saw Jessie raise her eyebrows sky-high and lower her chin. All she needed were half glasses at the end of her nose and she would be the spitting image of the quintessential librarian. "Okay, it's not my problem."

Why did she insist on worrying about what others thought? These decisions were based on what he had done; they were the consequences of his actions, not hers. It was time she took control of her life.

"I want to leave him, I want to find out who is following me and why, and I want to know what happened to Rebecca all those years ago," Rose declared. "Even if it turns out that David killed her."

"So, you're willing to entertain the thought that he might have?" Jessie looked surprised.

"Yes, I've been growing less sure with every piece of evidence that shows up. Given everything that's happened I would be a fool not to at least consider that I may have never really known him," Rose admitted quietly.

"Okay, then I'm going to text Collier to see if he can try and track down who that GPS belongs to," Jessie picked up her phone and tapped away.

While Jessie was preoccupied chatting with her friend, Rose decided to make the most of the opportunity to take some time off for herself. She wandered into the kitchen, leaned up against the counter in front of the sink, and stared out at the darkening sky. How many times had she looked out like this? Hundreds? Thousands? She always found the view out her back window relaxing. The sight of the carefully manicured lawn, the swaying of the large weeping willow that was located along the back fence. There was a time when it soothed her worries; the time when she was worried Joshua was getting involved with kids at school who would lead him down the wrong path and when she ached for her daughter who was in the throes of teenage angst and heartbreak. She had stood here when she had learned of David's affair last year. She had taken strength from nature and the reassurance that life goes on and that some things will always stay the same.

That peace was missing tonight. She pushed herself away from the counter and began wandering aimlessly through her home, as though in search of the life she thought she would always enjoy. In the kid's old bedroom that her grandchildren claimed when they stayed over, she ran her fingers along pictures of Joshua and Kayla. Joshua grinning in his track and field outfit, his medal hung proudly around his neck. Kayla, a sweet cherubic baby, lying on a furry white rug.

Their life happened and they were happy. They had raised a family together and that couldn't be taken away. Some of the memories were tarnished, but they could never be fully destroyed, no matter what David had done. He couldn't take away her family.

"Why?" she whispered as she sat on one of the twin beds and pulled a stuffed animal to her chest. "Why weren't we enough? Why wasn't I enough?"

What would make a man take the chance of throwing all this away, and for what? Sex? It made no sense. He had everything he could ever want. He had a good job, a loving wife, and a growing extended family. Why would he risk all of that?

Tears rolled down her cheeks and she sobbed into the animal. When her tears had slowed, she sniffed and listened to the quiet house. Jessie must still be talking with her friend. It had grown darker outside, and a heavy silence hung over the house. She made her way out of the bedroom and down the stairs before turning the front light on. She peeked into the living room and saw Jessie curled up on the couch, her eyes closed and her breathing low. Picking up her cell phone from the coffee table where she had left it before she began wandering around the house, Rose looked over and smiled at Jessie with fondness. She took the blanket that was at the end of the sofa and carefully pulled it up over her shoulders. Just as she finished tucking her in, Jessie stirred and looked up at Rose in confusion.

"Sorry, didn't mean to wake you up." Rose apologized.

"Don't be silly. If I slept much longer, I'll have a killer kink in my neck," Jessie said as she rubbed her eyes. "I remember when I could sleep on the ground with some rolled-up clothes for a pillow and be fine the next day. Now? I pull a muscle just rolling over."

"Oh, come on, you're not that old," Rose said.

"I spoke with Collier, and he is going to get right on trying to trace that GPS," Jessie filled her in. "He says we need to cross our fingers and toes so that he can get a name for us."

"Good, well I think I'm going to go to bed," Rose said. "The spare room is made up so feel free to crash there whenever you're tired enough."

"Thanks," Jessie looked at her sister-in-law hesitantly, as though she was weighing her words carefully. "Rose..."

Rose raised her eyebrows questioningly.

"I'm sorry about everything; you don't deserve any of this."

Rose felt the tears well up in her eyes again and she took a deep breath to calm her emotions. She had cried enough in one day to last her a lifetime. "Thanks, Jessie, now I'm going to get some rest. We have a busy day ahead of us tomorrow."

"We do? What are we doing?"

"Taking back control."

Chapter 41

Present Day

"The first thing we need to do is see if we can figure out this birth certificate," Rose stated, setting down a cup of coffee on the table in front of Jessie. She stood with her mug in her hand, allowing the steam to warm her face, and blew on it gently and carefully.

She had slept surprisingly well last night, and she was feeling refreshed. As painful as finding out her husband was having an affair, on some level, she felt as though part of her had been released. It was as though the tie that bound her to David had been severed. As long as she didn't linger on the betrayal and the pain of imagining him with someone else, she felt as though she had regained a piece of herself that had been lost for a long, long time. Although she had thought about it deep into the night, she had been unable to pinpoint exactly when she had lost that piece. What she had realized was that it had happened gradually, over the years of their marriage. She had invested so much in him and their marriage that she had denied parts of herself in order not to lose the dream she had of who he was and who they were together. She wasn't sure how she was going to turn things around, but she had woken up determined to try.

"I thought you didn't think it had anything to do with anything," Jessie asked. "Do you have an idea, an avenue for us to check out?"

"Nope, I just know that is the only unanswered question right now. It might have nothing to do with anything or everything to do with something," Rose responded with a small smile on her lips.

"You look much better this morning," Jessie commented. "More rested and sure of yourself."

"I am. Last night I was devastated and broken, but the more I thought about it, the more I realized that I wasn't really surprised. At least not as surprised as I should've been," Rose explained. "Deep down I've known for a while that something just wasn't lining up and hadn't been for a while."

Jessie reached over and placed her hand over Rose's. "I'm glad you have some clarity, even if it's still painful."

"Yeah, me too," Rose whispered. Then, she mentally shook herself and looked her sister-in-law in the eyes. "Do you recall anything else at all about the birth certificate or what your mom told you when you found it?"

"I don't. Mom wasn't exactly the type of person prone to confide in someone or explain things. Don't get me wrong, she was a great mom, but when I left home, I started realizing that I knew very little about what made her tick. I started seeing her as a real person, you know? And I realized I didn't know who that person was."

"That's not uncommon; to grow up and reassess how you view your parents," Rose said.

"Yeah, but it was more than that. I knew we had a whole other extended family on her side, but we never saw them, she never talked about them or anything. Whenever I asked questions, she would just brush me off and say she was busy, or she would talk to me about it later."

"David always told me there wasn't much family on your mother's side."

"Well, it's true. In fact, I don't recall ever meeting anyone from her side," Jessie confirmed. "I always thought it was odd but what can you do? Families can be odd."

"You're preaching to the choir," Rose smirked. "I've created quite the family for myself."

With her coffee mug halfway to her mouth, Jessie paused and looked at Rose, a serious expression on her face. "You do have quite the family Rose, and nothing David has or hasn't done can change that."
"I'll try to keep that in mind."
"Now, the birth certificate. Why don't you go grab it and we can take a closer look at it," Jessie said.
"Funny you should mention that" Rose said as she stood up and reached for the paper on the kitchen counter. "I have it right here."
Setting the thick, yellowed birth certificate in front of Jessie, Rose sat back and watched her examine it closely.
"Michael John Cordell," Jessie murmured. "Who are you and do you have anything to do with Rebecca Evans?"
"What about your dad's side of the family? Would they know anything about this?" Rose asked. They had been so focused on his mother, that they hadn't bothered to consider their father.
"I don't think so. I have some cousins but they are even younger than me. Their mother, my aunt, died in a car accident when the boys were pretty young and the only other family member is an aunt who is quite elderly and is in a home the last time I heard," Jessie explained.
"So, cousins that are younger than David, a dead aunt, and an elderly, potentially dead aunt," Rose summarized what Jessie had said. "Not many options for who the birth certificate may belong to."
"Or potential mothers of Michael Cordell," Jessie said.
"Yeah, we don't even know who we are looking for: MJ or MJ's parents," Rose said.
"MJ?" Jessie laughed. "The mysterious Michael Cordell has a nickname now?"
"Sure, why not?"
"Hey, I'm good with it. And you're right, we don't know what or who we're looking for at this point,"
"I googled his name but couldn't find anyone that was a fit for age, ethnicity, and stuff," Rose said. "I also looked into getting a copy of

the long-form birth certificate that has the parent's names on it, but
you can only get one if you can prove you're a close relative."

"What the hell? I thought in the age of the internet people had no
privacy, why can't we find anything out about this guy? We have his
full name, date of birth, and the place he was born, for heaven's sake."

"There seem to be lots of sites online where you can look up things,
but I don't know which ones are credible and which ones are just
scams."

"Why don't we see if we can find a private investigator that can look
into it for us?" Jessie suggested.

"I suppose," Rose was disappointed. She had hoped Jessie would
know a friend of a friend who could find something out for them.
The desire to just get things moving was strong and she had hoped
they could do something about the birth certificate today.

"I tell you what, how about I phone around and see if I can get a
recommendation for a good investigator and maybe we can work on
getting him hired and started today?" Jessie suggested.

They spent the morning doing research online and calling Jessie's
friends and they soon had the number of a reputable private
investigator. They called and shared the name on the birth certificate
with him, then made an appointment for later that afternoon to
discuss what he had found out.

"Well, that was quick!" Rose exclaimed as she hung up from her
conversation with the PI. "He didn't think it would take long for him
to find out what we need!"

"I'm a bit surprised too, to be honest," Jessie agreed. "And I didn't
want to say anything and slow things down, but I can't make it this
afternoon, you will have to go."

"What? We're in this together!" Rose heard something dangerously
close to a whine in her voice.

"I know, and we will, but I told Collier I would take him to his dental appointment. They are giving him meds to knock him out and he needs someone to drive him home, I can't back out now!"

"Aaaargh!"

"Now, now, you're a big girl, you can handle this one thing by yourself," Jessie teased Rose. "Then you can come back and tell me everything you find out."

~~~~

Sitting across the desk from a slim young man dressed in a buttoned-up white shirt and loose tie, Rose couldn't help but think that this private investigator looked more like a financial planner. She hadn't realized until he walked into the office how much she had been influenced by TV. Without thinking about it, she had imagined an older man in scruffy, unkempt clothes. Maybe even with a cigarette or cigar. She experienced a moment of internal embarrassment that she had pictured him as some kind of old-fashioned gumshoe-type character.

"It didn't take long to run the name through our sources and get some information for you," he told her. "There was a Michael John Cordell born in that County and on that birthdate. He was born to a woman by the name of Helen Cordell, father unknown."

"I'm confused, that is my mother-in-law but my husband has the same birthdate," Rose rubbed her forehead, a frown forming.

"That would make sense because this Michael John Cordell was a twin, so by the sounds of it, your husband and this man are brothers," He nodded his head as he peered at his computer. He didn't seem in the least surprised that he had dropped this news on her. He acted like he had just told her the weather forecast.

"My husband is a twin? But... Why?" Thoughts were flying at Rose and she was having trouble thinking coherently.

"Why what Mrs. Slater?"

"Sorry, I just don't understand why the boys were separated. I assume she had him before she was married as her married name was Slater. Did she give him up for adoption? But why only one?"

"I'm not sure what the reasons were behind it, but he was adopted by Nancy and Charles Kowalski and his name was changed to James," He finally took his eyes off the computer screen and turned in his chair to face Rose.

"Do you know where he is now?"

"I'm sure I could find out given a bit more time," the private investigator replied. "I would probably need another day or so."

"Oh, okay, yes then if you could do that..."

~~~~

Rose left the investigator's office in a cloud. She went to her car and sat staring out of the windshield for a few minutes. It made no sense. Why would his mother give up one child but not the other? Why had she never told them, not even David? And who was this mystery twin and where was he now? Most importantly right now, did this have anything to do with Rebecca's murder? She felt a headache coming on and she knew she had to find someone to sit down and discuss this with; someone to brainstorm ideas and possibilities.

She grabbed her cell phone to call Jessie, but it went directly to her voice message. After leaving a message for her to call her when she could, Rose hung up and called Barry's number. Whether it had something to do with the murder or not, their lawyer needed to know about this. There was no answer on his cell and when she called his office, she was told he was in court.

"Damn it!" she exclaimed. She needed to talk to someone. But as Jessie said, time for her to be a big girl. The last few days had shown her quite clearly that she relied on other people for a lot of things in her life. It wasn't necessarily a bad thing, especially when it came to support and encouragement, but she needed to start taking more ownership of her decisions. David had always been the one to decide what they were doing next; whether they were going to turn left or right in life. Now that he wasn't with her day to day and making the decisions, she realized how much she relied on him.

With a renewed sense of determination, Rose put her car in reverse and pulled out of the PI's parking lot.

~~~~

When she arrived home, she poured herself a glass of wine and sat down at the kitchen table to wait for Jessie to call her. The news that David had a twin somewhere was still throwing her and she reached for her laptop to do some research. She googled 'twin DNA' and her eyes immediately widened. Ever since she had heard about the twin, something had been niggling at the back of her mind and now it was right in front of her. The overwhelming majority of identical twins have the same DNA. As the puzzle pieces clicked into place, she felt her heart pound faster. At first, she had thought that if he had a twin that could explain the eyewitness who saw 'David' with Rebecca the day she died but now she knew it could also explain the DNA found on her body. Could David's twin be the killer? Half a glass of wine into her thoughts, she found herself almost giggling. An evil twin? Her life had become a second-rate soap opera. She had thought her life couldn't get more surreal when the police showed up at her door and took her husband away in handcuffs. But everything that had happened since that day had only added to the sense that she was standing in a rowboat in the middle of the ocean.

She was startled out of her thoughts when the doorbell rang. Lately, anytime someone came to her front door it was to either harass her with horrible deliveries, bully her with intrusive questions or arrest her husband. It wasn't surprising then that she felt anxiety rising in her as she walked to answer the door. The light on the new security system panel that was on the wall next to the front door was flashing and it reassured her to know it was activated.

Grabbing a hold of the doorknob, she started to twist it while taking a last-minute peek through the peephole. She froze. Then she stepped away from the door slowly, her breath caught in her throat, and her eyes wide.

"Damn," she muttered.

Chapter 42

Present Day

The sound of the doorknob being jiggled back and forth broke Rose out of the cloud of shock that surrounded her. Turning on her heels, she ran to the kitchen and grabbed her cell phone and then returned to the front door.

"What do you want?" she asked.

"Can you open the door so we can talk?"

"No, I'm sorry I can't," Rose couldn't believe she was issuing an apology.

"I just want to talk to you about David,"

"Please leave, you can visit David in jail,"

"I will go and see him, but I wanted to talk to you as well," The doorknob jiggled again and this time it sounded as though the whole door was being shaken as well.

"Leave now or I'm calling the police," she said, trying to keep the shakiness out of her voice.

"What for? I haven't done anything wrong, I just want to talk to you, open the door!"

Rose decided it was best not to engage in a conversation with him any longer, so she moved away from the door, sitting down on the bottom step of the staircase. She decided if he didn't go away in the next three minutes, she was going to call 911. Why she decided on three minutes, she had no idea, but she looked at her phone to note the time and then she waited. A minute had passed when she realized that it was dead quiet at the front door. Rose swallowed hard. Had he left? She slowly walked back towards the front door and looked outside. No one was there. She leaned up against the door, her body going limp with relief. Whether he just wanted to talk or not, there was no way she was going to let a stranger into her home.

Her eyes flew open wide at the sound of glass breaking at the rear of the house. She ran. At the same time, she began punching in Jessie's number to her cell, an instinctive reaction to needing help. She came to stop just before the kitchen, her back up against the wall so she could peer around the corner to see if he had broken in. As her gaze scanned the room, she landed on the intruder standing near the back door. Her eyes met those of her husband.

~~~~

"I just want to talk to you," the man said, his hands held up, palms towards her.

"How did you get in?" Rose asked, her eyes darting around the kitchen.

"I had to break the small pane near the back door, I'll pay to have it fixed,"

"Oh," Rose held her cell phone tightly. "Why are you here, why do you want to talk to me?"

"Sit down and we can talk, okay?" he gestured toward the kitchen table. Rose took a wide berth of him and sat on one of the chairs. When he pulled out a chair, Rose quickly cleared Jessies number off her phone and punched in 911.

"What did you just do?" he asked, frustration evident in his tone.

"I've called 911,"

"Why? I told you I just want to talk!"

"You broke into my home!" Rose spat back at him. "I don't want to talk to you and you can't just break into someone's home and force them to talk to you."

Rose could hear the 911 operator picking up the call.

"This is 911 what is your emergency?"

"A man has broken into my home," Rose stated, looking him in the eyes. He reached over and grabbed the phone from her hand and hit the red button to disconnect the call.

"That isn't going to stop them from coming here," Rose told him.

"No, but it gives me a bit of time. I would have liked to be able to talk to you without the pressure of the police arriving at any moment but so be it. I assume you know who I am?"

"Michael John?"

"James Daniels. But yes, I was born Michael John Cordell," he said.

"What do you want to talk to me about?"

"I wanted to see if there is anything I can do to help David."

Rose stared at him in surprise. Of all the things she had expected him to say, this hadn't even been on the list. She looked at him closely, marveling at how much he looked like her husband. Except there was a darkness to this man's eyes, an almost cynical knowing look to him that was completely at odds with her husband.

"Turn yourself in," Rose finally said.

"For what?"

"What do you mean for what? For murdering Rebecca of course,"

"What are you talking about, I never even met her, how could I have killed her?" he sputtered. "Don't try and lay that on me!"

"It makes perfect sense; you were seen in town with her on the day she died and your DNA was found on her after she was dead."

The man who called himself James and who looked so much like her husband and yet oh so different, settled back in the chair and stared at her before very quietly saying "No, they saw David with her and found David's DNA on her."

The two of them looked at each other unblinking, as though trying to read each other's minds.

"David didn't kill her," Rose said.

"How do you know that?" He asked as though he wanted to understand, as though he was amazed that she honestly believed her husband incapable of murder.

"I just know it, he isn't capable,"

"We are all capable,"

"Not David,"

"Even David," he slapped his hand on the kitchen table as he said it and then stood up. "Well, I can see I have worn out my welcome here, I have to be going."

"If you are so innocent, why don't you wait for the police to come? You can explain to them that it was David, not you. You can tell them your alibi for when that poor girl was murdered."

"I don't think so," he strode away from here and toward the front door, but he had miscalculated the amount of time it would take the police to arrive. When he opened the door, two squad cars were just pulling up. Rose stood behind him, her hands crossed over her chest. "It's time you came clean James, it's time to pay for what you've done."

~~~~

Jessie stared at her sister-in-law with her mouth agape. She had arrived about fifteen minutes after the police had hauled away the brother she didn't know she had and was listening to Rose explaining her afternoon.

"So let me get this straight, my older brother is an identical twin and my mother gave one of the twins up for adoption, but not the other. She never told us about it and now you think my brother David is not guilty of murder but that my until now unknown brother is the monster who killed that girl?"

"Yup, that is it in a nutshell," Rose took a deep breath, raised her hand's palms upwards and shrugged. "What can I tell you, it's been an eventful afternoon."

"I'll say! So, they are talking to him at the police station right now? If, as you say, identical twins almost always share identical DNA and they look alike, how will the police know which one of them is guilty?"

Rose sat in silence, unsure what to say. The truth was, she wasn't sure if there was a way of figuring it out. Except for one thing. "The only thing is if James can't provide a reasonable alibi, and David can find people who were with him in the theatre, that would help."

The two women sat quietly, each of them lost in their thoughts. They were in a state of uncertainty, not sure what was going to happen. Would the appearance of James mean anything to David's case? Or would they even have a case now?

Rose picked up her cell phone off the coffee table and called Barry. He was available now and she filled him in quickly. There was silence at the other end of the phone until finally she heard him mumble "Well, shit,"

"Yes, exactly. Do you know what this will mean to David's situation" she asked.

"To be honest I'm not sure. I need to chat with the prosecutor and make sure he is aware of these latest developments. I've never had this type of a situation arise before, I'm going to have to do some research and find out what this means."

"Okay, well, can you please, please call me as soon as you find anything out? Both Jessie and I are going crazy here not knowing what this means."

Rose served dinner later than usual and it consisted of sandwiches and some canned soup. There had been a time when she would have felt bad not providing a full hot meal for company but somehow, she couldn't even muster up any concern over it tonight. When they had finished eating, they placed the dishes in the sink and went to sit in the living room.

"This has been a crazy, unbelievable week," Jessie said as she ran her fingers through her hair. "People think all the traveling I do is exciting, that beats nothing the suburbs can come up with!"

Rose laughed and raised her glass of wine in Jessie's direction. "Honestly, it isn't usually so... dramatic!"

Jessie stood up and turned on the gas fireplace before stretching out on the couch opposite Rose.

"From what I can gather, it may come down to which of the two men can come up with the most evidence to support their case. The DNA and the eyewitness point to either of them but as we said, the alibis could be helpful. Has anyone ever tried to track down any of those boys that David went to the theatre with in Rutledge? That would strengthen David's case."

"I don't know, I assume the police would have looked into it at the time, but I suppose that is something that should be in the files the police have from the investigation."

"That could take forever, is there any way we could find out who was there?" Jessie asked, sounding like she was asking herself the question rather than Rose.

"I don't know how, I don't think I've even heard their names,"

"We could ask David if he remembers," Jessie pointed out. "Why don't we go to the jail tomorrow and talk to him about it."

"Before or after we tell him there's someone out there walking around who looks exactly like him?"

"Maybe before, while he can still think straight," Jessie chuckled. A silence fell over the two women, each of them lost in their thoughts and feelings about this newest development.

"You know this is messed up, don't you?" Jessie said with a deep sigh. "Either way you look at it, I'm here trying to figure out how to prove that one of my brothers is a killer."

Rose couldn't imagine what emotions Jessie was going through right now. While she was stunned that there was a brother she knew nothing about, and that there was a man who looked identical to her husband, it wasn't the family she grew up in. Jessie must be thinking back on her entire childhood, wondering if she had missed something or trying to see if she could see where her mother had been lying to them.

"I'm sorry all of this is happening Jessie,"

"Yes, well, I can't say it isn't shocking but, in the end, I want what is best for David, for you and your family," Jessie stated emphatically. "And that starts with finding someone who can verify David's alibi."

Before she could respond, Rose's phone rang and she picked it up without looking at the call display.

"I know who you're looking for," a voice said quietly.

"Pardon?" A frown creased Rose's forehead and she looked up at Jessie. The discussion she had been having with Jessie and the words that were just spoken whirled in her mind and she felt a sense of disorientation. It was as though the voice on the other end had simply continued the conversation she had been having with Jessie.

"You heard me, I know who it is," The voice continued, and Rose tapped the speaker button on her phone so Jessie could hear what was being said as well. The voice of the person on the phone sounded tinny and almost unisexual, as though it was a computer-generated voice intended to disguise not only their voice but their gender as well.

"Who is what?" she asked.

"Send your friend to meet me by the gas station on the corner in fifteen minutes and tell her to come alone," the voice said. "I have some documents she might find interesting and that will help you too."

Rose had tilted her phone so the display became visible and she saw that the number displayed was an odd assortment of numbers and letters. Obviously, a fake phone number.

"Why my friend?" she asked, trying to stall and see if she could get more information out of them.

"Because this involves her and her brother," the line went dead in Rose's hand.

Rose and Jessie stared at each other in silence, both unsure how to process what had just happened. Finally, Jessie spoke.

"Well, I guess I better get a move on if I want to be there in 15 minutes."

"I'm coming with you."

"No, you aren't."

"I'm not going to let you go alone," Rose pushed back despite the firmness of Jessie's voice.

"Don't argue with me, Rose. He said to come alone and so I'm going to go alone. I don't want to take the chance that we miss out on some valuable information. The gas station has bright lights and security cameras, I'll be perfectly safe."

"I don't like this," Rose responded, her voice full of worry.

"I know but it's what we have to work with right now."

Jessie slipped into her shoes and grabbed her coat and purse from the sofa.

"Wait!" Rose shouted as she ran into the kitchen. Jessie could hear a commotion, the sound of things banging around, and then a breathless Rose returned. Holding out her hand, she passed Jessie a can of bear spray. "Take this in case you need it," she told her sister-in-law. "I heard it's stronger than pepper spray and you can hit someone with it who is further away from you."

"I'm sure I won't need it, but thanks," Jessie waved the can in thanks and was out the front door. Rose went to the window and watched her pull away. She had an uneasy feeling about Jessie going alone. But what could anyone do? As she pointed out, she would be in a pretty safe place. And now she was armed.

Chapter 43

Present Day

Jessie was sitting in the parking lot at the gas station, looking around nervously. She had no idea who she was looking for, or even if the person was a man or woman. There was a knot of tension sitting in the pit of her stomach and her heart was pounding. She looked in her rear-view mirror when she saw headlights turn into the parking lot. She watched as the car parked and a woman jumped out of the passenger seat, followed by two teenagers from the back seat.

Jessie leaned back in her seat. She drummed her fingers on the steering wheel and looked up and down the road that ran in front of the station. Every time a vehicle approached, she held her breath, waiting to see if they slowed down, preparing to turn in. Five minutes went by, and Jessie reached to pull her phone out of her purse to see if there were any messages from Rose. Maybe the person had changed their mind. She rummaged around in her purse for a minute before growing frustrated and dumping the contents on the passenger seat. No phone.

Shit. For the first time since leaving Rose's house, she felt vulnerable. Even in a well-lit parking lot with people coming and going and a can of bear spray beside her, she felt increasingly uneasy and exposed. Something just felt wrong.

~~~~

Pacing around the living room, Rose reached for her phone on the coffee table, and she noticed that Jessie's phone was sitting beside it.

"Damn it," she said. Jessie was on her way to meet this person, whoever they were, and she could not contact anyone. Should she go after her? But what if the person saw her and lost the opportunity to potentially find the identity of Michael Cordell? No, Jessie would kill her if she showed up there; if she was in a public place, she would be fine.

Just as she decided to sit and wait, a loud bang came from under her feet, and the house went dark.

~~~~

Before she had a chance to consider what she was doing, Jessie threw her car in reverse and backed out of her parking stall. She had been waiting for close to fifteen minutes and whoever had called should have been here already. Something was wrong and she didn't like the cold feeling of dread that was spreading throughout her belly. Someone had been following Rose. Someone had put a bug in Rose's car. Someone had hacked into Rose's computer. Why did someone want to talk to her and not Rose?

Maybe they did.

She pressed down on the accelerator, heart pounding and her eyes darting along the road, looking for any sign of someone driving away from Rose and David's area.

"Damn it!" she pounded the steering wheel in frustration as she came up behind a slow-moving Honda Acura. "Speed it up!" she yelled at the car in front of her. What had she been thinking? Why didn't she let Rose come to the gas station with her? At least they would have been together. Strength in numbers and all that.

She turned off onto Rose's street and came to a stop in front of the Slater home. It was dark, every single light was off. She didn't need to double-check to know that the other houses on the block had lights on and therefore electricity. Something was very, very wrong. Rose wouldn't have gone to bed and turned all the lights off, not when she was so anxious about Jessie.

She walked up the sidewalk to the front door of the house. She reached for the doorknob and then realized the door itself was open a few inches. She pushed it open wide without entering the house.

"Rose! Are you okay, Rose?" she shouted, making sure she was loud enough to be heard upstairs. The house was silent. She felt around on the wall to the right of the door and flipped a switch. Light washed over the hardwood floors and bathed the walls. She looked around carefully, alert for anything out of the ordinary.

"Rose! Where are you? Answer me!"

She stepped cautiously into the entryway. She found herself trying not to make any noise with her feet, and immediately felt foolish. She had already announced herself by yelling out twice, what harm would some footsteps do? Arriving in the living room, she flipped on the lights and gasped.

The room looked as though it had been ransacked. The cushions from the sofa were strewn all around and a glass vase lay in shards on the floor, beside the coffee table where it had once sat. The two glasses of red wine had spilled onto the cream-colored area rug, making it look as though it was doused in blood.

Seeing her cell phone on the floor, she picked it up and quickly sent a text to her friend, Collier. She gave him Rose's address and that she thought something was very wrong. If he didn't hear back from her saying everything was okay, could he come look for her?

Jessie left the living room and began frantically running in and out of each room in the house, desperate to find Rose. When she had checked the upstairs and the main floor, she turned to look at the door that led to the basement. Inhaling deeply, she resolutely headed for it. She walked down the stairs carefully, not wanting to slip and end up on her back at the bottom. She would be no good to Rose in that condition.

She reached for the chain that she knew hung in the middle of the room, attached to a single light bulb. It swung wildly from side to side, casting ominous, swaying shadows from one end of the basement to the other. Her eyes swept the room, coming to rest on an old sofa and chair set. Bile rose in the back of her throat as she saw a head of hair leaning up against the chair's armrest. In the darkness of the basement, it was hard to tell exactly what color the hair was, and Jessie approached it carefully, the blood rushing to a pounding crescendo in her ears.

"Rose?" Her voice was barely above a whisper.

She reached the back of the chair and now she could make out a shape lying on top of black garbage bags that she knew were filled with Kayla and Joshua's old clothes. A memory flashed across her mind of Rose rolling on the floor laughing at some long-forgotten joke she'd told her the day they cleaned out the trunks of kids' stuff. They had been drinking wine and reminiscing about a time when the kids were just babies. Pushing the thought aside, Jessie squeezed her way between the sofa and the armchair so she could get a better look to see if it was Rose and if she was okay.

She reached out and touched the hair, gently calling Rose's name. The hair rolled onto the floor and Jessie let out a horrified scream. When it hit the floor, it made a hollow sound and bounced across the concrete, coming to rest with its face staring lifelessly toward the sky.

Jessie began to shake and cry as she looked down at the mound of clothes she had mistaken for a body. Moving away from the furniture, she approached the head and with her foot gave it a swift, angry kick. The hairdresser's head that Kayla had played with as a child made a cracking sound as it collided with the far wall.

"Fuck!" she screamed. The relief she felt in discovering that Rose was not dead was replaced with an anger that coursed through her veins like molten lava. She ran up the stairs, through the front door, and jumped into the car. She was about to phone the police when her cell rang.

"Hello!" she answered brusquely, ready to brush off whoever was calling.

"Hello Jessie," the odd genderless voice greeted her.

"Where the hell is Rose?"

"Now, now calm down Jessie."

"Don't tell me to calm down you miserable piece of shit, where is Rose?"

"She's fine, you don't have to worry about her at all," the voice continued. "We're just out enjoying the night air."

"Let me talk to her!"

"I'm afraid that isn't possible at the moment, but you're welcome to come join us if you want." The voice was beginning to take on an almost sing-song quality and Jessie felt the hair on her arms begin to rise.

"You better not harm a hair on her head!" Jessie shouted, feeling helpless and unsure of what to do; should she insist on talking to Rose or should she keep this person talking and hope to figure out where they were?

"Come join us Jessie, we're going somewhere to park, and it is such a beautiful night to watch the sky."

"Where are you taking her?"

"Oh Jessie, I'm so disappointed you don't remember my spot. I thought you and Rose appreciated the solitude and beauty of nature."

Her heart skipped a beat. Had this person taken Rose out to where Rebecca had been killed? That meant they knew where she had died. That meant she was probably speaking with Rebecca's killer.

Then, in a voice that was now firm and no-nonsense, they said "Come alone. If you tell anyone where you're going, you will be

responsible for what happens to her. Remember, I have my eyes and ears on you. I will know if you don't obey."
The line went dead.

~~~~

Rose opened her eyes, confusion and pain meeting her consciousness. She tried to move and felt something tug around her neck and her waist. What was going on? What had happened? She tried to open her eyes but there was darkness all around her. Then the darkness filled her eyes, and she fell unconscious again.

~~~~

"Rose honey, time to wake up."
"Hmmmm..."
"Rise and shine, beautiful, you're going to miss all the fun!"
Her mind swam in circles, looking for something to grasp ahold of something that would stop the rising nausea.
"Rose!"
Her head was suddenly jerked upwards, causing her eyes to fly open as she gazed into the darkness. She filled her lungs with air and exhaled slowly a couple of times as the bile in her stomach subsided and her eyes were able to focus. She realized she was looking up at the sky, a dark sky full of twinkling stars. The scent of woods and night air filled her nostrils. Her thoughts cleared and she was able to think straight. But she was still so confused. Why was she staring at the night sky and why was she outside?
Suddenly, the memory of what had happened hit her as swift and painful as a punch to the gut. She had been in her home when the lights went out and someone had grabbed her arms, wrestling her to the ground. No matter how hard she fought, she was helpless against the strength of the person attacking her. Then her mouth

and nose were covered, and she thought she was being suffocated until she smelled a sickly-sweet scent and felt the world dissolve into blackness.

"Oh good, you're back," a voice whispered in her ear. She tried to turn around to see who was talking to her, but it was then that she realized she was secured to a tree. The tree was not large, but it was solid and there was no bend to it. There was a rope wound around her waist and neck, and duct tape secured her hands and ankles.

"Who are you? What do you want?"

"Is that any way to show your gratitude? After all, I did to bring us together?" The person spoke quietly and in an almost whispery voice that caused a shiver to run down her spine and she felt a coldness coil in the pit of her stomach. Her legs were weak, and she felt the acrid taste of vomit at the back of her tongue.

"Please, whatever you want, just don't hurt me, please. I'm a mother and a grandmother, my family needs me," Rose began to plead. Pride meant nothing to her when faced with this living nightmare.

"Oh honey, I think your time is just about up, you've had more than your fair share of time with them," they said with an edge to their voice.

Oh god, what was happening? Who was this madman? She looked around, the moon was full and high in the sky, bathing the trees with light. The wind passed through the trees, causing shadows to dance on the ground. The beauty of the night was in stark contrast to the terror she felt coursing through her veins. There was a niggling at the corner of her brain, and she wondered what it was until she saw the way a stand of trees looked, the way they clumped together to form a familiar silhouette. She was on the edge of the clearing where Rebecca had been murdered. Her legs went weak, and she felt the pressure of her weight on the ropes that encircled her. No, no, no...

"I don't understand," she whimpered. "Who are you?"

"I'm the one whose life you stole," they whispered in her ear as they wrapped their arms around her and the tree at the same time, their hands resting on her waist.

"I don't know what you are talking about, I don't understand," Rose willed herself to remain calm, taking deep breaths to keep her mind as clear as possible. "How could I have stolen your life?"

"You stole my life when you married David of course," Their fingers gently traced a line up and down her forearm and up toward her shoulder.

"But that was years ago, we have been married for years, how is that stealing your life?" Rose wanted to keep them talking, as it would give her more time. Time to do what exactly she wasn't sure, but it was the only thing she knew to do at this point.

"I was supposed to be with David, not you! There is no way he could ever be happy with you; he's always wanted me!"

"How, how did you meet David?" she asked.

"Oh, I don't even remember the first time I met David, he's a man I've always known," they responded. The sound of their laughter caused bumps to rise on Rose's arms and a sick feeling grew in her belly. This person was insane, completely stark raving crazy.

"If you have always known him, that means you knew him first. Why didn't David decide to spend his life with you then instead of me?" Rose knew this was a dangerous question and that it might make this person angry, but it might also make them angry enough to make a mistake.

"You think you're so smart, don't you Rose," The voice rose and Rose was almost positive it was a woman talking. The angrier she got, the less she seemed able to keep her voice steady and neutral.

"I'm just curious, that's all, I didn't mean anything by it," Rose tried to sound as unconfrontational as possible. She had a response from her captive and now she knew it was a woman, but she didn't want to push her luck by getting her even more angry. She heard some rustling noise behind her and then a soft chuckle.

"It looks like we have company,"

Rose felt a rush of hope, could someone be here to help her? But the woman didn't sound concerned.

"Who?" she asked.

"Oh, just someone else I need to get out of his life," was the chilling response.

Thoughts were sailing in and out of her mind faster than she could grasp ahold of even one of them. Who was she talking about? What was she going to do with the person once they arrived? And what was she planning to do with Rose? She didn't have much time to contemplate her fate before she heard more rustling in the trees.

She stepped away from Rose and the tree, moving quietly and surefootedly. Rose lost sight of her when she blended in amongst the trees about ten feet ahead of her. She was left standing, immobilized, and tied to the tree, helpless. She wasn't sure what was happening, but she knew it couldn't be good. Something was happening that she just didn't understand.

The sound of trees moving, twigs snapping, and muffled curses reached her ears. A second later, she spotted the woman, her back to Rose, and she was pulling an unconscious figure into the opening. Oh god, was it Jessie? Her breath caught in her throat, and she had to remind herself to breathe. The woman was tying her feet together and then rolled Jessie onto her stomach and tied her hands behind her back. Although she didn't move, Rose assumed Jessie was still alive, otherwise, she wouldn't bother tying her up, would she?

She tried to get a look at her face as he came towards her, but her head was down, and she had pulled a hood from her shirt up over her head. Who was this woman who had gone to such trouble to get both her and Jessie out here alone? In the exact spot where Rebecca had been killed. Did she have a vendetta against David? A wave of terror washed over her. If this was all about David, then her children might not be safe. Or her grandkids. A whimper escaped her lips, and it was all she could do not to burst into tears at the overwhelming helplessness that washed over her.

"Tears won't work on me, so save them," The woman said as she walked up to Rose and then raised her head and looked into Rose's eyes.

Chapter 44

Present Day

"Who are you?" Rose asked the woman standing in front of her. The woman was about five and a half feet tall, was dressed from head to toe in black, including a black hat on top of dark auburn hair.

"I'm the woman who's going to be comforting David," she replied, one side of her mouth lifting in a sneer. "I've been waiting a long time for this but I'm going to be at his side as he mourns the loss of his wife and sister."

"I get why you want me out of the way, but why Jessie, she hasn't done anything," Rose wasn't sure whether this woman had mental health issues or not, but maybe they could reason with her.

"David listens to her and cares what she thinks, she'll only get in my way," the woman explained. "David needs to look to me, because I love him and I know what's best for him."

"But you can't keep everyone away from him," Rose pointed out. "He has children, and friends..."

"I'm not concerned about that, once he relies on me, he'll see that he doesn't need anyone else," she said with a shrug.

A moan came from behind her, and she spun around. Jessie was coming around. What was this woman going to do with them now that she had them both here, tied up and at her mercy? She obviously wanted them both dead, but how? and when? Would they have time to talk her out of it or was she planning on doing it quickly?

"Ou shon a mmish," Jessie tried to yell but it came out muffled and slurred, like someone who had been to the dentist and whose lips were numb.

"Now now, don't be such a potty mouth!" As she was speaking, she walked over to Jessie and looked down at her, the moon shining brightly on her face and Jessie stared up at her.

"Okay, let's move you," she said. "Now, upsy-daisy, on your feet." She helped Jessie stand up and then shuffle towards Rose.

"Why are you doing this? If David wants to be with you, he would," Rose asked. "Why do you need to kidnap us?"

"Listen, this wasn't exactly my first choice either, but when he refused to put me on the visitors list at jail, I knew it was time to do something drastic. I'm not some dirty little secret who has to be hidden away or denied completely!" Her voice was beginning to get loud again.

"You're the woman who my husband is having an affair with." Rose stated. She seemed to forget the feelings of fear she had been experiencing as anger overtook her. How dare David bring this crazy woman into their lives.

"Don't make it sound like I'm some fly by night slut," a deep scowl appeared between the woman's eyes and her lips clenched. "He was mine first!"

"Wa?" Jessie asked. Whatever had been causing her to slur seemed to be slowly dissipating. The woman looked over at her, frustration evident on her face.

"You don't remember me do you Jessie?"

Jessie stared at the woman as though trying to figure out who she was, but finally shook her head no.

"It's Kim? Meadowland?" The woman seemed to be breathing heavier than before and her jaw was clenched tight. Jessie's failure to know who she was seemed to be making her fume. Suddenly, realization seemed to dawn on Jessie and her eye widened.

"Yes, that's right Kim Borden," she said when she saw the recognition in Jessie's face. "Tell Rose I knew David first, I knew him before even Rebecca did!"

"Yes, tha's right," Jessie said. "Rebecca's friend."

"So, Kim," Rose began, hoping beyond hope that she could still reason with the woman. "Knowing David first doesn't mean anything; it isn't about who knows someone longer."

"Oh no? I beg to differ. Not only did I know David before you, but he also chose me back then. And he will do it again." Kim's hands were clenched at her side, her stress evident.

"You dated David in high school?" Rose asked. She had always been under the impression that Rebecca was the only girl he had a relationship within high school.

"We didn't date, we fell in love," Suddenly, Kim's demeanor changed completely, her face softening and her eyes taking on a faraway look. "We had one amazing night together and he was going to break up with Rebecca. We were going to be together."

"Then what happened?" Jessie asked.

"Then Rebecca got his hands on him, like she always did. She must have convinced him not to leave her, and she always got what she wanted!" The angry Kim was back. "Do you know he even denied we had that night together? I wrote him while he was at that camp, I wanted to know when he was going to finally break up with her. He said he didn't know what I was talking about! How could he do that to me?" She was pacing back and forth in front of them and becoming more and more upset.

"What a bastard!" Jessie said, although her voice held little conviction.

"No! don't say that about him," Kim strode up to her and pressed her face close to Jessie's. "It wasn't his fault; she was the one who made him stay with her! He was going to break up with her, I know he was, but when they came here, she threw herself at him. They had sex right in front of me!"

Rose felt something shift as what Kim had just said sunk in. David had brought Rebecca here and Kim saw them? That would mean that Kim would know how Rebecca died. She glanced over at Jessie and saw the look on her face that told her Jessie was thinking the same thing.

"Was that the day Rebecca died?" Jessie asked quietly.

"Of course, when else was she here?" Kim looked at Jessie as though she was a bit slow. "She was supposed to be coming to pick me up but I was early. I was waiting for her when I saw her and David meet on the street. She couldn't wait to get him alone and he was no match for her."

"Did you follow them?" Rose asked, hoping she would continue talking.

"Of course, I saw that they were heading here so I cut through the fields. I got here just in time to see her throw herself at him. He just wanted to talk, but she knew she had to use her body to get him to stay."

Kim was shaking with anger and Rose didn't think it was because she remembered the anger, but because she was reliving it as she spoke so she kept quiet, wanting Kim to keep talking. If she was talking, there was hope. Jessie seemed to have the same idea as she kept quiet.

"I tried to reason with her, I told her that he loved me, but she laughed. She laughed," Kim was staring off into the distance as though she had forgotten that Rose and Jessie were even there with her. "She said I was crazy and that there was no way David had slept with me. She refused to listen to me. I had to shut her up."

The silence was heavy as the enormity of what Kim had just said hit both of the women. It wasn't David or James who had killed Rebecca. It was Kim. And now she wanted to kill them too.

"Did you know David has a twin brother?" Rose finally spoke up. "Maybe it wasn't David at all."

Kim spun around, her eyes wild and her lips pulled back to bare her teeth.

"Shut up! Don't try to screw with me. You are just as bad as her, do you think I'm stupid? I grew up in Meadowland, David did not have a twin."

Rose realized she would never be able to convince this woman of something she herself had just found out today. She eyed Kim warily as she began to walk around the clearing, suddenly deep in thought as she ran her hands through her hair and sighed deeply. While she was lost in thought, Rose looked over at Jessie, and she spoke under her breath so quietly that Jessie could barely hear her.

"Let me do the talking, don't antagonize her, and do what she says," Rose whispered.

"What can you do? You're even more immobile than I am," Jessie pointed out.

"Never mind, I can't explain right now," Rose told her sister-in-law. "Just keep your wits about you and wait for a sign from me."

"Now what are you two gabbing about without me?" She was striding quickly towards them; her tone was playful, but her body language was purposeful and aggressive.

"I just wanted to make sure she was okay," Rose spoke up before Jessie could.

"She's fine," Kim said. "It's getting late, let's get this over with."

She walked around behind the tree, keeping her eye on Jessie while she worked at the knots that held Rose in place. First, she undid the rope around her waist. When it fell to the ground, it brought Rose little relief as her ankles were still bound by duct tape. Then Kim worked at the rope around her neck. Having these removed alleviated the constrained feeling and she felt as though it was easier to breathe somehow, even though she still had her hands bound around the tree.

She moved Rose away from the tree and then produced a roll of duct tape from her pocket which she used to secure her hands in front of her body. As the blood flowed more freely into her hands, they began to fill with pins and needles. Rose winced at the pain and rotated her shoulders to help work the stiffness out. Kim then edged her towards a fallen tree so she could sit down.

"Where are you going?" she asked.

"Jessie's first," she said, not looking Rose in the eye.

Rose felt terror rise within her. She couldn't let her take Jessie.

"Wait!" she called out as she began walking in Jessie's direction.

She stopped and looked back at Rose.

"I want to show you something that will prove what I said," Rose tried to keep her voice as normal as possible, hoping that the tremor she heard in it was not obvious to Kim. She hesitated, looking at Jessie who was standing, quiet and unmoving and then back at Rose.

"If you are so sure that it wasn't David's twin you slept with, then you won't be afraid to see what I have," Rose said, a challenge in her voice. Kim walked towards her, she lifted Rose into a standing position and looked at her carefully. She glanced over her shoulder and made eye contact with Jessie.

"It's in my pocket, the left front one," she instructed Kim who stepped closer and reached toward her pocket.

Rose simultaneously brought her hands forward swiftly towards her chest and her head down onto Kim's head. At the same time, Jessie threw herself forward, catching Kim as she let out a shout. Jessie hit Kim's body with hers on her left side and she went over sideways onto the ground. There was a loud whooshing sound as Jessie landed on her. It took a moment for Rose to register that she had just had the wind knocked out of her.

Rose shuffled quickly to Jessie, holding out her hands for her to work on the duct tape. Luck was on their side as she had been careless and, in a hurry, when she had bound Rose's hands in front of her and even working at it with her hands behind her back, Jessie was able to catch an end that hadn't been pushed down completely. Jessie yanked at the piece of tape as forcefully as she could with her bound hands. She had to try a couple of times as she couldn't get ahold of the piece easily, but finally, she heard it tear.

"Once more," Rose said frantically. The amount of writhing Kim was doing on the ground was starting to slow down and Rose was afraid she was going to regain her wits and strength before they were able to get free. As Rose flung the tape off her hands, she began working on Jessie's. It was easier now because her own hands were completely free, and she could see what she was doing and soon Jessie's hands were free too.

"Get off of me you bitch!" the woman screamed. "I'm going to kill you!"

"I don't think so!" Rose cried out, just as she worked her one foot free from the tape. She pulled her foot back and kicked her hard in her side. She heard a sickening thunk sound as a rib gave way, but she didn't have time to dwell on that. She was on her knees, going through her jacket pockets, trying to locate the roll of duct tape.

"Here it is!" Jessie cried out, as she reached out to pick it up off the ground. It had dropped out of her pocket. Just as she leaned over to reach for it, Kim gave another agonizing groan and grabbed her hand. Without another thought, Rose landed another kick to her side. She screamed in pain and Jessie picked up the tape and quickly secured her hands behind her.

Sitting on her to make sure she didn't try anything again, Jessie tossed the roll of tape to Rose so she could do her ankles.

Winded and in shock, the women moved away without taking their eyes off her. She lay on the ground, her hands and feet bound, moaning in pain. After a moment of silence, Rose turned to Jessie and said, "What now?" Before Jessie could answer, they heard what sounded like a herd of animals running through the underbrush towards them. The women grabbed each other, their hearts pounding. Suddenly, the clearing was ablaze with light and they heard someone shout through a bullhorn.

"This is the police, do not move!"

~~~~

After the police had secured the area, a couple of figures came down the trail towards them. It was Jessie's friend Collier and David's lawyer Barry.

"Oh, thank God," Collier said, grabbing Jessie and pulling her into a bear hug. "I didn't know if we would make it in time."

Rose looked at Jessie, the confusion evident on her face.

"I left a note on your front door before I left," Jessie said. "I had told Collier if I didn't call him back that he was to come to your house. The note told him where I was going and to call Barry."

"Telling me to call Barry was quick thinking," her friend said. "I can't imagine trying to convince the police myself that you were in danger and that they should bring out a team to help you."

"You wouldn't have been in time if it hadn't been for Rose," Jessie said. "She was ready to take me out to the back forty and shoot me, but she took her down."

"I didn't do it on my own," Rose said. "And Barry, thank you so much for helping to get the police here."

"No problem. Do we have any idea what this was all about? Or who that woman is?"

Rose and Jessie exchanged a look.

"How much time do you have?" Rose asked him.

Chapter 45

Present Day

They gathered at Kayla's house so the police could process the scene in Rose's home. While Kayla had been shocked to see Jessie and Rose show up on her doorstep, accompanied by a police officer, she was soon hustling around making them hot beverages and wrapping them in warm blankets. Rose refused to explain what had happened until Joshua arrived as she didn't want to have to tell her story twice. She knew she would be bombarded with questions she couldn't answer, and she wanted to get it all over with at once. While they waited, she and Jessie sat side by side on the couch, their fingers entwined, drawing warmth and strength from each other. They had been through a very traumatic experience together and it had created an even deeper bond than had existed before.

While they were waiting for Joshua to arrive, Kayla's phone rang. It was Barry, wanting to speak to Rose. After a brief exchange, she told him to come over and speak to them all at once. He had been to the police station and learned a bit about what was happening and wanted to share it with her.

It seemed like a lifetime before both Joshua and Barry arrived looking anxious.

"Mom, are you okay?" Joshua immediately went to Rose. "Kayla said something happened to you tonight. What were you doing in a forest at night?"

"Shhhh... sit down and be patient and we'll tell you what happened; at least as much as I can," she told him.

"And hopefully I will be able to fill in some blanks," Barry added as he took a seat in the chair across from Rose.

Jessie began to fill them in on what else had been happening to her since their father had been arrested.

She explained what had happened over the last several hours—everything from discovering their father had an identical twin to how someone had called, and she had gone on a wild goose chase while someone kidnapped Rose. She explained how she had left the note for Collier after someone called and told her where Rose was being kept. By the time she was at the point in the story where she had come to and found Rose tied to a tree, Joshua looked as though he was ready to faint.

Rose relayed the rest of the story, making their escape sound easier and less violent than it had been.

"And this is where I come in," Barry said. "I have received some information from the police. After we heard from this woman, we had a chat with both your father and his twin. It turns out in fact that it was the twin that had slept with Kim more than 30 years ago. He pretended to be David and made a lot of promises, including that he would break up with his girlfriend for her. According to him he was a quote stupid jerk unquote who would have done anything to get in a girl's pants back then."

Barry seemed to be taking more than a little pleasure in having the entire room hanging on his every word. "So, from what I can tell, this Kim woman spent the last few decades believing she had slept with David and that Rebecca was the only thing standing in her way. While she isn't outright confessing to murdering Rebecca, I think it will happen soon, she seems like the type who wants to talk."

"She just randomly tracked us down and decided to kill Mom and Aunt Jessie?" Joshua asked, disbelief evident in his tone. Jessie and Rose were quiet for a moment, debating how to tell them that their father had an affair.

"I know this is a lot to digest and we're not entirely sure about all the details, but things will become clearer in the coming days," Barry responded, a kind smile on his face as he looked at Joshua and then looked knowingly at Rose. He had bought them some time to let the kids process things.

"An identical twin? Why didn't he know anything about it? Why didn't you know anything about it Aunt Jessie? How is this possible?" Kayla asked.

"There are still some gaps but apparently he was told that his birth mother could only keep one of the two and she chose to give him away," Barry explained. "It must have done a real number on him and he struggled for many years."

"So why did he show up now? Has he always known where David is?" Rose placed her elbow on her lap and rested her forehead in her hand. She was beginning to develop a headache from all the excitement of the evening and now the confusion of this explanation.

"No, he said he saw David on the news when he was arrested for the murder of Rebecca. He was able to track him down."

They all sat in silence, each of them caught up in their own thoughts, working through what they had just learned. Finally, Kayla spoke up, her voice excited as she realized what this meant.

"When can Dad come home?"

"We will have to go before a judge and there's some paperwork to do, but I'm thinking within a day or two," Barry told them, grinning from ear to ear.

"Oh, thank goodness!" Kayla threw her arms up dramatically. "Then life can get back to normal!"

Rose felt Jessie's hand squeeze hers and she wondered if her life would ever be the same again.

Chapter 46

Present Day

It had been two weeks since David had been released and Rose still felt unbalanced. David had been so happy to be home that he had gushed over how wonderful it was to have a hot, private shower and how good her cooking tasted. He went out for walks every day and sometimes even in the evenings. He said he would never again take for granted his ability to come and go as he wanted. By the time he realized his wife was unusually quiet, he had been home for days. When he questioned her about it, she said she was processing everything that had happened. And that was true, she was.

They had learned that David's mother had given up one of her twins when they were born because she was young and unmarried. She had come from a strict, conservative family who had disowned her when she became pregnant, and the father had long moved on to what he considered to be greener pastures. Jessie had shared that she felt this accounted for her mother's sadness; giving up her son and being unable to talk about it with anyone. Both David and Jessie realized that they were probably half-brother and half-sister rather than sharing the same father, which they had always assumed. But they also agreed that they had no interest in finding out for certain. Given the role that DNA had played in David's incarceration and Jessie's subsequent capture by his twin, they knew they wanted nothing else to do with any testing. They were brother and sister and that was enough for both of them.

The more they learned about how David's twin James had grown up, the more they felt for him. He had been adopted by a couple named Charles and Nancy Daniels. They quickly changed his name to James and raised him in a harsh and unloving environment. Why they ever wanted to have a child was a mystery Rose would never understand. They were cruel and abused their adopted son his entire life. Rose couldn't help but wonder how David would have turned out if he had been the one who had been adopted.

"Why are you so deep in thought?" Rose jumped, David's question surprising her as she stood staring out the kitchen window.

"You scared me!" She had noticed that she was still pretty jumpy and her therapist reassured her that once she had processed everything that had happened over the last little while that it would go away.

"Sorry, didn't mean to,"

"I was just you know, thinking about things," Rose said as she reached for the dishcloth. "I was just thinking about how some people can have such a crappy life and turn out okay and others have a good life and turn out crappy."

"That's true," David said, picking up a coffee mug to dry. "But most of us grow up in okay homes and turn out to be human."

"I suppose,"

"You've been very withdrawn; I know you've been through a lot while I was in jail. I can't pretend to understand how it affected you. I know you say I've said it enough, but I am so so sorry about... everything."

"I know you are," Rose gave him a sad smile. "I'm just not sure..."

"What aren't you sure about?" He waited for her to answer and when all she did was stare down at the bubbles in the sink, he spoke up again. "You aren't sure about me?"

"I'm sorry too David, I want to just pick up where we left off, but I can't act like nothing has happened. I can't just accept your apology and move on from your affair."

"Okay," he said quietly. "So where do we go from here?"

"I don't know. I really don't. I'm working through some stuff with my therapist and I hope I'll get some clarity soon, but I just don't know."

They stood at the sink in silence, each of them absorbed in their own thoughts until David placed his hand on Rose's arm.

"Take as much time as you need, I'm not going anywhere and I want you to know that I'll do whatever it takes to make you happy again, if you decide you want me to."

"I appreciate that, thank you,"

"I know it's a bit ridiculous to take until my age to really understand that my actions have consequences and I know I might lose you because of my actions. That's a consequence for me, but it's also a consequence for you and for our family. I'll never take that for granted again."

He took Rose in his arms and they stood holding each other in the kitchen that had borne witness to years of their family's tears and laughter.

Don't miss out!

Visit the website below and you can sign up to receive emails whenever CARLA HOWATT publishes a new book. There's no charge and no obligation.

https://books2read.com/r/B-A-BXIW-KOJPC

BOOKS 2 READ

Connecting independent readers to independent writers.

Did you love *For Love's Sake*? Then you should read *For Crime's Sake: When True Crime Kills*[1] by CARLA HOWATT!

[2]

True Crime was her life until it killed her.

When well-known true crime YouTuber Natalie Baker, host of 'For Crime's Sake,' is found dead, her sister Rebecca has a lot of questions for the local Sheriff. Questions he doesn't want to answer.

Did she get too close to her cold case?

The Sheriff insists her sister died in a double suicide, but why was it no one had ever seen her with the man she was supposed to love? At least not until their bodies were found on the floor of her home.

And how was her death related to a missing baby named Sarah Jane Montgomery?

1. https://books2read.com/u/bzKpzZ

2. https://books2read.com/u/bzKpzZ

A psychological thriller that is guaranteed to have you questioning reality.

Read more at https://www.facebook.com/CarlaHowattAuthor.

Also by CARLA HOWATT

For Crime's Sake: When True Crime Kills
For Love's Sake

Watch for more at https://www.facebook.com/
CarlaHowattAuthor.

About the Author

Carla Howatt lives in Alberta, Canada where she helped raise three children, two husbands and a few pugs. A communicator at heart, Carla is also a proud introvert, port inhaler and dark chocolate hunter.

Her pets Carrera, Mercedes, Enzo and Mufasa keep her laughing and her husband keeps her shaking her head.

Read more at https://www.facebook.com/CarlaHowattAuthor.